"Such a sharp tongue you possess, Katharine. No soft and gentle wife will you be, I vow."

"*No* wife will I be. I will not wed you!"

"I will give you a choice. You may don the wedding gown I have brought—" Senet nodded at the heap she had thrown to the floor "—or you may be married as you are, in your chemise."

"You are deaf, dumb, blind and senseless!" she shouted furiously, her hands balling into fists at her sides. "I will not wed you!"

"I give you the span of a minute to make your decision."

"You, a knight of the realm? You would not parade any woman before her own people so nearly undressed. And certainly not the woman you mean to have as a wife," she said with disdain.

"Nay, *I* would not subject you to such a humiliation, but *you* are the one who will conclude the outcome."

Dear Reader,

As the weather heats up this month, so do the passion and adventure in our romances!

Susan Spencer Paul brings us another tale in her fabulous medieval BRIDE SERIES, all loosely related—and very hot!—stories of stolen brides. You may know Susan from her mainstream historical novels written as Mary Spencer. *The Captive Bride* is the story of Senet Gaillard—Isabelle's tortured brother from *The Bride Thief*—who meets the *one* woman who can mend his broken heart, Lady Katharine Mathus. But first he must storm her castle and "force" her to marry him!

Lord of Lyonsbridge marks the *twelfth* book for the talented Ana Seymour. In this unusual medieval novel, a sinfully handsome horse master teaches a spoiled Norman beauty important lessons in compassion and love. And don't miss Linda Castle's new Western, *Heart of the Lawman*, about the power of forgiveness. Here, a single mother, upon release from prison, is drawn to her child's guardian—the same man who mistakenly imprisoned her....

Finally, we have a wonderful marriage-of-convenience story set in Oregon, *Plum Creek Bride* by Lynna Banning. When a German nanny travels to the West to care for a baby girl, she arrives to find a grieving widower—the town doctor—and teaches him how to love again.

Whatever your tastes in reading, you'll be sure to find a romantic journey back to the past between the covers of a Harlequin Historicals® novel.

Sincerely,

Tracy Farrell
Senior Editor

SUSAN SPENCER PAUL

THE CAPTIVE BRIDE

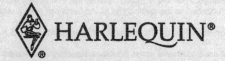

HARLEQUIN®

TORONTO • NEW YORK • LONDON
AMSTERDAM • PARIS • SYDNEY • HAMBURG
STOCKHOLM • ATHENS • TOKYO • MILAN • MADRID
PRAGUE • WARSAW • BUDAPEST • AUCKLAND

ISBN 0-373-29071-3

THE CAPTIVE BRIDE

Copyright © 1999 by Mary Liming

Visit us at www.romance.net

Printed in U.S.A.

Books by Susan Spencer Paul

Harlequin Historicals

*The Bride's Portion #266
*The Heiress Bride #301
*The Bride Thief #373
Beguiled #408
*The Captive Bride #471

*The Bride Series

SUSAN SPENCER PAUL

who also writes as Mary Spencer, lives in Monrovia, California, with her husband, Paul, an R.N., and their three daughters, Carolyn, Kelly and Katharine. She is the author of twelve historical novels set in a variety of time periods, and especially loves writing about the medieval and Regency eras.

Dedicated to my wonderful Liming sisters-in-law,
Jeanie, Lori, Nancy and Barbara,
with all my love

Prologue

France, March 1437

Sir John Fastolf was sitting with his booted feet propped on a trunk when the flap to his tent opened. He looked up from the missive he was reading and saw the tall man standing outside in the heavy rain. "Ah, at last. Sir Senet. Come in and be welcomed. Luc—" he turned his attention briefly to his busy serving boy "—bring Sir Senet some wine." Then he waved to his visitor. "Come in, man. No need to stand in the rain. Come in and sit down."

Senet ducked and stepped into the tent, removing his helmet with one hand as he did so. When he lifted his head it was to meet Sir John's greeting smile with a somber gaze.

"Have you word from London, my lord?" he asked, standing in his place and dripping water on the rug that had been laid on the ground.

Sir John nodded. "This morn. I sent word to you as soon as I had it in my hands. The battle has gone hard, I take it?" His knowing gaze moved over the other man's dirty, much worn armor.

Senet's expression gave little away. "As ever, my lord."

"Yes," Sir John said with a sigh. "As ever. I shall miss your good services when you've gone, Senet. You're one of the finest soldiers I've had the pleasure to command. Sit down and we'll share a goblet over your good fortune."

Senet's gaze sharpened. "The king has approved my request?"

"His regents have, rather. You'd have made no headway without the aid of your sister's husband, Sir Justin Baldwin. It was he who convinced Duke Humphrey to consider making you this boon. I needn't tell you how unusual this is, given the fact of your father's treason."

"Have I made no reparation for that?" Senet demanded.

"Quite obviously you have," Sir John told him, "else you'd not have your family lands returned to you. There is a condition, however, before you may take repossession of Castle Lomas."

"Condition?" Senet repeated warily. He pulled the gauntlet from one hand and took the goblet the boy Luc brought him. When Sir John motioned again for him to sit, he carefully took the chair opposite his host.

Sir John accepted a goblet as well, sipping from it slowly before answering.

"Circumstances have fallen in a fortunate manner for you, Senet. I doubt the request to regain your lands would have been considered, much less granted, if Sir Richard Malthus hadn't died without leaving an heir. It was Malthus, you recall, who was given the deed and title to Lomas after your father was executed for treason. There is only an unmarried daughter now, Lady Katharine, twenty and one years of age, who has seen fit to run the estate since her father's death in any manner she pleases—which does little to endear her to Duke Humphrey, you may be sure. But that was as Malthus wished, at least until the girl should be properly wed. Sir Justin petitioned for you in the matter, and the king's regents have agreed. Your lands will be returned to you in full as soon as you've taken Lady Katharine to wife.''

Senet stared at him, his fingers tightening upon the goblet he held. Sir John held his hands up, as if warding off what he thought must be an objection. ''I know she is somewhat older than what most men seek in a wife, but I am assured that she is both hearty and hale and descended of a long line of good breeders. 'Tis unlikely that you would have any trouble in getting an heir off her.''

''Has Lady Katharine agreed?''

Sir John smiled grimly. ''Unfortunately, no. It appears that she's received the news of your proposed marriage with little enthusiasm, and has denied the request based on a formal betrothal her father arranged between herself and a wealthy baron, Lord Hanley. Lord Hanley, however, disappeared more than three years ago while on a religious pilgrimage, and has long been presumed dead. Still, Lady Katharine insists that the betrothal be maintained and has refused any and all proposals of marriage. Duke Humphrey, understandably, is exceedingly displeased with the girl, and has granted you permission to…encourage her in the matter. Only make certain that you bring the lady no harm, nor any of those in her care.'' He set his goblet aside on a nearby table and sat forward. ''And now, Senet Gaillard, I have the unhappy task of releasing you from any further duty here in France. You're to leave for England as soon as possible and make for Lomas.''

Senet nodded, his expression as sober and unremarkable as if Sir John had merely spoken of the weather.

"What of my friends? Sir Kayne—"

Sir John held up a staying hand. "He and Sir Aric and John Ipris are to go with you. I would not separate you from your comrades at such a time, and they have served England as well as you have done these past several years. To ask more of them now would be unjust. You are all released from duty to return home and lay your siege upon Castle Lomas."

Senet drained his cup and set it aside. Standing, he took up his gauntlet and helmet. "Lomas is mine by right of birth," he said evenly. "Lady Katharine is another matter. If by wedding her I reclaim what is rightfully mine, then you may be certain, my lord, that she will be my wife. Regardless of what her wishes may be, or how stubborn she may prove. She will wed me, even if I must lock her away to make certain of it. I promise you that on my very honor."

He set his helmet upon his head with an easy, long-practiced motion, and tugged on his gauntlet. Making a curt bow, he bid Sir John good day, then turned about and left as abruptly as he had arrived.

Chapter One

England, July 1437

"It is unacceptable."

Katharine put the missive aside with finality. The gaze she set upon the man standing before her was unwavering. "You may tell Duke Humphrey and Sir Senet Gaillard that my decision on the matter remains unchanged. And," she added distinctly, "unchangeable. I will not accept Sir Senet for a husband. If Duke Humphrey finds this distressing, then I pray you will remind him that I am already betrothed."

"He has not forgotten it, my lady," Sir William told her with a slight bow. "But Lord Hanley has been presumed dead these past three years—"

"He is not dead!" Katharine rose from her chair. "I will not have you, or anyone else, saying so." She gripped her skirt in a tight fist as she moved nearer the man. "The pilgrimage he's undertaken has merely lasted longer than expected. If any ill had befallen him or his companions, I would have had word of it."

"The trouble, my lady, is that you've had *no* word from

him. Nor has anyone else. It is only logical to assume the worst."

"Not at all," she countered. "Lord Hanley is an exceedingly devout man, and would not be given to such worldly concerns as writing mere missives when he is instead giving worship to God. He wished to make this journey before taking on the duties of marriage and so asked me to wait for his return. I will do as he requested and fulfill the promise I gave him. Surely Duke Humphrey would not want me to do otherwise."

"My lady, only hear me—"

"There is nothing more to say," she said brusquely. "You may convey my sentiments to Duke Humphrey exactly as I have expressed them, and tell him that I pray he leaves me in peace."

The man hesitated.

"Are you quite certain that this is what you wish, Lady Katharine?"

"Quite certain."

He looked behind her to where three other ladies sat watching the proceedings.

"There is no one who can change your mind?"

The ladies to whom he looked variously cast their eyes to the floor, and Katharine replied, "No one."

He bowed. "Then I will thank you for receiving me, and bid you good day."

Katharine nodded. "Mistress Ariette will escort you through the hall." One of her ladies, a diminutive young woman, rose silently from her chair. "Godspeed to you, my lord."

She collapsed into the nearest chair the moment he quit the room.

"May God forgive me," she murmured, drawing in a

deep breath and crossing herself, "for speaking so many falsehoods." The breath was released in a rapid *whoosh*.

The remaining women quickly surrounded her.

"Oh, my lady, you were wonderful!"

"Thank you, Dorothea." Katharine accepted the goblet of wine that was pressed into her shaking hand. "I thought my knees would give way before he finally left. Did he believe it, do you think?"

"He must have done so," Dorothea answered, fanning her mistress with a small square silk linen. "You were most convincing."

"Indeed," said the other maid, younger than the other two. "You made Lord Hanley sound almost a saint, and that was not easily done."

Katharine smiled. "I nearly choked on the words. If that pompous fool ever does return alive from his travels, I can only pray he'll never hear of what transpired this day."

"He might insist that you wed him."

"May heaven forbid it!" Katharine said fervently, and her ladies nodded.

A soft voice came from the doorway. "My lady?" Ariette had returned. "He has gone."

"But he'll be back soon," Katharine said with a frown. "Or if not him, another of Duke Humphrey's messengers. The king's regent has a never ceasing supply of them, so it seems. This makes the sixth we've dealt with thus far, not including the visit Sir Justin Baldwin paid."

"Perhaps the duke himself might make the journey," Dorothea speculated.

"I shouldn't be surprised." Katharine stood and walked back to where she'd left the missive. Unfolding and laying it upon the table, she flattened it with both hands. "I must find the means to keep Lomas without fettering myself in the doing. Surely there is some way to manage it."

"I don't know why you won't at least *see* Sir Senet," the youngest girl said. "'Tis rumored that he's very handsome, as well as a brave knight who has attained much honor. And Lomas would have been his by right if naught had happened to change the matter."

"I've no care for either Senet Gaillard's looks or his attainments, Magan," Katharine told her distractedly, studying the page before her. "His father was a traitor to the throne, and I'll not be wed to such a one. And as to Lomas being his—I should have to be dead first."

"Oh, my lady, please don't say that," Ariette begged. "The duke may force you to wed the man. Or he may grow even angrier and make Sir Senet lord here without the necessity of marriage. Then we would all of us be beneath his hand. Even you."

It was true, Katharine thought unhappily, and might very well occur, especially if she continued to turn aside the proposed marriage. And it was something that might already have occurred to Duke Humphrey, regardless of whatever crimes Senet Gaillard's father had committed. The past lord of Lomas might have been a traitor to the crown, but Sir Senet, if all that she'd heard was true, had more than proven himself loyal to both king and country. He'd killed his father's own people in the war with France—his own people, since he was so closely related to French royalty, in order to prove himself.

But none of that mattered to Katharine. She had no wish for an arranged marriage. Indeed, she had no wish for marriage at all. It was naught but a chain to women, a path to lifelong servitude. Even the betrothal that her father had arranged to Lord Hanley, whom she despised, had been awful to her. When he had decided to go on his pilgrimage, Katharine had been utterly relieved; when he'd evidently disappeared on that same pilgrimage, she'd thanked God for unexpected mercies. Not that she wished harm upon Lord Hanley, but she'd been her own mistress at Lomas since even before her father had died, and had no wish to be otherwise. If she married Lord Hanley or Sir Senet, or any man, she would suddenly become as she had once been—powerless and, worse, unable to do so much as speak her mind on how best to manage Lomas for the benefit of both the land and the people. She had seen that fate befall her own mother before her father had been gifted with the estate and title that belonged to Lomas, when they had lived at court in London. It was as if her mother had merely become a shadow, necessary only to make certain of the comfort of others, but nothing more. And like a shadow she had eventually faded beneath such a lack of identity. Katharine's father hadn't even realized that his wife was slipping away until it had been too late. She would never forget how stunned he'd been at her mother's death, how unforgivably surprised.

"I will think of a way to keep it from happening," Katharine vowed. "I must. Even if I cannot hold off marrying forever, at least I may buy enough time to find a husband of my own choosing."

"I cannot see what good that will do," said Dorothea. "They are all the same, are they not? And perhaps you may find one who is even worse than Sir Senet. Only think of Lord Hanley."

Katharine gave a slight shudder. "You speak truly, though few men could be a worse prospect for husband than he." She grew thoughtful. "But it would be convenient, would it not, if I truly had a betrothed? Someone who would convince Duke Humphrey and Sir Senet and any other suitors that I am soon to be wed so that they may leave me in peace."

"But you *are* betrothed," Magan told her. "To Lord Hanley. And it would be impossible to procure him, would it not?"

"Yes, and may God be praised for it," Katharine said with a nod, "but I doubt that any of Duke Humphrey's messengers would recognize Lord Hanley if they saw him. He was not given to visits at court, and was somewhat solitary. Would it not be most convincing to my case if he should suddenly return from his pilgrimage?"

Her ladies gaped at her, until Dorothea said, "My lady, you cannot intend to practice such deceit."

"Can I not?" Katharine's lips curved into a smile. "I am a woman sorely pressed, and capable of attempting anything at all. Indeed, the more I think of it, the better I like the idea. I need only find the right man to lend me aid in such a scheme, and all will be well."

"My lady, this is madness!" Ariette protested. "Only think. You would have to marry this man—a stranger. How can that be any better than wedding with Sir Senet?"

"I can't think I should have to do any such thing," Katharine replied evenly. "If I can only convince whoever will help me to temporarily play the part of my betrothed, then he may leave Lomas unfettered—and much the richer—once Duke Humphrey has been convinced. I'll have no further need of him."

"Will you not?" Ariette pressed. "And what will happen when the duke discovers you never wed? He'll be angrier than before, and will have you punished for such a lie."

"Hmm." Katharine tapped the tip of one finger against her chin, thinking of this. "You speak truly, Ariette. And it would be just as well to have the matter done with so that we need not worry over any interference in future. But the answer to that is simple, as well. I must only find a man who will wed if enough money is offered and who has no more interest in maintaining a binding union than I. Someone who will gladly be on his way once the ruse has met its goal.'' She smoothed her hand over the missive once more. "I believe I know the perfect man."

"Who, my lady?"

She straightened. "Kieran FitzAllen."

A collective gasp rose among the others.

"But, Lady Katharine!" Magan cried. "He's your own cousin!"

"My half cousin," Katharine corrected. "And distantly removed, at that, as well as basely born. Duke Humphrey has probably never even heard of him, or known of his existence. He'd pass perfectly as Lord Hanley, without a moment's question."

"But he's...he's..." Ariette began, faltering.

"A rogue," Dorothea stated sternly. "A complete scoundrel in every way. He's ever in trouble, and well you know it. I can't believe anyone would mistake such a coarse man for Lord Hanley."

"And I can't believe you should wish to *wed* him," Magan said. "Despite that he's the most handsome of men, he would likewise make the most unreliable of husbands. Only think of all his...women." She reddened just speaking of it. "How could you possibly wish to be united to such a man?"

"Easily," Katharine said with a wave of one hand. "Oh, Kie's a troublemaker, I grant you, but his heart is good and his pockets empty. 'Twould be a simple matter to coax him to the idea, and he'd leave Lomas readily enough when the time came. He's never wished to marry any more than I have. I can't think why it's not occurred to me before now that we might lend each other aid in the matter."

"He'd be a burden about your neck for the rest of your life," Dorothea declared. "Always showing up when he was in trouble or needing money. You'd never be rid of him."

"I won't care for that, so long as he never attempts to lay claim to Lomas. And that," she said with certainty, "is something he would not do. You know how he disdains responsibility." She grinned at her ladies. "'Tis why he's always roaming about, hither and yon, is that not so? Nay, Kie will give me no trouble. He'll make the ideal husband, if I can but convince him to come to Lomas to hear what I propose."

"I doubt you could even find him," Ariette said with a sniff. "He only shows up when he wants something."

"Unkind!" Katharine charged. "And untrue. You know very well that he comes often only to visit. We've always gotten along well, and I have counted him among my truest friends. If he has needed aid on occasion, I've been more than glad to lend it. He's never grown wearisome in his company, at least, as Lord Hanley was given to do."

"And what of Lord Hanley?" Magan asked. "What if he should one day return from his pilgrimage? What a fine road of trouble that would be, were he to find you wed to another who'd taken his name."

Katharine shook her head. "He'll not return. Not after so long. And if he should—" The idea made her feel slightly ill. "At least I would be safely wed to another. If I lose Lomas for the deceit, I would not also have to suffer in being his wife. But come. We waste precious time. Magan, bring parchment and ink, and I will write a missive to Kieran. If only he can be found in time, we may

be ready to receive whoever else Duke Humphrey deigns
to send. Even Sir Senet Gaillard, should he be so bold as
to come to Lomas uninvited. But I cannot think he would
do anything so rude, unless he is more treacherous than
his father was.''

"Oh, my lady," Magan said, pleading, "I beg you to
think of this matter again. It can bring naught but disaster!''

"There is no more time for pondering. Indeed, we
would do far better to spend our time in prayer, and ask
God to aid us in finding my cousin. Knowing how he
wanders, that in itself may require a small miracle.''

It looked the same as Senet had remembered it. The
valley spread out below was the most beautiful he'd ever
seen—although he knew, in truth, that only he would
think it so. But the land surrounding Castle Lomas was
ripe with crops—wheat, oats, beans—while farther away
it rolled gently, dotted with oak trees. Farther still the trees
grew together more thickly, forming a forest. A small,
constant river meandered through the middle of the valley,
bordering the castle gates on one side. He remembered
fishing in that river, and riding through the oak trees and
forest, and hawking with his father in the fields on cold,
early mornings. His mother had liked to sit atop the castle
walls on pleasant nights and gaze out at the stars, pondering their distances and trying to figure the numbers in
her brilliant mind. His sister, Isabelle, had played with
him in the garden in the inner bailey when they were
children, although she was older than he by some few
years.

How very long ago it seemed, when he had believed
that Castle Lomas was a place of complete security. He
had thought he would live there forever and one day be

lord, that he would bring his own lady there as wife and raise his children in the castle where he himself had been born.

It had gone away so quickly, all of it. The land, the castle, the title—even his parents. His father had found it more difficult to give fealty to his family than to France, the land of his birth, and so had turned traitor when England had sought the French throne. Even after England had secured the throne he'd continued plotting treason, and when the betrayal had been discovered, Lord Lomas had been promptly executed. Castle Lomas, the lands and the title had been stripped away, claimed by the crown as forfeit for the crime. Senet's mother, an English noblewoman, had died soon thereafter, of a broken heart. His sister, Isabelle, had been given into the care of their mother's half brother, Baron Hersell, and had been made to labor as little better than a lowly servant. Senet himself had become a slave to the man who had been fostering and training him for knighthood, but who would no longer countenance to train the son of a traitor. For years Senet had labored as if he were an animal, and had prayed daily for death, finding the thought of it far preferable to the life he had. His father's deeds had taken away everything, even Senet's claim to honor.

When he was sixteen he'd been miraculously rescued by Sir Justin Baldwin, the man who had saved Isabelle from Baron Hersell and taken her as his wife. Sir Justin had given him a home, a family, and had trained him for knighthood. In his selfless, gentle manner he had also given Senet something far more—the courage and the means to fight for his honor again. And Senet had done just that, serving England for the past ten years in its bloody, hopeless war against France, proving his loyalty time and again on the battlefield. Whatever his father had given away to France, Senet had taken back again, not letting himself think too long or too hard on who it was that he killed, or that his enemy might also be of his own, half-French blood.

And now he was nearing the last of it. His final goal. Castle Lomas would be his before the day was out, as it should always have been, and he would have his honor restored in full.

"The king's messenger is returning." Kayne, standing beside him, pointed to where the small figure of a man on horseback moved across the valley floor. "I wonder if Lady Katharine's response was any different today than it has been these past many weeks."

"It matters not," Senet said. "Today is the finish of her wavering, whether she said 'nay' or 'yea.' Today I will have Lomas, either by reason or by force, and tomorrow, by the same reckoning, Lady Katharine will become my wife."

"What I wonder," said Aric, standing on Senet's other side, "is if she's ugly. A woman that age, twenty and one, and unmarried—there must be a reason for it."

"It matters not," Senet repeated. "I've no care for what she looks like, even if she should be an ugly hag. She will be my wife. Tomorrow."

"'Tis indeed a goodly land," Kayne remarked, crossing his arms against his chest. "I can understand why you longed for it. But, God's feet, what a price you've been made to pay."

Aye, he'd paid a price for it, Senet thought, in blood, with his very soul. Nothing would take it from him now.

"I give you good day," a voice behind them greeted, accompanied by the sound of a horse's hooves.

"John, well met." Senet moved to hold that man's

horse as he dismounted. "How is it that you've returned before the king's messenger? Did all go well?"

With a good-natured smile, John Ipris joined his friends at the edge of the hill, his stance leisurely and relaxed compared to the ready manner of his warrior companions.

"I've completed my survey of the castle proper, Senet, if that is what you mean. As to Lady Katharine—from what I overheard of her conversation with Sir William, your suit has not yet met with acceptance. She invoked the name of Lord Hanley again and insisted upon her loyalty to him."

"'Tis an admirable quality in a woman," Kayne said. "Loyalty."

"And not often found in the fairer sex," Aric added somewhat bitterly. "She's a fool to waste the virtue on a dead man."

"If what John says is true, and we will discover the full of it when Sir William arrives, then we must fall upon our next planned course of action."

Kayne sighed. "I had prayed it would not be so. I am heartily weary of killing."

"As am I, my friend," Senet said soberly, "but it will not come to that, if we are careful. John can tell us what weaknesses Lomas possesses, if they are any different from what I have remembered, and we will easily take it. Indeed, I have no wish to bring harm to any in the castle. Certainly not to my future wife or those belonging to her."

Aric chuckled. "'Twould not be the most befitting way to begin a marriage."

"She'll have every opportunity to give way in peace," Senet said. "Just as soon as the attack has begun."

"And what if she will not do so?" Kayne asked.

"Then I'll know what manner of woman I'm taking to wife, will I not? And she," he continued evenly, "will discover what manner of man she shall have for a husband."

Chapter Two

The battle for Lomas was a brief one, in part because it came without warning—so shortly after Sir William had departed—taking Lady Katharine by surprise, and in part because it was so well-executed that none of the men-at-arms had a chance to obey their mistress when she gave the order to defend the castle. Still, Senet admired the effort those same men had put forth before being subdued. Lady Katharine might know little about keeping a castle safe at all times, but she clearly possessed enough intelligence to make certain of the loyalty of those beneath her hand.

No one was killed, a fact for which Senet was fully grateful. Kayne had spoken truly—they were all weary of killing. Ten years of it was sufficient for any man. Kayne, especially, was near the edge of enough.

The fighting men of Lomas were corralled in the inner bailey, looking about in a bewildered way at the smaller force that had so readily bested them. It was proof once again of how invaluable John's remarkable skill in memorizing exact details was. He'd shown them the way to steal into the castle without detection, his facile brain remembering each entrance as if he'd held a map in his hands. But it had ever been thus with John, since Senet had known him. Indeed, his own rescue from slavery had been made possible only because of John's amazing skill.

Apart from their ease of entry into Lomas, there had been the actual fighting that had made the difference in their quick victory. Months it had been since he and Kayne and Aric had fought side by side, and yet it was as if it had merely been days. They each knew what the other would do and how he would act without having to think on it. It was what had given them such strength during all their years in France—an instinct that proved the difference between life and death. The small forces Duke Humphrey had lent Senet to aid in his conquest had merely filled in the missing spaces.

It was over now. Castle Lomas was in his hands again, at last, and Senet stood before the men of the castle and addressed them as rightful master.

"I am Senet Gaillard," he said loudly enough for all to hear. "Some of you will remember my father, Ignace Gaillard, who was the lord of Lomas for many years before he was tried and executed as a traitor to England. I am his heir, and have proven myself loyal to the throne. The crown has therefore declared it right and fitting that I should regain the estate which my family held for four generations before it fell into disgrace. This is my inheritance, given by God and king, and I am your rightful lord. Any man among you who finds it impossible to vow his fealty to me may take his things and leave. Whoever stays will make his pledge of loyalty on the morrow, before the priest and Lady Katharine."

"We have vowed fealty to Lady Katharine!" one of the men shouted, and the others murmured and nodded. "'Tis she whom we serve!"

Senet exchanged a brief look with Kayne, who shook

his head. That soldiers should declare for a woman over a proven fighting man was almost beyond belief.

"And where is your lady, then?" Senet demanded. "I do not see her here, to guide or support you, or even to do her duty and make terms for you. Is this the woman you wish to serve?"

"I am here, Senet Gaillard."

The strong but clearly female voice came from behind, and Senet turned to see the speaker standing on the arched walkway above him, gazing down into the bailey. Their eyes met and held, and he realized, with a distinct certainty, that he was looking upon his future wife. Lady Katharine.

His first thought—an unsettling one—was that she was going to prove a handful. There was a defiance in both her stance and expression that boded no good for either of them. His second thought, even more disturbing, was that she was an uncommonly beautiful woman, tall and elegant and admirably formed. Her eyes were green—he could see the vivid color even from the distance at which he stood, and her hair, which was partly covered by white silk, was a mixture of gold and red. The stubborn set of her lips detracted only slightly from what he perceived to be a heart-shaped face, delicate and lovely and fully at odds with the bold manner in which she held herself. She looked like more of a battle-ready Valkyrie than a soft female. But she wasn't soft—she'd proven that time and again by her actions during the past two months—and it was a fact Senet knew he had best remember if he wished to master the woman. And he would master her. He had not thought, since he was a much younger man, that he would marry, but if he must do so, he would at least be lord of the union.

"Lady Katharine," he said, inclining his head toward

her slightly. "We are honored by your presence. Do you come to speak terms for your men?"

"For all of my people, aye," she stated, and he noticed for the first time the three women standing behind her, each as unfriendly in their manner as she was. "Come to the great hall, Senet Gaillard," Lady Katharine said curtly, making it a command, not an invitation. "I will receive you there."

Chin high, she turned about and strode away, leaving everyone present with the clear impression that she yet held herself as the lady of the castle. Senet allowed the behavior for the moment. It was an insult to him as the new master of Lomas to be treated with such contempt—she'd not even deigned to address him by his knightly title—but he was the one who had time on his side. For Lady Katharine, both time and power had slipped away; Senet could afford to be generous if it would in any way soften her before their marriage. It was a false hope, perhaps, to strive for some measure of peace with his wife. It didn't particularly matter if they remained enemies, but he would rather gain her willingness and friendship than forever be wary in her presence.

"Kayne, Aric," he said, glancing at his friends. "Attend Lady Katharine with me in the hall and we will make our terms. John, go and fetch Clarise and escort her safely to the castle. Bring her to the hall as soon as may be."

"God in Heaven," Ariette murmured as she followed her mistress into the hall. "He's even more handsome than rumored. Did you see his eyes? So blue and clear. I've never seen the like before."

"And his hair!" Magan said, scurrying beside her. "Black as coal, and straight and fine as a woman's. I couldn't help but stare, though I tried not to."

Katharine had made the same attempt, but had found it impossible. Senet Gaillard must have been fashioned by the very devil to appear as he did. His coloring alone made it impossible not to look at him; those icy blue eyes seemed almost inhuman against the black of his hair. But he was very much a real man. A real, large and muscular, thoroughly masculine man. She'd seen the intention in the expression that his handsome face had held. There was no softness in him whatever. He meant to give up nothing, to take what he wished. It was to be battle between them. He'd clearly understood it, just as he had clearly understood her open disdain for him and his men.

Lifting her sweeping skirts with a tight fist as she moved toward the great hall's dais, Katharine said, "His eyes and hair have naught to do with the man. He is our enemy. Don't let his outward appearance cause any of you to forget that. Has the missive gone out to Kieran?"

Dorothea nodded. "The messenger was able to get away before the fighting began—but only just. I fear he will not find Kieran FitzAllen in time. What if Sir Senet should demand that you marry him at once?"

With a graceful gesture, Katharine turned about and sat in the large, thronelike chair that had served as her father's seat of judgment. "He may demand as he wishes, but it will avail him nothing. I do not intend to wed him. And I certainly do not intend to cede Lomas to him. At least not forever."

She couldn't lose Lomas. It was all she had, all she'd ever had that truly belonged to her. And she had managed both the land and the castle successfully, putting the full of herself—all of her heart—into the task. Her father had been Lord Lomas in name only, never having much interest in the details involved in maintaining such an estate, preferring instead to busy himself with the grandeur of his title and fortune. *She* was the one who had labored so hard on Lomas's behalf. *She* was the one who had devoted her every waking hour—and hours when she might have been sleeping, too—to the welfare of the people who had lived beneath her father's hand. She wasn't going to give over all she'd striven for, or the people she'd striven for, to the son of a traitor.

The doors to the great hall opened and Sir Senet Gaillard walked through. He was yet dirty and sweat-soaked from the battle, and carried in one hand his sword and in the other his helmet, as if he were still ready to fight. He advanced toward her unsmiling, and Katharine felt a strange, unbidden clutching sensation in her heart, something akin to fear, she thought, although she wasn't afraid of him in the least. She forced the odd feeling away and made herself meet his gaze directly. Walking behind him were two other men, one as blond and fair as day and the other as dark and formidable as Senet Gaillard was, though far less appealing in face.

They stopped directly before her. Senet Gaillard alone took one step closer.

"Lady Katharine," he said, and again she felt that strange sensation thrumming deep within. "As you have seen fit to ignore the edicts of the king's regents to receive us peacefully, I have come in the only manner left me. Having taken Castle Lomas by force and possessing it fully, I make my formal claim to the land, the castle and the title, as well as to all those people, moneys and chattel belonging to them. Including," he said more slowly, "yourself."

What on earth was wrong with her? Katharine wondered. It was impossible that she would be affected simply because a man was so handsome. Indeed, she had known many men who were far fairer to gaze upon than Senet

Gaillard, yet not one of them had produced as much as a quickened breath. The sight of Senet Gaillard, the sound of his voice, affected her horribly. Not only was her heart pounding in her chest, but she had somehow suddenly gone dumb. All of the biting words she would have said faded away. She struggled to speak, even to think of how to answer him, and felt utterly foolish.

He stood where he was, waiting, finally arching one eyebrow upward questioningly.

"Do you concede, my lady?"

"In the matter of the castle, I have little choice," she said at last, striving to make her voice calm and steady. "You have taken it by force, without due consideration for any of my requests for peace. For the time being, I concede it to you. Howbeit, as I have already informed Duke Humphrey, I am betrothed to be married, and will honor the promise I have already given Lord Hanley in the matter of marriage. As I understand that you cannot attain Castle Lomas, the lands or title without a marriage between us, I have faith that you will find your rule here to be of very short duration. If such as that appeals to you, please be content to pursue your pretense until the day of the arrival of my worthy betrothed. After he has come, I pray you will leave Lomas peacefully and with respect for what the law holds as true in these matters.

"In the meantime, my ladies and I will abide above-stairs, out of your way. I ask that you and your men leave us unmolested, in peace and privacy, as your knightly vows will require of you. I appeal to your knightly status, as well, in your dealings with my people, including the servants of this castle, whom I demand be treated with forbearance and kindness. I will not take it lightly should one of them come to any harm while you play out the farce you have brought upon us. That is all I have to say."

She rose from the chair. "My ladies and I will leave you now to enjoy the temporary victory you have attained."

"Nay," Sir Senet said. "You will not go. I have heard you out, Lady Katharine. You will now allow me the same courtesy."

"I allow you nothing," Katharine told him coldly.

His somber gaze never wavered. "Then I will force you to it, my lady, if that is your preference."

Her eyes narrowed. "You are truly your father's son, Senet Gaillard. I had heard it was so. Is it your intention to rule Lomas with threats?"

"It is my intention to be lord here. The manner in which I rule will be determined, in large, by you, Lady Katharine. I have said that you will listen to me, and you will. I would prefer not to use force. Be seated again."

Katharine lifted her chin. "Nay, I will stand. Speak what you must."

He drew in a long, taut breath. Katharine could see a muscle twitching in the tight set of his beard-stubbled jaw.

"I would that you sit."

Katharine strove to keep from fisting her hands. She was so filled with anger at the beastly man that she felt as if flames must surely be about to spout from the top of her head. How dare he speak to her as if she must obey him! She was the mistress of the castle, and he nothing better than a false usurper.

"My ears," she replied tersely, "work just as well whether I sit or stand, Senet Gaillard." One of his companions, the handsome, blond-headed man, cleared his throat in an obvious effort to keep from laughing. Senet Gaillard gave him a sharp, quelling look. Katharine straightened her shoulders to stand taller. "I am not so poor a maiden as to wilt beneath the force of your words, or those of any man. Speak, and then leave my ladies and me in peace.''

She thought she heard a weary sigh emanate from his stern mouth. He set the tip of his sword on the edge of his booted foot and relaxed his posture as if he were, indeed, most weary.

''Very well, Lady Katharine. I'll speak to you plainly. Lord Hanley has been presumed dead these past two years, and your betrothal to him, in the eyes of the throne, the church and the law, is therefore made void. As the lord of Lomas, I have been commanded to take you as wife to make certain of your future, also to protect and keep you. We will wed on the morrow. I advise you to make yourself ready. The ceremony will be performed after morning mass. Afterward, your men will vow their fealty to me as their lord, and to you as their lord's wife.''

Her heart began to beat more painfully in her chest, and Katharine lowered her gaze briefly, struggling to maintain at least an outward composure. The man clearly meant what he said, and looked fully capable of carrying out every word. If she showed the slightest weakness before him now, she'd be finished before she'd even started.

The doors to the great hall opened and several armed soldiers entered, followed by a tall, slender man whom Katharine had seen only hours before in the company of the king's regent, Sir William, when he had come to deliver Duke Humphrey's missive. She had assumed that he was one of Sir William's men, but it was suddenly clear that he was one of Senet Gaillard's minions. He approached the dais where Katharine sat, leading on his arm a young, very beautiful woman who appeared to be rather frightened by her surroundings. Senet Gaillard turned at the girl's approach and reached out a hand to draw her near.

"Here you are, Clarise. Come. Don't be afraid." To Katharine he said, "Lady Katharine, I make known to you Mademoiselle Rouveau, a gentlewoman beneath my care. I desire that she be given an appropriate chamber and a maid to attend her needs. At once."

Katharine didn't think she'd ever been so angry in all her life, and trembled with rage.

"How pleasing your proposal is, Senet Gaillard. You speak of marriage in one breath and present your whore to me in the next! Do you dare to bring your leman here and ask *me* to take care of her? You may take yourself off to the devil, sir! You, your men and your woman with you!" It was bad enough that he had taken her castle by force and meant to take her by the same means, but to so openly humiliate her was beyond belief!

The beast only stood where he was, frowning at her in a calm, albeit bemused, manner.

"She is not my leman," he said, "but a lady of gentle birth. I will not have her insulted or mistreated, certainly not by my own wife. While she lives beneath my hand, you will treat her with every respect."

Katharine had had enough. She speared the frightened girl with a look of thorough disgust, almost gratified to see the shaking creature cringe behind Senet Gaillard's muscular form.

"If I treat her to anything at all, Senet Gaillard, 'twill be pity, for she appears to be much in need of it. Keep her out of my way if you wish her well."

"I do not intend to do so," he told her. "I mean to give her over into your care. You will do as I have said and make her comfortable here. It is your duty as my wife."

"I am *not* your wife," she said from between set teeth. God's feet, but she hated the man! On the day he was thrown off of her lands she would give the biggest celebration Lomas had ever seen.

At that, he at last began to look aggravated. Lifting the tip of his sword from his boot, he took a step toward her.

"But you will be on the morrow," he told her softly, for her ears alone. "I had hoped for matters to go well between us, Lady Katharine, to make a friend rather than an enemy of the woman I take to wife. That is still my desire. Is it yours?"

"What I desire," she began hotly, "above all things, is for you to go to—"

"Because I should very much dislike having to bow you to obedience," he interrupted smoothly, "and would advise that you instead offer it freely. You will not like the taming to be had at my hands, Lady Katharine. I promise you that. If you make peace with me, however, I equally promise that you shall never come to regret it. I repay honor with honor."

"And dishonor with dishonor?" she asked tartly.

He inclined his head. "If that is the way you will have it. Either way, you will be my wife, and I will be the lord of Lomas."

She was silent for a long moment, meeting his gaze fully. At last, her features softened, as did the posture with which she held herself. She lowered her lashes and attempted to look meek, although she was certain she had never felt the emotion before.

"Of course, my lord," she said finally, keeping her voice low and feminine, purposefully deferential. "It will be as you say. I admit that I do not wish to marry you, or any man who is not of my choosing, but there is clearly no other course for me but to accept the situation. If you will but be patient in allowing me time to become used to the fate that has befallen me, I will consider it a great kindness. I have not been used to living beneath the command of any man.'' She lifted her eyes to his. ''Including my father. I have ruled here as mistress since I was but fourteen years. It is not my nature to be...obedient.''

He appeared to consider this, and at last gave a slight nod. ''I do not desire a dog for a wife, nor a slave, but only for you to know that I will be master here. In every way. So long as you give me no cause to do otherwise, you will be treated by myself and my people with every respect due to the lady of the castle. Indeed, save that you will have a husband to answer to, I do not intend that your life at Lomas should change overmuch. I will be patient with you.''

''You are good, my lord,'' she said, trying not to choke on the words. ''I am most grateful. Forgive, I pray, the lack of welcome you have received at Lomas. I shall strive to remedy the situation at once. Be pleased to make yourself and your men comfortable.'' With a hand she indicated the entire hall, where chairs and tables were available for many. ''I shall instruct my captain of arms to answer to you directly.''

''He will answer to me as his lord,'' Senet Gaillard stated.

''Yes,'' said Katharine. ''Of course. And I shall have my servants lay out food and drink sufficient to refresh your forces. As to your own comfort, my lord, a suitable chamber will be prepared.''

''The lord's chamber will be made ready,'' he corrected. ''I will abide there.''

Katharine had to draw in a slow breath to maintain her appearance of calm. To think of such a man occupying the chamber next to her own renewed her outrage altogether. But when she spoke, the words were carefully polite and contained.

"It shall be as you have said, my lord. Give me but an hour, and I shall send a servant to escort you there."

"There is no need." He sounded almost amused. "I was born at Lomas, and remember very well where my father's chamber is. Do you abide in the mistress's chamber that adjoins it, my lady?"

She understood the intent that lay behind the question, and felt her skin heating. "Yes," she replied tightly.

He regarded her steadily. "It is well. I will leave you now with the request that you see to Mademoiselle Rouveau's needs directly. Her comfort is to be your utmost concern."

Katharine's jaw ached from the force with which she made herself keep silent. The tiny creature who was still cowering behind Senet Gaillard dared to peek up at her, revealing a face that was delicate and beautiful, hair that was the color of dark honey and eyes that were large and blue. Katharine felt like a clumsy, ugly giant before the girl's dainty perfection.

"Certainly, my lord," she said at last, even managing to smile at him. "You will be well pleased, I vow. Everything shall be just as you wish."

He moved even nearer, and Katharine resisted the urge to step back. He was very tall, she noted, as well as muscular. He even made *her* feel small, which, considering her unfashionable height, was no simple feat.

"We will do well together, Lady Katharine," he said softly, and she felt again that unbidden sensation deep in her belly. "I shall repay you tenfold for your kindness and obedience. I vow this before God." Reaching out suddenly, he grasped her hand before she could pull it away. Lifting it slowly to his lips, he gently kissed her fingers, never moving his remarkable blue gaze from her face. "This marriage is not of our choosing, but we can make of it an agreeable union. You'll never regret being my wife. I'll make certain of it.''

He released her and turned away, striding out of the hall with his men at his heels, leaving Katharine staring at the place where he at last disappeared. Only the girl remained, standing some feet away and watching the women on the dais with such pathetic trembling that Katharine felt a reluctant leniency toward her.

A hand touched her arm, and Katharine turned. "What was that about?" Ariette whispered as Dorothea and Magan gathered close. "I've never seen you act so meek and mild before.''

Katharine smiled. "Pray God you never see such again,'' she said in a low voice. "But I'll do whatever I must to save Lomas, even if it is to act the fool. Don't forget that it is the man I marry who will gain Lomas, not the man who merely takes it by force. If all goes well, I shall be a wedded woman within the week, but Senet Gaillard, for his every effort, will not be my husband.''

"But, my lady—!''

"Hush!" Katharine demanded in a whisper. "We cannot speak safely here. And there is much to prepare for. Come, let us play out this farce as long as we must to keep Senet Gaillard from discovering the truth.'' With a welcoming smile fixed on her face, she turned again to face the waiting French girl. "Mademoiselle Rouveau, be pleased to come with my ladies and me.'' Katharine began to descend the dais stairs. "You will be weary from your journey and desirous of rest.'' She extended a hand to have the girl follow her. "Come. We will have you comfortable shortly, I vow.''

Chapter Three

From the long table set on the dais, Senet looked about him with approval. Lady Katharine had somehow done the impossible in the five short hours since he'd spoken with her, which was proof, he realized, of just how capable a female she was. The great hall of Castle Lomas had rapidly been prepared for a feast, and both food and drink of amazing quantity and fine quality had been set out for all to enjoy. That she had managed all this with such short notice was a miracle in and of itself. He'd assumed that he and his men would be fortunate to enjoy a thin stew and bitter ale. This, instead, was just the sort of feast that a woman might spend weeks preparing to honor the arrival of her future husband, in celebration of their coming marriage.

Musicians strolled among the impatiently waiting feasters, singing merry tunes to both entertain and appease until Lady Katharine and her ladies should arrive and signal that the festivities could properly begin. Servants continued to bring trays out of the kitchens, bearing a variety of meats, breads, vegetables and cheeses, so much food that Senet could hardly imagine it all being eaten, even by the hundreds of hungry people sitting at the tables spread out across the hall. Where had it all come from? He couldn't remember Castle Lomas being so prosperous as this when his father had reigned there as lord.

Seated in the place of honor at the head of the table, surrounded by his men, Senet felt a deep sense of gratitude regarding his future wife's conduct, and an equal appreciation for the grace with which she had accepted defeat. She'd clearly arranged the grand feast as a way of making apology for her earlier behavior, and he would not only accept the gesture, but publicly honor her for it, just as soon as she and her ladies arrived to take their places on the dais. He would gift her with his deepest bow, he decided, and then, before seating her beside him, he would take her hand in his and lift them, clasped, for all those assembled to see. It would be a gesture of their coming union, and of the deep respect he bore for her as one who had not only managed the lands and castle well in the past, but who would, with him, continue to do so in future.

The idea of ruling Lomas jointly with Lady Katharine pleased him more than he'd thought it would. Until this day, his only object had been to regain what was rightfully his, but now, having it again, claiming his lordship over Lomas, he realized how unfit he truly was to manage the estate. A great many years had passed since his father had taught him about the duties of being a lord, and although he believed with time he would regain the sense of them, he was grateful that Katharine would serve not only as his wife, but also as his guide.

Such a wife she would make! he thought for perhaps the hundredth time since setting sight on her. So proud, she was. So intelligent. And, yes, stubborn and haughty, too. She was like a wild falcon that needed a firm and knowing hand to master her—to bring out the best in her.

He'd already proved that he was more than capable of mastering her this afternoon, when a measure of firmness had caused her to choose the better course between her dangerous pride and the wisdom of being reasonable. Life with Lady Katharine would never be dull, he thought with a smile, sipping at the wine in his goblet. For that, he was strangely glad.

He had not thought to marry. Not for more than ten years, when his heart had learned that it was far better to shut itself off from love than to be vulnerable to the pain that love, and its losses, could bring.

Just thinking of his beautiful Odelyn, even now, brought grief welling up, despite the years that had passed since her death and his fervent struggle to press the memories away.

She had been very different from the kind of female that Lady Katharine was. Odelyn had been sweet and gentle and giving. God alone knew how her tenderness and patience had worked to bring him out of the darkness that had been the legacy of his years of slavery. If not for her, Senet had no doubt that he'd yet be living in that darkness. He'd built all his dreams about her, every plan for the future, and when he had lost her everything had faded away to darkness again. But it had been a different sort of darkness, for at least he had her memory to light his way. A distant illumination tempered the shadows—distant, aye, but there all the same, always there, and it was for that lone sweet, ghostlike presence that he'd pressed on.

Katharine Malthus was nothing at all like Odelyn. There was nothing gentle or sweet about her, or even tender, at least not insofar as he'd yet encountered. Lady Katharine would have frightened his delicate Odelyn with her height and severe manner, even with her stark beauty.

But Odelyn had been so young when she'd died, only just out of childhood. As he'd been. Katharine was a woman full grown, in face, form and clearly in mind. A woman he wanted in every way that a man could want a woman. The knowledge brought him no little discomfort. He'd not expected to experience such…outright lust for the woman he took to wife. Lady Katharine deserved better from him than that. He'd desired Odelyn, but had always practiced a certain restraint with her. Restraint, with Katharine, disappeared. She was far too challenging to inspire such feelings.

"Will she appear any time within the next fortnight, do you think?" Aric, sitting beside him, muttered. "It's been over an hour that we've sat here and waited."

"Having spent the past several hours laboring on our behalf to arrange this feast," Senet said, "as well as making our chambers ready and directing that pallets be set out for the men, it may be expected that Lady Katharine and her women require some few minutes to make themselves ready."

He was looking forward to seeing her again, he realized with some surprise. Anticipation was foreign to him, but she was a lovely, mysterious creature, and he wanted to know more of her. To speak to her, and see if he might coax her to smile at him again, as she had briefly done earlier.

"Calm yourself," Kayne advised Aric, sitting on that man's other side. "Ladies are given to much concern over their appearance, especially in such times as these. Lady Katharine is to be wed on the morrow, after all, and will wish to present herself to her future husband in her very best raiment and looks."

"She doesn't require much help for that," John Ipris put in. "She's remarkably beautiful, is she not? Not in the least an ugly hag." He gave Senet a teasing grin. "You're a fortunate man, Lord Lomas."

"Hah," Aric said. "A beauty she may be, but her tongue is sharp enough to slice a man in two. I don't envy you in the least, Senet."

Clarise, sitting beside John, leaned forward to say, in English, rather than French, "But she was very kind to me, m'lor, after you had gone. Lady Katharine and her ladies. They were all very...happy, *oui? Très joyeuses.*"

"There you have it," Kayne said. "The lady of the castle has clearly decided to make the best of the situation, just as you have done, Senet. All will be well."

"Just as soon as the lady decides to make an appearance," Aric said irately. "God's feet, Senet, send someone to tell her to make haste. You're master here, now. Will you let her keep you waiting so long and looking a fool?"

Senet supposed it would do no harm to send one of the servants to request that Katharine hurry to present herself. The feast could not properly begin until the blessing had been given, and the priest could not give the blessing until the lady of the castle was in her place. Lifting a finger, he beckoned a serving maid to attend him.

"Go up to my lady's chamber," he instructed, "and give her my compliments. Tell her that I desire she join us within the quarter hour."

"M'lor?" Clarise leaned forward again, looking past John. "M'lady is not in her chamber."

Senet and the men surrounding him all turned to look at her. Clarise blushed hotly beneath their steady regard.

"I went to speak with her," she explained slowly, striving to make her English perfect, "before coming to the hall. And the chamber, it was empty. I think she must be with her ladies." She was thoughtful a moment, before saying, "I mean to say, in the chambers of the ladies?"

"I understand, Clarise," Senet told her. "You're certain she was not in her own chambers?"

Clarise shook her head. "I called for her. There was no one, m'lor. I thought it very strange, for there were many clothes, lying all places...*partout, oui?* It was a great disorder."

"I don't think that she means Lady Katharine's simply a poor housekeeper," John said, turning a wary gaze upon his friends.

Senet was already on his feet, with Kayne and Aric following him. Racing up the stairs he told himself that he was wrong, that she was merely somewhere in the castle, in one of her ladies' chambers, just as Clarise had said, but his heart knew the truth even before he pushed open Katharine's chamber door.

Breathing hard, he took in the sight before him. It was exactly as Clarise had described it. There were clothes everywhere. Fine clothes, and shoes, too, as if the women had been in far too much of a hurry to hide their escape.

"Where could they have gone?" Aric said, surveying the chamber through steely eyes.

"They can't have left the castle," Kayne muttered. "There were guards at every door. It would have been impossible for that many women to slip out. And certainly not Lady Katharine, with her great beauty. There is no place where she might go unnoticed."

Senet walked slowly across the room, to a tapestry that covered one wall. Reaching up with both hands, he yanked the elegant cloth from the wall, exposing the hidden door.

"Lomas is ridden with tunnels, secret and mazelike," he said in a low voice. "She must have forgotten that I know this castle far better than she, or anyone else, could." He turned to look at his friends. "Tell Sir Alain to get the horses and men ready, Aric." A hard, grim smile that they knew well formed on his lips. "We're going hunting."

The Bull and Dog was, to Katharine's mind, a thoroughly sorry refuge, but it was likely the only roof they'd be able to buy to cover their heads for the night. She'd paid the innkeeper dearly to give them the lone private room the dwelling possessed, as well as to put a guard over their horses until morning. It was small comfort set against the smells and vulgar sounds the inn's patrons filled the place with, but it was better than sleeping in the rain, which had begun to pour an hour earlier.

In the filthy, tiny chamber that the inn's only whore had vacated for their use, Katharine and her ladies sat on a single pallet and tried mightily to eat, but the greasy stew the innkeeper's wife had brought them was difficult to identify and harder to stomach.

"Is it squirrel, perhaps?" Magan asked, lifting out of her bowl a hunk of something that still had hair on it.

"Let us pray that it is," Dorothea replied. "Squirrel would be far preferable to what I think it is."

Ariette let out a sudden scream and threw her bowl across the room, splaying the contents across the wall and floor.

"What in the name of all heaven—!" Katharine was across the room at once, peering at the discarded bowl and its spilled contents in the dim candlelight light before lifting a foot to squash what was crawling about among the stew's other, more lifeless ingredients.

"I'm sorry!" Ariette cried, clutching her cloak tightly about herself. "It was *moving*."

"'Twas only a roach," Katharine said calmly, returning to sit beside the other women. "I've killed it, though God knows what good it will do us. The room is crawling with them. And other vermin."

Exchanging glances, Magan and Dorothea put their bowls aside and discreetly scooted away from them.

Katharine set her hands on her indrawn knees and leaned her head against the wall. "How weary I am," she murmured. "I realize this is no fine place, but at least we are dry, and so are the horses."

"Yes," Magan said, "we must be thankful for that."

"Yes," Ariette agreed quietly, without enthusiasm. "Although 'tis cold in here as it is out of doors."

"We'll be fortunate if those leering brutes in the tavern don't come bursting in all together, intent upon the most lecherous sort of evil," Dorothea said. "They were loud enough in their thoughts when we entered this place."

"Oh, my lady, will they?" Magan asked with open fear. "They did seem so very rough and crude."

"If they do," Katharine said from behind hands that rubbed at her face, "we'll fend them off. You have your daggers, do you not? Don't hesitate to make use of them, for I assure you I'll have mine well blooded before one of the wretches can so much as set a finger to me. And if they do attempt to enter this chamber, 'twill be for our gold, most like, rather than our persons."

"That is even worse," Dorothea said dryly. "We need our gold far more dearly than we need our virtue. *If* we're to make our way without starving to death," she added when her companions looked at her.

"I think this a complete madness," Ariette stated, drawing her cloak still more about her. "We'll never find Kieran FitzAllen, and if Sir Senet should find us..." She left the dire thought unfinished.

"We *will* find Kieran," Katharine said insistently. "If not us, then the messenger who left Lomas will do so, and then Kie will come looking for us. Somehow we'll come across each other. It must be so."

"You try to convince yourself, my lady," Dorothea said, "but if Sir Senet finds us first, we'll be fortunate to live through the beatings we'll be given."

"I know," Katharine admitted morosely. The idea of running away from Lomas had seemed such a good one earlier, in the light of day and in the face of her fury at Senet Gaillard, but now, sitting in this dank hovel with the prospect of a long and sleepless night looming ahead—and a longer, difficult journey, as well—it wasn't quite so appealing. "But that son of a traitor—that *usurper*—will not find us so easily. The feast will delay him from discovering that we've gone, and the rain—thank a merciful God for it—will wash away the tracks we've made."

Dorothea shook her head. "That won't stop a man like Senet Gaillard."

Katharine thought of the man, of his ice-blue eyes and black hair. Of the hard face that had been without emotion after the victory he'd won at Lomas.

"No," she said softly, "I cannot think it will. I admit that my scheme to get away from him is perhaps a foolish one. I should never have let you all come with me."

"We would never have let you go alone," Ariette told her.

"Oh, no, dear lady," Magan agreed. "How could we forsake you in such a desperate time? I do not care what Sir Senet may do to us. Truly."

Poor little Magan, Katharine thought with affection, setting an arm about the trembling girl's shoulders. She was far too young for such a frightening adventure.

"But I care, Magan," she said. "And if, may God forbid it, he should find us, you must be obedient to his command and let me draw his wrath down upon my own head."

"No," Dorothea said firmly. "We are not such poor friends as to desert you."

"'Tis not right, Doro, for any of you to suffer for my sake. I am older and stronger, and the lady of Lomas, besides. You will do as I say and let me handle Senet Gaillard in my own manner. I do not ask it. I command it. But we will have no worry for that now. Let us rest as we may this night and pray that our journey to discover Kieran FitzAllen finds success."

They huddled together, sitting upon the pallet with their backs against the wall, and fell silent, not daring to lie down for fear of the vermin that crawled about the place. The loud din made by the patrons in the tavern continued unabated for hours, eventually lulling them to sleep. Katharine struggled to remain awake, to make some kind of guard for them against intrusion, but exhaustion overtook her and she drifted into uneasy dreams of Lomas, and of cold blue eyes in a hard, starkly handsome face.

His voice brought her awake with a start and a gasp. She flung her head up too quickly, striking the mortared wall and sending a shock of pain all the way down to her sleep-numbed toes.

"Search the tavern." The command was loud against the clattering of boots and swords, of tables being overturned and dishes breaking on the floor.

It was yet dark outside, and so cold that Katharine's skin burned with it. The lone candle that had earlier given them light had long since burned to naught, but the moment the door was flung open they would be discovered.

"Up!" she whispered fiercely, shaking the others.

"Up! Magan! Ariette! Doro—" Her hand searched about in the dark for the third girl. "Doro!"

She wasn't there, Katharine realized with growing panic as the searching men grew closer and louder.

"Oh!" Magan cried, scrambling to her feet as Katharine pulled her up from the floor. "It's Sir Senet!"

"God save us!" Ariette murmured with pure fright. "Where's Doro?"

"Gone," Katharine said, quickly feeling for the leather pouches that she'd tied about her waist. "Out that window, most like. And taken half the gold. The fool! She's gone in search of Kieran on her own. Ariette—" she pushed the older girl toward Magan "—go with Senet Gaillard and his men. Give them no trouble." She began to climb out the window. "Take care of Magan."

"But, my lady—!"

Katharine was out the window just as the door burst open. She heard one of Sir Senet's men shouting, "My lord!" and waited to hear no more. She started running, headlong, into the dark forest, picking up her skirts to race as fast as she could away from the sounds of Ariette and Magan screaming. He wouldn't hurt them, she told herself. He wouldn't. He'd taken Lomas without killing even one of her men, without causing any great injuries— surely he wouldn't beat two innocent women for crimes that were not their own.

She was the one he wanted—no, needed. Because without her he couldn't have Lomas. Now it came down to which of them wanted it more. She would run all night if she had to. She would find Kieran if she had to cover every square inch of England on foot, alone.

The woods were filled with a fine, chilling mist that made it hard to find her way, and caused each desperate breath to ache like a frozen knife plunging in her chest.

She stopped, after several minutes of panicked flight, and rested against a tree, panting harshly, trying to decide which direction to go. She was cold, so cold, and wet from the fog and mud. All around her the trees dripped with the rain that had fallen. In the distance she heard shouts, the sounds of horses whinnying and stomping. She wondered how Ariette and Magan had fared at the hands of Senet Gaillard and his men, and sent up a silent prayer that all was well.

Dozens of horses drew nearer in the dark, their hooves muffled in the mud. And then there were voices. Men's voices. *His* voice, above all the others. Katharine pushed from the tree and started running again, cursing the darkness that made it so difficult to see her course.

"Kayne!"

It was Senet Gaillard, she realized with panic. Right behind her. She began running faster.

"Here!" a man's voice shouted in reply, coming from Katharine's right.

She veered left, stumbling and crying out, then picked herself up and threw herself onward. Suddenly she heard muddy footsteps, and a man appeared out of the mist. The blond man who had stood beside Senet Gaillard that afternoon. Kayne.

"Lady Katharine!" he shouted, putting his arms out as if to catch her. Katharine stopped and stared, gasping for air. He was panting, too, moving toward her more slowly. "My lady," he began in an unsteady tone. Katharine ducked her head and rammed him with all her strength, sending him flying backward into the mud. The look of utter surprise on his face would have made her laugh if she'd had the leisure. As it was, she jumped past his inert body and ran on into the darkness. But her freedom was short-lived. Within steps she heard Senet Gaillard behind her, cursing as he closed upon her, and then his hand was on the collar of her surcoat, dragging her to a stop. Katharine whirled about with a fist, striking him in the face, nearly gaining her freedom again. But he held on and dragged her, struggling, into the mud.

"Foolish...woman," he managed to growl against the flailing blows she landed.

"I will *not*," she panted, "wed you!" A particularly strong slap stung against the side of his face, almost knocking him away.

That was when she realized he'd been striving to be gentle with her, for all at once her hands were clasped in a viselike grip and pressed into the mud, and her struggles stilled almost instantly by the hard strength of his body, which he nearly smothered her with, lying atop her. She felt unutterably stupid, as helpless as a child, and could have laughed at how she might ever have believed she could fight her way free.

He brought his face near her own and spoke in a tone that was full angry. "I offered you peace. I would have taken you for my wife with every respect owed to the lady of Lomas. You have made the offer forfeit. Now, Lady Katharine, I have hunted and caught you fairly, and you are my captive. I owe you nothing."

"Bastard!" she snarled. "Nothing is just what I want of you! Son of a traitor!"

"Prisoners do not speak in such a manner to their captors. Not without punishment. That I will save for later. For now—" He sat up, dragging her with him. "Kayne!" he shouted into the darkness.

"Here." Kayne came walking slowly through the mist, and several other men appeared as well.

"You have taken no harm?" Senet asked his friend.

"Only to my pride," Kayne replied with an embarrassed laugh. "And my clothes are muddied, but nothing more."

"Bind our prisoner's hands. She cannot be trusted."

Kayne rubbed the back of his blond head, hesitating. "Senet…"

"Bind them!" Senet commanded, pulling a knife from the belt at his waist. He roughly grabbed the hem of Katharine's surcoat and, ignoring her cry of fury, cut away a strip of cloth. "Here." He tossed the cloth to the other man, who had knelt behind Katharine and taken her hands. While he tied them together, Senet cut another, longer strip. He dangled it in front of Katharine's face. "Shall I use this to silence you? Or will you keep still of your own accord? For I tell you now nothing will anger me so well this night as any more of your foolish prate."

"Use it," she dared with ill-concealed hatred, "and prove to my people what manner of man you are. Traitor. *Usurper.*"

His icy eyes held no emotion as he deftly set the gag about her lips, tying it securely so that she could say no more.

"Those are better titles than the one you now bear, my lady," he told her softly, close to her face. "Titles you have taken of your own will. You are my prisoner, Lady Katharine." His cold gaze held her own. "My captive, and, by God above, I vow that I shall treat you accordingly."

Chapter Four

He carried her back to Lomas tossed over the bow of his saddle, ignoring her squirming and muffled complaints. After a while she subsided, and the only thing he worried about was what deviousness she might be plotting. But perhaps Lady Katharine was too weary for any further adventures, for they arrived at the castle before dawn without mishap.

She renewed her struggles when he lifted her from his horse and carried her past the many servants who were yet awake and waiting for their return. They stared, murmuring, as he strode by them and started up the stairs. When he passed Katharine's chamber and continued upward, her eyes widened and she made a long protest of, "Mmm-mmm!"

"That is the chamber for the lady of the castle," he told her, understanding her complaint. "When you are the lady of the castle, as my wife, you will return to it. In the meantime, you will be kept in the north tower." She began to struggle in earnest, and squealed furiously beneath her bonds. "Aye, you understand me well," he said with satisfaction, hefting her wet, muddy person higher in his arms with ease. "There are no tunnels there from which you may escape. How foolish you are, Katharine, to think I would not find you out. I know every secret Lomas possesses, and probably many that you've yet to discover.''

The chamber he took her to was almost as dark and dismal as the one at The Bull and Dog, although certainly cleaner. Katharine had never allowed any part of the castle to be let run with vermin. He deposited her on the stone floor, which was barren even of straw, and, without a word, turned about and walked out, locking the door behind him.

Katharine lay in the darkness, too exhausted and miserable to be angry. He had left her to die, to lay upon the cold floor in wet clothing without heat or comfort, to freeze in the chill of early dawn. He'd not even removed her bonds, or the gag about her lips. She would die in silence, immobile.

She was almost too frozen to think, but she tried to send up silent prayers for Dorothea, Magan and Ariette. God alone could keep Dorothea now, wherever she was. It had been beyond foolishness for her to go off alone as she had, but Katharine could both admire and love her for it, and be thankful for the friendship that had caused her to attempt such a dangerous task. A woman traveling without escort on England's roads was in no way safe. Robbers, thieves and worse would be glad of such easy prey—although Doro, cunning and brave, would certainly make any attack of her person a difficult chore.

In a way, Katharine was more afraid for Ariette, and even more for Magan. Ariette was tiny and delicate, and could so easily be harmed, while Magan was young and readily frightened. When they had left The Bull and Dog, Magan had been tucked under the arm of the dark, hugely muscular Sir Aric as if she were a child's doll. She'd

looked utterly terrified, and Sir Aric, scowling and unfriendly, had done nothing to reassure her. Poor, dear Magan. Katharine could only imagine how difficult the return
to Lomas had been for her in the company of such a
brutish man. Ariette had fared somewhat better, riding
with Sir Kayne who, unlike his friends, appeared to take
his knightly vows seriously in being courteous to ladies.

What would happen to them if she died? Katharine
wondered. Would Sir Senet treat them well? And the people of Lomas? He might know the secrets of the castle
itself, but how could such as that benefit the castlefolk
and townspeople? He wouldn't know about the agreement
she'd worked out between the dye merchant and the
town's weavers; it was so uncertain that one wrong word
would have the two sides warring again. And what of the
new children in the convent? Senet Gaillard would not
know of all that she'd promised to the tanner in exchange
for leather for shoes for them, or to the cobbler for making
them. The children *had* to have new shoes before winter.
She'd promised them—indeed, all of her people—so
much. They depended on her, day by day, to keep everything moving along, if not smoothly, at least in the right
direction. To make certain there was food enough in the
winter, and labor enough to bring in the harvest each fall.
And pleasure faires in the spring. So many matters were
beneath her command. So many things that Senet Gaillard
would let go by, just as her father had done, while he
played at being lord of the castle.

Exhaustion made it impossible to keep her eyelids
open, and Katharine at last relented and let them drift shut.
Sleep pressed heavily, a dark, alluring blanket, but before
she could give way to it the door was unlocked and
pushed open. Light spilled into the room, along with
voices.

"Bring everything in. The pallet goes there by the wall. Make a fire in the hearth. Quickly."

The chamber came alight and alive as what seemed like a dozen or more men entered.

Sir Kayne knelt beside her, concern filling his handsome face. "Lady Katharine."

"Leave her to me," Senet Gaillard said curtly. "And save your pity for Mistress Dorothea, who for the sake of this lady has exposed herself to every manner of danger. If John doesn't find her soon, she may not live to see Lomas again. Now, be pleased to leave me with my lovely betrothed. Aric will need your help with the other women."

Sir Kayne set a warm, comforting hand briefly against Katharine's cold cheek. "John will find her, my lady," he murmured, then stood and, with the other men, left the room.

Katharine heard the door shutting, then Senet Gaillard's footsteps moving back toward where she lay. She was shivering too hard to protest when he pulled her into a sitting position.

"Kayne means to reassure you," he said as he cut her bonds away. She gasped when the gag about her mouth fell to the floor. "But it is his misfortune to be possessed of a kind nature."

"He is," she said, fighting the cold pain that gripped her, "a ch-chivalrous kn-knight."

When her hands were released she nearly fell forward on her face. Senet's arm circled her waist, pulling her up.

"And you think I am not?"

"Wh-what will h-happen to D-Dorothea?"

He hesitated, then said, "John will find her, if any man can do so. He possesses a rare gift for finding the lost, for finding anything or anyone. I make no promises, but you may be easy at least that all is being done that can be done for Mistress Dorothea's sake.''

"Th-thank God."

"He will certainly be the one to thank, should she survive your thoughtless care," he said, leaning her back until he could reach the laces of her surcoat.

"No," she protested weakly, trying to push at the knife as he began to cut her dress away.

"You wish to lie in wet clothing and take ill?" He put the knife aside in order to pull the dress down her arms.

"Aye!" she said defiantly, forcing the words past chattering teeth. "M-mayhap I will be f-fortunate enough to die—p-p-please God—and be free of you! L-leave my chemise!"

"It is too wet. And filthy." He began to strip it off, as well.

"No!" She was shaking violently from both cold and shame. "P-please."

He paused. She could feel his indecision.

"Please," she whispered.

He swung her up into his arms and carried her to the fire, setting her before it and saying, "Can you sit while I fetch a blanket?"

She nodded. But her muscles were not as convinced. The moment he let go of her she rolled down to the floor and lay there, helpless and weak as a babe, until he returned and pulled her up to sit.

"Sleep will do you good," he muttered, setting the blanket about her shoulders. "Now you shall have your modesty while I rid you of this foul garment. Don't squawk at me, woman. I'm not the one who sent you out into the mud and rain, whatever you see fit to tell yourself. Hold still." He took the back of her chemise and, with an easy motion, tore it apart. Katharine made a sound of protest, but he ignored it and pulled the garment from her body.

"Now," he said, tossing the ruined chemise away, "to wash you."

She was too weary to argue when he lay her down once more, still wrapped in her blanket and near the warmth of the fire. He rose and brought back a bucket and cloth, then knelt and drew out one of her arms.

"What have you done with my ladies?" she murmured as he dipped the cloth in the bucket. "Ariette and M-Magan?"

He glanced at her as he began to wash the mud away. The water, to Katharine's surprise, had been heated. She closed her eyes and murmured with utter pleasure as the warmth soothed her chilled flesh.

"I gave them over to Sir Aric and bid him do as he pleased. By now I imagine he's beaten them both senseless."

Katharine's eyes grew wide and she tugged to free her arm. *"No..."*

"What? You're not troubled for them, are you? Not when you took them out into the night for such adventure? What did you think to do, Katharine?" He drew her other arm out to give it the same cleansing as the first. "You knew you could not run from me forever."

She was silent, and gave him a stubborn glare.

"It is no matter," he told her. "I shall have Aric persuade Mistress Magan to give me the truth. It should not take long. She's terrified of him." He shoved her arm back beneath the blanket and moved down to wash her legs.

"How did you attain knighthood, Senet Gaillard?" she asked with all the hatred she felt for him. "Beating in-

nocent women to your own purpose? You're an animal,
and no better, I vow.''

The warm, damp cloth in his hand slid slowly upward
from her foot across the curve of her calf, to her knee.
The touch was so pleasurable that Katharine had to bite
her tongue, hard, to keep from murmuring with it. All the
while, the man held her gaze.

"An animal," he repeated thoughtfully, drawing the
cloth back toward her foot in a slow, gentle caress. His
other hand, holding her ankle, spread its fingers wide over
her flesh, pressing soothingly against the aching muscles
there. He dipped the cloth into the water again, then
brought it back, hot and new, to bathe her frozen toes.
The pleasure was so intense it was nearly painful. Katharine drew in a slow, steadying breath.

"Aye," she said unevenly. "To treat w-women so."

He set her leg on the floor, beneath the cover, and drew
out the other. Dipping the cloth into the heated water
again, he said, solemnly, "One day, Katharine, I vow, you
shall say otherwise."

They were silent again. Her eyes drifted shut with the
tingling sensation of warmth returning to her limbs, and
weariness tugged mightily, but she murmured, "I meant
to find Lord Hanley. To wed him before I might be forced
to marry you."

"Lord Hanley?" he said with a measure of surprise.
"Did you think to go all the way to the Holy Land?"

"No," she said wearily.

Silence again, until he tucked her finished leg into the
covers. "It is a grave sin for a man to love his wife, or
for a woman to love her husband," he told her. "Has not
the church declared it so? We must give all our love to
God. Perhaps I do you a kind service in forcing you to

wed with me, rather than this Hanley, whom you appear to hold very dear. You love him?''

"Yes," she lied. "With all my heart. And I find no sin in it, nor in anything so pure and abiding."

He moved to wash her face. The cloth stroked gently over her forehead and cheeks, across her nose and lips and chin, then moved down to her neck.

"I once loved in such a manner," he said at last, his voice soft and careful. Katharine couldn't keep the surprise she felt at such words from her expression. "You think it impossible?" he asked at the sight of her raised eyebrows. "I assure you I speak the truth." He turned to toss the cloth into the bucket. His voice, when he spoke again, was void of emotion. "I loved well and deeply, and with this same abiding passion of which you speak. The church would have found me a very great sinner."

"Why did you not take her to wife?" Katharine asked. "If you loved her so well, surely you would not have given her up for the sake of Lomas?"

He shook his head, busying himself with picking up her torn clothes and making a pile of them. "Nay, not even for Lomas would I have given my Odelyn up. Nothing could have parted us, save death." He turned to look at her. "She was foully murdered shortly before we were to marry, and I have grieved her every day these ten years past."

Katharine touched her lips with her fingers, unable to find words to say for the pity she felt—for him, her basest enemy. Her weariness had surely robbed her of sanity, she thought, for her to feel any manner of sorrow for a man she so fully hated.

He stood with the clothes under one arm and the bucket in his hand.

"And so you see, Lady Katharine, that we are two of

a kind, for our hearts have been given to ones forever lost to us. You may at least take comfort in the knowledge that I shall never attempt to win your love. Your devotion to Lord Hanley may remain hallowed and untouched, just as mine for Odelyn ever will.''

She gripped the blanket tightly about her shoulders. ''It matters not,'' she told him. ''I will never wed you of my own free will.''

He began to walk toward the door.

''There is wine and food by your pallet, and a dry chemise that you may don. The pallet and fire should keep you warm enough through what remains of the morn.''

''I will not wed you!'' she repeated fiercely.

He ignored her and unlocked the door. ''Sleep,'' he advised. ''We will be wed this evening, when you have had sufficient time to rest.''

''We will *not*, sir,'' she stated.

''Katharine,'' he said, making her a mock bow at the open door, ''we will.''

Chapter Five

"A wager," said Sir Aric, "that she'll not come of her own accord."

"She'll come," Senet said, sitting calmly in the lord's chair in the great hall. He was flanked on either side by Aric and Kayne. Farther away, in his finest robes, sat Lomas's priest, Father Aelnoth, waiting in stony silence for Lady Katharine to attend her own wedding. "She understood me well, I vow."

"I fear Aric has the right of it," Kayne murmured, his gaze moving slowly over the castlefolk who filled the hall, each and every one of them staring up at Senet with mute reproach. They clearly loved their lady, and had no wish to see her wed by force. "And I do not think it wise that you sent Clarise to tend her. You know what Lady Katharine thinks of her. You might have done better to let her own ladies help her to prepare."

"It is best, I find, to give no importance to what Lady Katharine thinks," Senet told him. "At least not until we've wed and she's had time to reconcile herself to her new state. At the moment, she's not capable of thinking rationally. As to her ladies—" he looked to where Mistresses Ariette and Magan were sitting, on the other side

of Father Aelnoth, their faces and bodies rigidly held
"—they are not to be trusted until they have made their
allegiance to their new lord."

"I cannot see Mistress Magan bowing to you for any
reason," Aric said irately. "She's a stubborn, mean-
tempered little wench. Put her elbow in my stomach when
I merely tried to set her on my horse, so she did." He
rubbed the offended area and cast a look at the female in
question. She took note and gazed back at him with narrowed eyes.

"Clarise returns," Kayne said, drawing the attention of
them all toward the stairs. "Alone."

Concern was written on the delicate girl's face as she
hurriedly moved toward them. Senet didn't wait for her
to cross the great hall, where all those waiting had turned
to watch her, but rose and strode to meet her halfway. He
took her hand before she could speak and led her back
toward the stairs.

"Lady Katharine will not come," the girl said breathlessly, in French. "She would not even dress. When I tried
to speak to her, she threatened to—"

"I'll deal with her." Senet cut her off in a low voice,
striving to maintain his outward calm for the benefit of
their avid audience. "You need never be afraid of Lady
Katharine, Clarise. I promise you this on my honor."

Kayne and Eric had joined them, and he set Clarise's
hand on Kayne's arm. "Take Mistresses Ariette and Magan to the solar and wait for me there. I will bring Lady
Katharine." He began to ascend the stairs. "And bid Father Aelnoth to prepare himself. We will begin the ceremony shortly."

Guards stood at the door of the chamber in which he'd
locked his bride. At the sight of him, they stood aside and
let him enter. The first thing Senet saw, apart from Katha-

rine standing by the room's small, lone window, yet dressed in her chemise, was the expensive gown he'd brought her as a wedding gift—lying on the floor.

"We will have an understanding regarding Mademoiselle Clarise," he said, shutting the door behind him.

Katharine lifted her chin and folded her arms. "Will we?" she asked insolently.

"Indeed, my lady, we will. She is to be treated as an honored guest at Lomas, by yourself, as my wife, and by every other person who bides on my lands, including your ladies. I will not tolerate the least slight toward her, and if she should even once be driven to tears—"

"Never have I met such a hypocrite," Katharine said, sneering. "Only a few hours ago you spoke so sweetly of the eternal love you bear for your departed betrothed, yet now you trumpet openly an even sweeter concern for your French whore. If you love her so well, Senet Gaillard, then pray, marry *her*."

He moved toward her slowly. She stood her ground, eyeing him with defiance. She was, he thought, a beautiful creature, with her long red-gold hair unbound, flowing down the length of her shapely body and past her hips. The chemise she wore was thin enough to tease and entice. He felt a shocking, overwhelming lust for her— something he'd not felt with the myriad other women who'd tempted him before. But just as he'd not let other women rule him during the past ten years, with passion or lust or anything so foolish, he would not let her do so either. He would be master at Lomas, and the sooner she learned that, the better for all concerned. Especially for her.

"If Mademoiselle Clarise should shed even one tear because of you, Katharine," he repeated, moving until he stood directly in front of her, "I will turn you over my knee and punish you."

She pressed her face closer to his, unafraid and daring. "If you think I should deign to waste my time in tormenting your witless little whore, then you greatly mistake the character of my mind. I would rather labor in the kitchens, on my knees, yet, than lower myself to so much as countenance her existence. Keep her away from me, and we shall have no quarrel."

He shook his head. "Such a sharp tongue you possess, Katharine." Setting a finger beneath her chin, he lifted it even higher. "No soft and gentle wife will you be, I vow."

She slapped his hand away. "*No* wife will I be. I will not wed you!"

"I will give you a choice," he continued in the same calm tone. "You may don the wedding gown I have brought—" he nodded at the heap on the floor "—or you may be married as you are, in your chemise."

"You are deaf, dumb, blind and senseless!" she shouted furiously, her hands balling into fists at her sides. "I will not wed you!"

"I give you the span of a minute to make your decision."

"You would not humiliate me so," she said with disdain. "You, a knight of the realm? You would not parade any woman before her own people so nearly undressed. And certainly not the woman you mean to have as a wife."

Senet felt the sharp truth of her words deeply, as if they were knives striking a wound. It would be the meanest manner of torment, especially for a proud woman like Katharine.

"Nay, I would not subject you to such a humiliation,

but if you are determined, so be it. You are the one who will conclude the outcome. Quickly, now, Katharine, for we will be wed, even if I must carry you naked before all those assembled below.''

"So be it," she said in a low, heated tone. "I take no responsibility for what you have forced me to, and my people will know the full of it. You may carry me naked before them and stand me in front of a priest, but I will not say the words, Senet Gaillard. I will *not.*''

He didn't think he had ever admired a woman so completely before now—certainly not since Odelyn had died, and never in this manner. Katharine was fierce as any warrior, her spirit strong and her determination true. The knowledge that she would be his filled him with exultation. Bending, he looped an arm about her legs and, ignoring her cry of surprise, lifted her over his shoulder. Senet walked out of the chamber and toward the stairs, deaf to his bride's loud fury and the ungentle blows she struck upon his back.

The great hall was filled to overflowing, Katharine saw as she descended the stairs carried like a sack of grain over Senet Gaillard's shoulder. And every single person present watched as he made his way, with her all but naked save for the thin chemise she wore. Gritting her teeth she put every ounce of strength she possessed into the fists she flung at him.

"Bastard!" she shouted furiously. "Bastard! *Bastard!* Oh, God." She gave up when they reached the bottom of the stairs, and sank her aching fingers into her unbound hair, letting herself go limp against the bouncing rhythm of his stride, wishing that she could somehow disappear. That her people should witness her shame was beyond repair. She would *never* forgive him. A loud murmuring rose up, and from somewhere to her left she could hear

Father Aelnoth making a feeble protest. Katharine shut her eyes tightly against all of it.

He carried her to the small garden solar just off the hall, where her ladies spent many hours plying their needles in the greater sunlight that the chamber's tall paned windows provided. He set her on the floor, and Katharine barely had a moment to collect herself and push her hair from her face before Ariette and Magan threw themselves at her.

"Oh, my lady!" Magan cried. "We've been so worried for you."

"Are you well, Lady Katharine?" Ariette asked. "Oh, here, please—" She began to pull the hair covering from her head, in order to set it over Katharine's shoulders.

"Nay, Ariette." Katharine stopped her. "Senet Gaillard wishes to humiliate me openly. Let him do so and prove what manner of lord he intends to be." She gave that man a defiant glare.

"Lady Katharine, you are overset," Sir Kayne said gently, untying the elegant cape about his massive shoulders. "None of us would ever allow such a thing." Keeping his eyes lowered, he quickly set the garment about her. No sooner had he done so than Senet grasped it and tossed it back to his friend.

"Lady Katharine chooses to humiliate herself, Kayne, and you'll not save her from such rash foolishness. She will wear my cloak when we wed."

"How many times must I speak the words?" Katharine demanded. "I will not—"

"Quiet, woman." Senet cut her off impatiently. "I can scarce think with all your noise."

Noise? Katharine thought with complete outrage. She'd acquaint him with noise. She opened her mouth, only to have him dismissively turn away.

"Aric." He said to that man, who was standing by the door, watching the scene with clear amusement.

"Aye?"

"Which of these women do you prefer? Mistress Magan or Mistress Ariette?"

"Senet," Sir Kayne said uncomfortably, moving nearer to the women as if to protect them.

"Which one?" Senet demanded.

Sir Aric's lazy gaze fell on Magan, and she pressed more closely to her mistress. Katharine set an arm about her, feeling the younger woman's violent trembling. She realized, with sudden clarity, what Senet Gaillard meant to do.

"You will *not*," she said.

He looked at her, his blue eyes cold, his handsome countenance as inflexible as stone. "I will."

Their gazes held for a long, silent moment, with only Magan's soft whimpering filling the room.

"She is my ward," Katharine said at last, striving to keep her tone even. "I have sworn to keep her beneath my protection until she marries."

"Then perhaps Aric had best take her to wife, rather than as a whore."

"You ask much of me," Sir Aric said over Magan's sudden wails. "I don't want a wife."

"There are compensations," Senet told him. "She comes with property and monies, a small but prosperous estate in Somerset, and full rights to several acres of forested land. All of it yours for the bedding of her."

Magan gripped Katharine with both arms, with fingers and nails, weeping violently, pleading for safety.

"You cannot do this!" Katharine shouted. "To violate one so innocent—and a lady born. She would be ruined forever, with no chance of gaining a respectable husband.''

Senet turned to look at her. "She is in your keeping, Katharine. Think of the way to make certain of her safety, for I assure you it is very simple."

She couldn't. God help her. She couldn't say the words to put herself into his keeping forever. He wouldn't do this horrible thing to Magan. It was impossible.

"Take her, Aric," Senet said, his voice hard and unyielding. "You may use my chamber if you desire privacy for bedding your newly betrothed bride."

"Very well." Sir Aric pushed from the wall. "But I'll have to tie a cloth about her mouth to keep her quiet."

"Tie her any way you please," Senet said above Magan's loud cries. "Only make certain that you finish the task. You may wed her in the morn."

A brief madness broke out as Sir Aric tried to wrest Magan out of Katharine's grip. Katharine started it by shoving Magan toward Ariette and then striking Sir Aric full in the face with her fisted hand. It was a good blow, knocking the huge man back a pace and stunning him. She would have hit him again if Senet hadn't picked her up off the floor.

"Leave him be, Kayne!" he shouted when his blond comrade began to pull his sword out of its scabbard. "You must stand with me in the matter. Give me your trust, my friend. I will not betray it."

"Sir Kayne!" Katharine cried, struggling against Senet's steely grip. "You are sworn to protect innocent maids!"

Scowling, Sir Kayne shoved his sword back into its place. "I never thought to see you torment a lady so, Senet. Any lady." He moved toward Ariette, and held her as Aric scooped a now screaming Magan into his arms and tossed her over his shoulder.

Ariette shrugged free of Kayne's gentle grip, covering her mouth with both hands, watching with wide-eyed horror as Aric carried Magan from the chamber. Her cries could be heard echoing throughout the great hall, becoming fainter with each passing moment.

"Oh, my lady," Ariette murmured, tears coursing down her cheeks as she pleaded with Katharine. "Oh, my lady."

Senet had put Katharine on her feet once Aric had carried Magan away, and now she shut her eyes and covered her ears, striving to drown out the sound of Magan's distress. But it was impossible. The girl's terrified visage swam before her, and her cries rang in her head.

"I give way," she said faintly, dropping her hands to her sides. She repeated it more loudly, turning to Senet with all her fury, "I give way!"

He crossed his arms and faced her.

"Your word, Katharine, that you will stand beside me of your own accord, before all those assembled in the hall, and become my wife. You will readily take your vows, in full voice and agreement, for all to hear. There will be no question of your willingness."

She nodded wearily. "Aye."

"You will cover your nakedness with my cloak, accepting this mark of my possession without protest."

Her eyes opened, but not to look at him. She stared at the floor beneath her bare feet. "Yes."

"When you have become my wife, you will instruct your people to make their pledge of fealty to me, their new lord. I want no discord in Lomas, and no false loyalties."

She swallowed, then released a long breath. He waited.

"It will be as you have said."

He nodded. "Kayne, go and tell Aric that he is to bring no harm to Mistress Magan so long as Lady Katharine honors her word. He is to keep her out of the hall until I send for them, when all has been done. I shall want Mistress Magan to make her pledge of fealty."

Kayne left the room without a word. Senet unclasped the cloak about his shoulders.

"I will take no blame for what you have forced me to, Katharine." He set the cloak about her shoulders. She gave no resistance when he clasped it. Indeed, she would not even look at him. "I meant to make you my wife with every honor that is your due. I will yet do so, if you will but let me."

She shook her head in stony silence.

"So be it," he said. "Mistress Ariette, wipe your tears away. Go and tell Father Aelnoth that Lady Katharine and I will present ourselves in but a few moments. He is to make all ready. Now."

"My lady…" Ariette murmured.

"Go, Ariette," Katharine said dully. "Do as our master has told you."

When she had gone, Senet lifted Katharine's chin with a careful finger, until her eyes met his own.

"Katharine," he said softly, "you fight against your own measure. Not mine. 'Tis the fool's way to spite yourself."

She shrugged free of his touch. "Better a fool of my own choice than a willing slave. You have forced me into servitude, Senet Gaillard, but nothing more will you have of me."

"I do not want you for a slave," he told her. "I mean to make you my wife, Katharine. To honor you as such."

Her voice, when she spoke, was low. "Wife or slave,

my lord, it makes no difference. They are the same." She leaned closer, gazing at him with eyes reddened and weary, yet still holding the light of defiance. "The very same."

The ceremony was brief, for which Katharine was grateful. She let Senet Gaillard lead her to the dais where Father Aelnoth waited, and, before all those assembled, she made her vows. She felt the eyes of her people upon her, felt, too, their deep regret and sorrow at the manner in which their lady was wed—in such a state of undress, without even shoes on her feet, her hair uncombed and unornamented. And wearing Senet Gaillard's cloak, which so clearly marked his victory and her defeat.

He stood beside her, holding her hand upon his arm, and solemnly repeated his vows. When the priest gave him the kiss of peace, he passed it to Katharine in a brief, firm meeting of lips. Then he surprised her, when Father Aelnoth asked whether he had any token to make proof of his pledge, by opening the leather pouch that hung at his waist and pulling out two gold rings, joined together, as was common, by a thin band of silver. He set the rings into Father Aelnoth's hands, and when they had been blessed, took them back and broke away the silver bond. Taking her left hand, he touched the smaller of the gold circles upon the tips of each finger, as Father Aelnoth spoke, "In the name of the Father, in the name of the Son, and in the name of the Holy Ghost..." until he reached her fourth finger, and slid the ring all the way on.

It was a beautiful ring, clearly crafted with care and made of such clean, pure gold that it shone almost white. She had not expected this of him, just as she had not expected the beautiful gown that Mademoiselle Clarise had earlier delivered to the north tower, and the surprise kept her silent as Senet Gaillard took her other hand and set the ring meant for him in it. Katharine's fingers curled around it. She could throw it in his face, if she liked. It wasn't part of the bargain they had made, and she had already peaceably taken her vows. To do this thing—to put the ring upon him as he had done to her—would only serve to make her appear compliant and willing.

The silence in the hall was thick with meaning, and Katharine slanted a glance at the myriad, wide-eyed faces staring up at her, waiting.

She lifted her gaze to Senet Gaillard's handsome countenance. He was waiting also, patiently. There was no sign that he meant to force her to perform the small service.

Katharine uncurled her fingers and reached down to take his hand. Her own hand trembled as Father Aelnoth began to speak, "In the name of the Father, in the name of the Son…" and she moved the ring from his thumb to his forefinger to his middle finger and finally, to the fourth finger, where she slid the ring on.

The hall resounded with a collective easing of breaths, and Senet took her hands in his, holding them tightly. Katharine could no longer meet his gaze. It was over. They were man and wife, and Lomas was his.

Chapter Six

"He took you walking on the roof? *That* was how he meant to terrify you?"

Katharine stood in the middle of her chamber, still wearing Senet Gaillard's cloak over her chemise, and stared at Magan in disbelief.

Magan, who was busying herself with arranging Katharine's brushes and combs on a table upon which a steel polished mirror was set, said, blushing, "I know 'tis difficult to credit, but Sir Aric was very kind. The moment we reached the roof he put me down and apologized...in a most heartfelt manner. He—he even knelt—" she blushed more hotly "—and took my hands and asked me to forgive him for any fright he may have given me earlier, at The Bull and Dog."

Utterly shocked, Katharine sat down on her bed and kept staring. Ariette, standing across the room, stumbled to the nearest chair and sat as well.

Magan turned to them with a fluttering of hands. "I tried to return to the hall to tell you, before it was too late, that it had merely been a ruse decided upon between Sir Senet and his friends, but Sir Aric said he could not let me do so. And he was so gentle, I vow. He is not at all what I thought him to be, and he was in all truth sorry for whatever insult he gave me earlier. He is a gruff gentleman, of a surety, and not easy in his manners as Sir Kayne is, but he was—''

"Very kind," Katharine finished for her. "God above, strengthen me, I pray." She set a fist against her forehead and closed her eyes. "He *lied* to me. He played me for the veriest fool!" She opened her eyes and speared Magan with a frigid look. "And now Lomas is his. Because of a *ruse* and nothing better."

"I'm sorry," Magan whispered in a tiny voice. "I tried to come back to tell you."

"You might have made mention of it before you took your vow of fealty," Katharine said, remembering the relief she'd felt when Sir Aric had at last escorted Magan back to the great hall. The girl had been unharmed, and Katharine had told herself that the sacrifice she'd made had been a worthy one. "You seemed willing enough to pledge your faith and loyalty in a man whom you *knew* to be a contemptible liar."

"I would never have done so if you'd not already been wed to him," Magan said, moving to kneel before Katharine. "Please believe me, my lady. I would not have served you so ill for any cause. But you had wed him, and in doing so made him the lord of Lomas. To have denied him my vow of fealty would have been as grave an insult to you as to him. How could I have done such a thing?"

"I suppose," Katharine said with a sigh, "that you could not. And it would have made no difference. My men, my soldiers, all of the castlefolk, had already made their pledges to Lord Lomas." Rising, she stepped away from the kneeling girl and moved toward a window to gaze out of it. Night had fallen, and yet the celebration taking place in the great hall showed no evidence of stopping. Music, laughter, the sounds of dancing all drifted upward in the chilled evening air. Her wedding feast. It would go on, most like, until daybreak. By morn all of the good wine would be gone, and most of the ale, too.

She had taken her leave before the celebration had begun, as soon as Magan had finished making Senet Gaillard her vow of fealty, or, rather, shortly after Senet Gaillard had given her his permission to depart.

That was as it would be from now on. She would have to ask for his permission to come and to go, to perform the least task that was not within the small powers he would cede her. Oh, Katharine had no doubt that he would want her to perform the usual duties of the lady of the castle, but that would be all that was left to her. She would be expected to oversee the kitchens and assign the servants their duties, to keep lists of stocks and supplies and make certain that none fell short, to direct her ladies in the making of tapestries and garments.

The knowledge made her want to weep. To live such an existence would be awful to her. For other women, perhaps, it was more than enough, but not for her. Never for her. She had *ruled* at Lomas, and, despite a few missteps, she had done well. Far better than both her father and Senet Gaillard's had done.

"Perhaps 'twill not be so bad as we believe, having Sir Senet as lord," Magan said softly, rising to her feet. "'Tis not what any of us would wish, certainly, but Sir Aric told me that Sir Senet's intentions toward Lomas are true and honorable. He means to rule justly, and to make Lomas as prosperous as it can be."

"'Tis already prosperous," Katharine told her. "I have made it so, and he is naught but a soldier, without experience in the ways of managing an estate such as Lomas.

His intentions matter for naught. 'Tis his actions, ignorant and ignoble, that will be the ruin of us. Has he not proven already that he cannot be trusted?'' She turned to look at the younger woman. "He lied to make me wed him. What more proof of his nature could you desire?"

Magan folded her hands together and looked at her lady in a direct manner. "You lied as well, my lady, to keep from being wed. It seemed necessary to you at the time, and so you told us, but I do not find your nature to be changed because of it, or suddenly made false throughout."

"It is not the same!" Katharine replied heatedly.

"It matters not," Ariette said, standing and moving to where Magan stood. "You are his wife, my lady, and we are his vassals. Lomas is his, and naught can be done to change that. And," she added more boldly, "I will tell you now that I think matters might have fallen far worse. Sir Senet was neither your choice nor ours, but he is, at least, a man of honor."

"Honor!" Katharine repeated angrily. "He lied to me! To all of us! And frightened Magan half to death."

"Because he wanted Lomas and you gave him no other road to take."

"*I—!*"

"Aye, my lady," Ariette said firmly. "He might have beaten you to his will, as many other men would have done, or taken you by force and shamed you greatly. The lie was wrong, I admit, yet he treated you with great honor while he wed you. He covered you with his own cloak—"

"To mark me as his possession!" Katharine cried.

Ariette shook her head. "To claim you, aye, but as his wife, to show that he held no shame upon you, and to cover your nakedness with his own garment. It was a sign of honor and respect. Could you not have realized it, when everyone else present understood what it meant?''

"It wasn't for that!''

"He brought you a beautiful gown to wed in, the finest gown I've e'er seen, and gave you a ring.''

"And he took a ring in turn,'' Magan put in, "which a man will seldom do, as we know only too well.''

"That matters not,'' Katharine said, "for I have no doubt he'll not wear it.''

"He would not have taken it, or gone to the effort of having it made, i'faith, if he did not mean to wear it,'' Ariette said. "Do you not see, my lady? He means to give you honor, as far as he may do so, and all that I have seen of him has given proof of that. He could have so easily shamed you before your people, but he did not.''

"How can you speak of him so?'' Katharine demanded. "After all that he has done? He took Lomas by force, and has threatened ceaselessly to beat us, or worse—'' she flung a hand at Magan "—in order to bend us to his will. He made me admit the reason for our flight earlier by saying that he would beat the two of you if I did not do so.''

"His words,'' Ariette said, "were at variance with his actions. Any other man would have beaten us all when we were found out at The Bull and Dog, but Sir Senet bade his men to treat us gently. Even Sir Aric, who perhaps may have handled Magan more roughly than was right, strove to be careful after she stuck her elbow in his side. Sir Senet himself took care of you in the tower, when he might have left you to suffer. Does it mean nothing to you?''

"Less than nothing!'' Katharine retorted hotly, feeling both foolish and childish. She had not let herself think of the kindness Senet Gaillard had shown her after her escape, of his gentle touch and manner. Her experience of men had taught her to expect so much worse, but he had surprised her beyond measure. She felt only confused— and frightened—feelings she loathed with every part of her being. He was her husband now, this handsome, bewildering man who had outmanned her at every turn, as no man had *ever* done to her before. The knowledge made her tremble deep within, where no one else could see— where she would make *certain* no one could see. "I am outnumbered. If Doro were here…"

"She would agree with all that we have said, and more," Ariette concluded firmly. "My lady, I honor you above all others, but I believe, in soothe, that Sir Senet means only well toward Lomas. Will you not, for the sake of your people, strive to make peace with him? Please, my lady?"

Katharine turned away in stony silence.

"Can you find Sir Senet so wanting?" Magan asked. "He was not your choice, but he is a most pleasing man, and I cannot but think that you would rather be wed to him than to Lord Hanley, or even Kieran FitzAllen, for all that your cousin is so handsome to look upon."

"I would rather be wed to no man," Katharine said, though much of her anger had gone. She had fought as well as she could, and was not such a fool as to continue fighting when the battle was over. "Leave me."

"Leave…?" Ariette murmured with confusion.

"Aye."

"But, my lady, we have not yet made you ready."

Katharine sighed and moved to the bed, sitting on it again. "Senet Gaillard wed me for Lomas, which he now has. Katharine Malthus he must take as she is. I will not make a greater mockery of this marriage than it already is. Go." She lifted a hand toward the door. "Return to the festivities and enjoy yourselves." She offered them a weary smile. "And if you can lure the so kind Sir Aric into dancing, Magan, I will give you my prettiest hair comb."

Magan blushed hotly. Ariette looked worried. "Are you certain you wish to be alone, my lady? Would you not have us wait until Sir Senet arrives?"

"I am not so timid a female to require such coddling, Ariette. Nay, go and enjoy yourselves. Have no fears for me, or for the lord of Lomas. I will fight him no more. For the sake of my—*his* people."

Ariette moved quickly to kiss her upon the cheek.

"Always your people, my lady," she whispered fervently, hugging Katharine. "Never believe otherwise."

She was relieved when they had gone, and glad for a small measure of peace. She did not know when Senet Gaillard would come, or even if he would come. Perhaps, having gained Lomas, he would prefer to celebrate the night with his mistress, rather than the ungainly wife he'd been made to wed. Katharine had no doubt that he would far prefer the delicate and pretty Clarise to her manlike self, and she almost hoped that he would go to her.

And yet, she was curious as to what it would be like to...procreate with a man. With *him*. The very thought made her face burn. She hated Senet Gaillard. Hated him as she'd never thought to hate anyone. But she could not deny that he was, just as Magan had said, a most pleasing man. His touch when he had cared for her had been gentle, and his hands moving upon her had been...very pleasant. She had heard, from some women, that it was a horrid thing, to have to lie with a man. From others, she had heard that it was the most delightful act possible. When she had believed she would never marry, Katharine had not let herself think too often on such matters, but she had yet been curious. Which was, she thought restlessly, standing and pacing about the chamber, perfectly natural. She and Doro and Ariette and Magan had talked about it openly sometimes, and laughed a great deal, too.

Katharine stopped in the middle of the room, tense with fear. It was supposed to hurt. And there would be blood. And it would mean, too, that his domination of her was final and complete. How could there be any pleasure in that? He already had Lomas, which was all that he wanted. If he forced her to lie with him, it would be only to make certain of his claim to the title and land so that none could contest that their marriage had not been made complete.

She cast a glance at the secret door behind the tapestry, but there was no hope of escaping there again. Senet Gaillard had set a guard to every hidden exit; still more guards stood outside of her door. She might attempt to sneak out through his chamber, for her own adjoined it with but a door between, but she didn't doubt that she would be caught before she reached the stairs.

With a sigh, she sat before her polished steel mirror and looked at her sorry reflection. This was what she had looked like on her wedding day. A wretched mess. Her hair was tumbled and unkempt, her face pale, and beneath her eyes were dark circles that made her look deathly ill. What a becoming bride she must have made. She suddenly felt like weeping with a horrifying tide of self-pity.

Well, she would make the best of things, Katharine thought, dashing the tears aside with a furious movement of both hands, for she was no weak woman to glory in morbid hopelessness. Senet Gaillard had bested her. So be it. Now she must think of what she would do, and discover if he might be bartered with. She lifted a hand to a long, intricately carved box set near the mirror, and—

after hesitating—opened it, drawing out a sharp and shining dagger, which she lifted into the light.

She had given her word that she would no longer fight Senet Gaillard, and that was a promise she would keep. But she would bargain with him yet and see what might be agreed upon. He was far stronger than she, and just as crafty, but this, she thought, turning the knife about to inspect it, would make the situation more equal.

"Surely you'll let us carry you to your bride," Aric insisted. "You'd not deny us the honor of doing so, would you? After all we've been through together? And 'tis our duty, as well you know, Senet."

Standing, Senet set his mug of ale aside. "I will go alone, Aric, for the sake of my lady. She would think herself very ill-used, indeed, were I to let her be so teased. And I've no mind to give Lady Katharine greater cause to be vexed with me just now." He smiled as the men around him laughed. "Stay and enjoy the feast, my friends." He briefly gripped Kayne's shoulder. "And keep any from coming abovestairs to disturb my lady and me. I will want all my patience to deal with her certain displeasure. Aric?"

Aric answered with a lazy smile. "Aye?"

"Take pity on Mistress Magan and dance with her."

The lazy smile vanished in the laughter that followed this, and Aric sat up more straightly, glancing about to where Magan sat with several of the castle ladies. She glanced back, then turned away, blushing.

"I do not dance," Aric said roughly. "I've never done so, as you well know."

"For such a pretty maid," Senet said, slapping his large and muscular friend on the arm as he walked past him, "you should make the attempt. I bid you good night."

Shouts and cheers from all those assembled followed him as he made his way up the stairs. He was certain that Katharine heard the noise and would be waiting for him, prepared for battle. He was ready for her anger, ready to coax and soothe and do whatever he must to get his beautiful wife to share a bed with him. The idea that she might refuse nagged at the edge of his thoughts, but he was far too happy to believe it would be so. After these many long, difficult years, Lomas was his, just as it always should have been, and he felt a deep, tumultuous joy at the knowledge. Nothing could go wrong on such a night as this. He'd find the way around Katharine's objections to becoming his wife in full, just as he'd found the way to gaining her agreement to the marriage.

It had been regretful that he'd been made to force her— he tried to shy away from that particular word, but could not, in truth, allow himself such an easy escape. Katharine was a proud woman, and he could take no pleasure in knowing that he'd used devious means to subjugate her. He regretted it, and deeply, but he would make amends now that Lomas was his. He would never again use such methods to bend her to his will. There would be only the truth between them, painful as it might be. She would want the truth, always. That much, he already knew about his noble wife.

There were guards at the door, and they moved aside without a word as Senet passed them. He stepped quietly into the entryway, noting the darkness of the main chamber beyond, and closed the door with care. He moved forward with equal care, half expecting some kind of attack. Katharine could not have escaped again through the chamber's secret door, for Senet had earlier locked it, but such was her determination that she was not beyond trying yet to gain her freedom of him. But she was not waiting in the shadows with some heavy object lifted high to smash upon his head. She was, so he could see by the small fire glowing in the hearth, lying on the bed, fast asleep.

He approached the bed with quiet footsteps, gazing down at his bride with a measure of wonder. How beautiful she was, her red-gold hair shimmering in the flickering light as if it were a river of molten fire, and her face, so perfect and lovely, framed against the white of the bedding. His gaze wandered over the body encased only by the chemise she had earlier donned, where his opened cloak revealed her full breasts and slender waist, the swell of her feminine hips and the line of her long legs. Her feet, which were as bare as when they'd wed, peeped out from beneath the thin cloth, as pretty as the rest of her.

He regretted, as he had earlier done, that he'd not somehow found a way to cause her to change her garments after their marriage and return to the festivities. Perhaps he would have found the way to make her smile, to dance with him, to forgive the manner in which he'd so falsely dealt with her. So beautiful a woman was his wife. How proud he would be to introduce her as such, to know that she was his. Lady Lomas. Katharine Gaillard.

He took a step nearer, meaning to speak her name and wake her—and then he saw, clutched in the hand that rested near her pillow, the glint of a dagger.

Katharine meant to fight him even in this, then. She thought him a brute. He had forced her to marriage; she believed he would force her to the marriage act, as well. But how weary she must have been to sleep beyond her fright of him, he thought, and felt a great wave of tenderness. She had been pushed beyond all measure in the past two days. All because of him.

Senet moved to a chair near the fire and began unlacing

his boots, setting first one, then the other, on the Italian carpets that covered the floor. He was weary, too, from all that had occurred. Yesterday morn he'd not yet possessed Lomas, while today he was not only lord, but also husband of a wife. A battle, a pursuit, an imprisonment and a marriage—within but two days. He'd not slept even a moment in that time. But no measure of weariness could push aside the heated desire he felt for his slumbering wife.

Standing, he pulled off his leggings and unbelted his tunic, pulling that garment off and leaving only his undershirt as a covering. Beyond that he would not frighten her, for God above knew how unsightly his scarred body was.

"Katharine." He said her name softly as he approached the bed, reaching out a hand to slip the dagger from her slackened grip. "Katharine."

Her eyelids drifted slightly upward, and she made a murmuring sound.

"Be easy," he went on gently. "I mean only to take this weapon. Have no fear, for I will not—"

She came all awake then, her fingers closing on the dagger even as his did. With a gasp, she rolled away, the knife yet in her hand. Senet watched, frowning, as she tumbled off the other side of the bed, her hair flying all about. She scrambled up to her feet, the knife held aloft, and stared at him wide-eyed.

"Katharine, you've naught to fear from me."

Panting for breath as if she'd run a great distance, she pushed the hair from her face and blinked rapidly in the dim light. It was clear that he'd waked her from a deep slumber, and given her a terrible fright. He could almost see the room through her eyes, blurry and unreal as she strove to make sense of where and what her situation was.

He'd had the same unnerving experience many a time while he'd been in France, being brought instantly out of exhausted dreams and into a murky nightmare of blood and war.

"You woke me," she stated at last.

"I did not mean to frighten you," he murmured apologetically, moving slowly toward her, his hands held palms out so that she could see he held no like weapon. Warily, Katharine backed away, unsteady on her feet. "I intended only to remove the dagger from your grip. You might have hurt yourself with it, even in your sleep."

She looked at him with a measure of open disbelief. "You wished only to take the knife? You do not mean to consummate our marriage?"

"Certainly I mean to consummate our union," he said calmly, "but it is not a matter for weapons, I vow. I will not hurt you in the matter, if I can avoid doing so."

"If you can *avoid* doing so?"

"I have never lain with a virgin," he admitted, taking another step closer, keeping his hands out, "but I am given to understand that there is sometimes a short pain to be endured by the woman in the breaching of the maidenhead. 'Tis unfair, i'faith, but 'tis as well a truth that cannot be other than accepted and overcome. I shall do whatever I can to make this as easy as possible, Katharine. On my honor I swear this."

The knife came up a little higher and he realized by the manner in which she held it that Katharine was skilled with the weapon, and that, despite her weariness, she could readily wound him.

"I wish to strike a bargain, my lord."

Senet fell still, not expecting this. "A bargain?"

She nodded. "There is no need to do this deed, for I cannot think you wish it. You desire to make certain of

Lomas, having done so much to gain it, and that is all. Let us make this bargain, then, and keep the truth between us alone. I will cut myself, here, you see?'' She set the knife against her forearm, causing Senet to take another step nearer in alarm.

''Katharine, do not—''

The knife whipped up sharply, fending him off. ''I have no fear of doing so, and no conscience against spreading the blood upon the sheets to make the trophy you require as proof of our final union. I shall never say otherwise, and will not contest your lordship of Lomas. It is far too late for me to regain what I have lost, and I have vowed this night to fight you no more. Now I wish only to live in peace.''

'''Tis what I desire, as well,'' he said honestly.

She shook her head. ''I do not mean at Lomas. I will leave on the morrow. My ladies will go with me, for I think they would be happier. There is a small estate that was left me by my mother, Caswell, which is my own inheritance and cannot be claimed by you as my husband. I will live there quietly and give you no cause for grief. You will need never consider me, i'faith, for I shall manage very well, as I have ever done, and you may live here at Lomas with your…with Mademoiselle Clarise and be fully content.''

Senet stood where he was, at last dropping his hands to his sides. He thought over her words carefully, striving to push aside the strange sensation of injury they wrought so that he might find the key to unlock this present difficulty. But the hurt lingered. Did she find him so abhorrent that she could not bear living with him as his wife? Or was it merely her disappointment in losing Lomas that made her want to leave? She had mentioned Clarise, but he strongly doubted that she was driven to suggest such a bargain out of jealousy—for that would require some measure of affection for him, and he knew very well that she would never care for him as she cared for the long-absent Lord Hanley.

Perhaps, he thought, she was simply afraid of what was to come. It was understandable, yet surprising. Katharine was the bravest woman he'd ever met, and he could hardly merit her being afraid of a little pain—not a woman who would so readily cut her own flesh to avoid being taken by a man. But mayhap that was the difficulty. He had already taken so much from her; how grave a humiliation she must think it to be forced to give more, even her own self.

He had formed some idea of wresting the dagger from her, but instead Senet turned away, offering her his back if she wished to make the attempt of plunging the weapon in, and strolled slowly toward a small table set with a silver brush and comb.

"I fear that I cannot let you leave Lomas," he said, taking up the comb to examine it. In the polished steel mirror set upon the table, he could see only a vague reflection of Katharine outlined by the flames in the hearth. Her hand was yet raised, as if she expected him to turn and jump at her any moment. He set the comb down. "I require your aid in the managing of the castle until I have better learned to do so myself. You will have a great many duties—"

"I cannot," she said harshly. "I have none of the skills you will desire in a wife."

He turned to look at her. "You malign yourself, Katharine. There is ample proof at Lomas that you possess every necessary skill. But I think you mean to turn me aside." He folded his arms across his chest and gazed at her directly. "Give me the truth. You're merely afraid of the marriage bed—'' he nodded toward that heavily curtained piece of furniture ''—and of what takes place there. That is all.''

She shook her head. "Nay, I am not."

He shrugged. "You are."

"I am *not* afraid," she insisted angrily. "I only wish to make this bargain, to leave Lomas and live in peace."

"Is that truly what you wish?"

"Indeed, my lord, that is all and everything."

He gave a slight nod. "Then I will make this bargain, in this way. Share that bed—and all that our marriage allows—with me this night. Remain at Lomas seven days and nights, sharing that bed with me, and if, at the end of that time you yet wish to go, I will send you on your way with every blessing and with all that you require. Moneys, goods, furniture, servants, cattle. Everything you want for your new household."

Her eyes narrowed. "You could not stay away from your—from *her* so many days, and I would insist upon it."

She meant Clarise again, he realized, and had to lift a hand to cover the smile that formed on his lips. Perhaps she *was* jealous, even if in small measure. How strange it was that the knowledge should give him such gladness.

"Well?" she demanded. "You have not answered me."

He lowered his hand and said, in all seriousness, "I will stay away from Mademoiselle Clarise while you are at Lomas. For the seven days and afterward, if you should remain. I give you my complete and solemn vow of this, with every honor that I possess."

"But you will want her," Katharine charged.

"Nay, I will not. I would not so dishonor you, Katharine, while you are a true wife to me. Neither by thought nor deed. I shall make this covenant with my eyes and mind and, aye, even my heart. You will have no cause for such shame at my doing. So long as you are here, by my side. I make no like promises should you go, and no man would judge me wrong in that.''

Slowly, she lowered the knife. "It seems a fair bargain," she said quietly, her voice filled with weary disappointment. "I believe you mean to keep it. I suppose, being a man, you must consummate the marriage." She turned to a small table and set the dagger upon it. "So be it. I will do as you say, though you must tell me, I fear, for I am not...I have no...experience in such matters."

Senet's gaze moved over her still-turned figure, from the top of her head down the fountain of her red-gold hair and lower to the gentle curves of her hips.

"You said you weren't afraid."

She stiffened and lifted her head. "I'm not. I will not screech and howl with maidenly fear, if that is what you expect."

He stood from the table and approached her with measured steps. She was yet turned away from him. "Almost since I have known of you, Katharine, I have learned not to expect anything usual. You are unlike any other woman I have ever met."

He lifted a hand to touch her shoulder and felt her first shiver, then fall very still. She swallowed loudly. "You have known many women, I think. You must not say after you have finished with me that I did not warn you of my many failings. But mayhap you have found no woman perfectly fitting since the death of your beloved."

The muscles in her shoulders were knotted with tension. Senet lifted his other hand and set his thumbs against the base of her neck, rubbing slow circles there.

"I have known women, i'faith, each fitting in her own

way, but none so beautiful and brave as you are, Katharine."

She uttered a dull, brittle laugh. "You think to weaken me with mockery, sir, but all for naught. I know I am not beautiful, nor will I believe any such honeyed words as you see fit to tease me with."

"You have not looked well into your mirror if you cannot see what is so plainly there, Lady Lomas, but if you want no honeyed words, I will not give them." His hands slid upward, to the taut muscles of her neck. "How closely have you been held by a man, Katharine?"

Her body stiffened at this, and she swallowed again. "I have embraced my father and uncles."

"And Lord Hanley? Did he not hold you closely?"

She shook her head faintly. He could hear the pace of her breathing quicken as his fingers slipped forward to caress the soft skin of her face, her chin, then over her neck again, down to the fine bones at her collar.

"No?" he murmured, bending close until his own breath brushed against her ear. "Come. Turn to me, Katharine, and I'll show you how 'tis done."

She was rigid as his hands guided her to face him, and she would not lift her eyes to look at him. Senet slid his hands carefully from her waist to the small of her back, gently urging her forward, against him. She drew in a sharp breath as their bodies touched, but he pulled her even closer, until she could feel him from her knees upward. It was not unlike embracing a piece of wood, but Senet held her fast, unyielding against her resistance.

"Don't be afraid," he murmured against her cheek. "Put your arms about me, Katharine. Hold me."

"I do not wish to," she said, "and I am not afraid."

He smiled, sliding a hand up to her shoulders to bring her breasts against his chest. "You must become used to what a man feels like. To what I feel like. Hold me. Tightly.''

Tentatively she put her arms about him and set her hands upon his back as if she expected to be burned, first touching then pulling away, then touching again and staying. There was no strength in her arms to hold him to her, but Senet's own arms kept them pressed tightly together. Her body was warm and feminine, soft and curving. He stroked his hands over her back, from her shoulders to her hips, and felt how firmly muscled she was. She was his lady warrior, not a frail, fainting flower who would ever need cosseting.

They stood thus for several long, quiet moments until she slowly began to relax. Her fingers moved over the garment he yet wore, finding the scars on his back, of which she began to make a slow exploration. It had long amazed him that women found the damned things so interesting to touch, but never to behold.

"You were beaten?" she asked, her fingertips following the line of a particularly long and bumpy scar, seeking the trail of it beneath the thick cloth.

"Aye. Long ago, when I was a boy." But that was the last thing he wished to think about now. To distract her, he said, "It was less fearsome than the first time I lay with a woman. I was far more afraid of what was to happen than you are now."

"I am not afraid," she said once more, but with less heat. "And I do not believe you were afraid. Men have nothing to fear by the act. 'Tis all pleasure for them, or so I have heard."

"'Tis a great pleasure," he admitted, gently massaging the small of her back, "for both men and women. I will always strive to make it a pleasure for you. But it is not something that can be forced upon another. 'Tis a pleasure that must be accepted...as a gift, else it will be as nothing. Or perhaps worse than that—a mere task to be borne. A wearying duty.''

"That is what is asked of a woman, is it not?" she charged. "To lie beneath her husband and receive his seed, then to bear his children. It sounds a wearying duty to me.''

He chuckled. "Aye, for many women I think it is just that. But it should be far more. I know that I am but a stranger to you, Katharine, and a man you hate, as well, whom you did not wish to marry, but I will give you pleasure, if you'll let me.''

"I have little choice in the matter," she said bitterly.

"You have every choice. I learned that well when I first learned of women. I was afraid that first time, just as I told you, but the girl who lay with me was most patient." His hands continued to caress and pet, and Katharine began to lean against him. "She was one of the serving girls in Howton Hall, the place where I was fostered to learn knighthood, and four years older than me.''

"How old were you?" Her voice was muffled against the cloth of his tunic, where she rested her head.

"Nearing my thirteenth year," he replied, lifting a hand to stroke her hair in a slow, rhythmic motion. "I was the most favored student among Lord Howton's fostered boys—this was only weeks before my father was found out as a traitor—and much cosseted. She came to me one night, where I slept with the others, and took my hand to draw me away to the kitchen, where her own pallet was. I was terrified of what she expected from me, for I had only the smallest idea of how to proceed. I was certain she would laugh at my lack of knowledge, and felt the greatest fool alive. 'Twas so far from being a pleasurable experience that I might rather have been tormented upon a rack. But she was patient, as I have said, and taught me not only how to give her pleasure, but how to receive it from her, as well. There is a little trick to the matter, you see."

"A trick?" She sounded wary. "To receiving pleasure?"

He nodded with his cheek against the top of her head, causing her head to nod as well. "A very simple trick. It is only this. No matter how afraid you may be, or how timid or shy, you must permit yourself to freely enjoy what is offered."

"It sounds foolish," she said.

"Nay, I will show you. Here." He slid a single finger down the curve of her arm, feeling her shiver in response. "Is that not pleasing, Katharine?"

She drew in a long breath before replying, "I suppose it is."

"But you did not permit yourself to enjoy it."

"I—" She paused, stiff and awkward in his grasp. "It is not easy for me," she said unhappily.

"Because you do not make it easy. Pleasure is yours to receive or turn away, Katharine. 'Tis your own choice, one I'll not take from you."

"You have already taken enough."

"Aye," he said softly, "this is so. Now I will only ask and offer, and you may answer as it pleases you."

They stood in a long silence, pressed together, swaying slightly back and forth. Senet's hands continued their gentle quest to both ease and arouse, and Katharine's hands, after a time, began to play lightly upon his scars again.

"Have you ever been kissed, Katharine?" Senet finally murmured.

Her fingers fell still.

"Nay?" he asked, truly surprised. "Not even by your

Lord Hanley? What manner of man was he, to treat you so ill?"

She lifted her face, glaring up at him. "He held me in the greatest and most sacred manner of respect, and loved me far too well to treat me lightly."

Senet laughed and slid his hands over the swell of her hips, bringing them against his own. She made a gasping sound as he pressed his arousal against her, but he only held her more tightly.

"He was not much of a man at all if he did not once try to kiss his own betrothed, and you so lovely a woman. But I will gladly remedy the lack."

He lowered his head and captured her lips before she had a chance to turn away, kissing her lightly, very gently. It was a brief kiss, followed by another, as tender as the first, and then another, and another. He gave her no reason for fright—she could have easily pushed from his grip. But she stood still, subject to his ministrations, trembling slightly and making a small whimpering sound when he set a hand against the back of her head, turning her so that he might kiss her more fully. Her hands, on his back, fisted in the cloth of his tunic and held tight, as if she required some measure of purchase to keep from falling. When he at last lifted his head and gazed at her, it was to find her eyes closed and her lips parted.

"Pleasure, you see?" he murmured. "'Tis yours to take. A very simple thing." He kissed her again as he bent to slip one arm beneath her legs and another beneath her shoulders. Lifting her, cradling her close, he carried her to the bed.

Chapter Seven

A very simple thing, he had said just before picking her up and laying her on the bed, but Katharine wasn't able to convince herself of it. Fear wasn't unknown to her, but this feeling of complete helplessness was. Senet was being purposefully gentle, for which Katharine was grateful, but he was still a big and powerful man. When he stretched out beside her—nearly half on top of her—she felt thoroughly engulfed by his solid, heavy strength and the vivid heat of his body. She experienced a moment of complete panic and felt her every muscle prepare to shove him away, but then his mouth was on hers again, soft and coaxing, and one of his hands lightly touched her stomach, making her tremble in response. The fingers of his other hand twined their way into her hair, caressing, soothing. His thumb stroked over her forehead in a gentle sweep, again and again as his lips moved over hers in soft, beguiling kisses that seemed to steal away all of her sense and reason.

Pleasure. Hers to take, if she wished it. Or hers to deny. Lying beneath him, feeling the sweet caresses of his hands and mouth, which only hinted at what more was to come, she understood what he meant. She might lie there as if made of stone and force the pleasure from her mind. It wouldn't be so simple as he'd made it sound, but Katharine knew that she was strong enough to do it. All she had to do was pretend that it was Lord Hanley rather than this handsome, bewildering man lying with her—she was certain she'd have no difficulty feeling a lack of anything with Lord Hanley. But she wasn't with him. She was with Senet Gaillard, her husband, whose skilled touch made her shiver uncontrollably and whose kisses made her crave more.

She wanted the pleasure he promised—wanted it beyond the fear her lack of knowledge gave life to. Unable to speak the words, to tell him what she wanted, she instead pressed against him and awkwardly lifted her hands to grip his shoulders.

He shivered, then, too, just as she had done, and groaned against her mouth. His body tensed and pushed and surged over her until she felt his arousal hard against her hip. She gasped, frightened anew, for he seemed to be ready to overwhelm her completely, but he murmured, "Shh, Katharine," and kissed her more gently, settling between her legs and then stilling his movements. All the while he stroked and soothed.

"Trust me. I'll give you no harm." One of his hands smoothed up her leg, beneath her chemise to caress her naked hip. "So beautiful you are, Katharine." He kissed away her protests. "Aye, beautiful," he whispered, his mouth moving down to her chin, her neck, burrowing lower to her breasts. His tongue touched the tip of one, over the cloth of her garment, and she shook her head and tried to push him away.

"Let me," he pleaded softly. "Katharine..."

The weight of his body left her so suddenly that she drew in a loud breath. "Senet," she managed to say in that one gasping breath. He was busy pulling her chemise off her body, ripping it in places when it wouldn't give easily. In but moments he was tossing the shredded garment aside, and gazing down at her in the flickering firelight. The look on his face was one of awe—as if she were truly lovely. But she knew she was not, and tried to cover herself. He took her hands and held them back.

"S-Senet," she said again, pleading, turning her face away. "Don't."

"Oh, Katharine." His voice was low and unsteady. "How can you not believe me when I say that you are beautiful? Why do you not believe me?" He bent nearer, placing kisses on her neck, her face. "Is it because you don't yet trust me? I'll show you how very beautiful you are, my little warrior...."

With his hands and his mouth he showed her, touching her breasts, kissing them, until she cried out with pleasure. Lower, he moved, kissing, touching, telling her over and again, "Here, Katharine, you are beautiful...and here... here...tell me you believe me...."

He wouldn't stop until she said the word, "Aye." Only then did he cease his sweet torturing and lift his head to smile at her.

"Aye," he repeated, "so beautiful you are, Katharine. Set your arms about me now. Hold me tight, for I mean to make you my wife in full. Here," he murmured against her lips, as his fingers teased at the center of her, "where you are ready for me. Open for me, Katharine. My wife. My beautiful warrior. We shall be one...yes...open..."

It hurt as he pressed his body into hers, but he kept murmuring against her ear, "Hold me tight, Katharine. *Tight.* This is our battle, which we shall fight together." He held her face in his hands and looked into her eyes. Katharine's arms were so fast about him that they ached with the effort, and she clenched her teeth. "Now, my brave wife," he whispered. "Hold on to me. *Now*." With a single, swift thrust he pushed all the way into her and held still. Katharine closed her eyes against the pain.

There was a brief silence, filled only by their harsh breathing. He made a groaning sound and set his forehead against her own. "There, Katharine. We are one. You're mine—forever now. And I'm yours." He kissed her brow, her cheek. "The pain...is it very bad?"

She opened her eyes slowly, blinking up at him. "'Tis not so bad," she murmured, licking her lips. "It feels so odd. Not what I thought." He was big and hard, filling her completely.

He moved, sliding up and down. Katharine's eyes widened. He gazed at her, breathing even more unsteadily than before.

"Does it hurt?" His voice was strained, taut.

She shook her head. "Nay, it feels...I can't..."

"Pleasure," he said, his own eyes closing. He moved again, that same sliding, and groaned. "I only want to give you pleasure." He began to move more strongly, breathe more harshly. "Don't let me...hurt you, Katharine...I'll stop..."

"It doesn't hurt." Each movement as he stroked into her grew easier. The pain of his intimate invasion eased, to be replaced by a new manner of tension. "I don't know what to do," she whispered, shifting restlessly beneath him.

"Hold me," he said against her mouth, between soft, heated kisses. "Move with me."

He showed her how, teaching her his rhythm until she began to understand why it was said that a man and wife became one. Pleasure—it wasn't something only he could have, or her—it was what they gave each other, together.

He coaxed and murmured and touched, and held her when the pleasure became so great that she cried out from it. It was a fearful thing, this pleasure he gave. Katharine shivered with it from her head all the way down to her toes, unable to stop herself. But he felt it, too, shuddering just as she did and murmuring her name. He lay atop her afterward, still at last, his body hot and damp. Katharine's hands had found their way up under the tunic he yet wore, and as she lay there, feeling sated and sleepy, her fingers moved lazily over the map of scars on his flesh. He had been beaten many times to be so badly marked. The thought of what he must have suffered sent an unwanted wave of pity through her. She didn't want to pity him, or care anything about him. Despite what had just passed between them, he was still the man who had taken Lomas—everything—from her.

Senet's face was pressed in the place between her shoulder and head, his breath hot on her neck, slowing each moment along with the beat of his heart, which she could feel against her breast. He was heavy on her, but seemed as incapable of movement as she. At last he murmured something incomprehensible and, with what seemed to be a great effort, rolled off her. One of his hands moved up to cradle her cheek, to turn her toward him. He was smiling, and Katharine turned away.

"Did I hurt you?" he asked, his voice heavy with concern.

She rolled to her side, away from him.

"No."

There was silence and stillness, and then his fingers stroked lightly over her shoulder. "You found pleasure, Katharine. I know you did."

Her face grew hot with the memory of how she had

moved beneath him, touched and caressed and pleaded
with him to do the same to her.

"Aye," she said. "I did as you said and took it for
myself. Now I suppose you mean to enslave me in such
a way. With this pleasure you hold so dearly. But perhaps
I will not let you take hold of me so easily as you did
Lomas."

His fingers fell away. With a sigh, he sat up and started
searching for the bedcovers. Pulling them up to cover
them both, he scooted up behind her, ignoring her attempt
to shrug him away, and set his arm about her waist to
draw her near.

"What I think, my little warrior," he murmured wearily, his body pressed against the length of hers, "is that
I am the one who is in danger of being enslaved. Go to
sleep, Katharine," he said, yawning, when she tried to
turn toward him. "In the morn I will hear all you wish to
say to me, and will listen, I vow."

He fell asleep almost at once. She could tell by the
deep, steady rhythm of his breathing and the way his body
leaned heavily against her own. Weariness tugged at her,
too, for the passing days had given her little chance for
rest. His arm around her was strange, but not uncomfort-
able, and Katharine was glad of the warmth Senet Gaillard
brought to her bed.

Music and laughter drifted up from the festivities that
continued below, and as Katharine closed her eyes she
thought that perhaps all was not as hopeless as she'd
thought. Senet Gaillard was lord of Lomas, but her people
weren't mired in the misery and fear she'd believed he
would impose. There was laughter and music, and even
if she hadn't wanted him for a husband, he wasn't the
tyrant she'd expected. He'd been gentle and kind this
night. He'd given pleasure when he might have simply

taken it. He'd promised not to lie with another woman—
if she stayed. If she stayed. At Lomas…and with him.

Light streamed through the parted bedcurtains when
Senet woke—a light which bespoke an afternoon sun,
rather than that of the morning. Years of soldiering had
trained Senet's senses to a fine pitch. His brain came alive
all at once, taking in his surroundings, searching for danger as well as for the answers to the moment's most necessary questions: where he was, how he had gotten there
and who else was with him. His body was far slower to
react, so that by the time his mind had reminded him that
he was at Lomas, had been married, had enjoyed a pleasurable wedding night and had slept in his wife's chambers upon her comfortable bed with her delightful body
in his arms, he had only begun to stretch and yawn.

Katharine was no longer beside him. Memory, returning as slowly as his body's movements, told him that she
had crawled out of his grasp an hour earlier. He vaguely
recalled telling her to stay, but she had resisted his feeble
attempt at keeping her and slid out from beneath the
covers. He'd regretted the loss of both her warmth and
her softness, for she'd made the most comfortable pillow
he could have imagined. He would have liked to make
love to her again with sweet, sleepy morning languor, but
had been far too weary to give chase. Moments after she'd
left the bed he had drifted back into slumber.

Now, much the better for the sleep he'd had, he opened
his eyes and rolled to his back, staring up at the bed's
canopy. It had been a long time since he'd enjoyed the
comfort of a feathered mattress and the luxury of warm,
heavy coverings. For too many years his bed had been a
pallet on the ground—or less, a mere blanket—and often
without help of a tent to keep either rain or chill at bay.

But he had endured it all just for this, to be back at Lomas again, to take his rightful place as lord. After ten years of striving it hardly seemed possible that he was truly here, and that all his plans had come to life.

The sound of footsteps alerted him that he wasn't alone. He sat up, pushing the covers aside.

"Katharine?"

Silence, then, "Aye."

He drew the curtains back even farther, peering out. "Where are you?"

"By the fire. It's late...too late to go down to break your fast. I have some bread and ale for you here."

Her voice was solemn, tentative. He remembered the bitterness she'd spoken with after he'd made her his wife. He had expected that, for Katharine was too strong a woman to fall at any man's feet, no matter how carefully he might have bedded her. But such as that he could readily face. This manner of temper was something altogether different—Senet wasn't certain what to make of it.

He stood, the floor cold beneath his feet, and found his leggings where he'd left them the night before. Pulling them on, he walked around the bed to the fire.

Katharine was sitting in one of two chairs, fully dressed. Her hair, he saw, was unbound and wet. She was leaning toward the warmth of the flames to dry it, but her contemplation was given to a nearby clothing chest where the gown he'd brought her as a wedding gift now lay, neatly folded by one of her maids.

"I bid you good morn," Senet said as he approached. Katharine looked around at him, unsmiling.

"'Tis past midday," she told him.

He smiled. "Then I bid you good day. You are well, I see."

"Very well." With a hand she indicated a small table

where a tray bearing a mug, cheese and a small loaf of bread was set. "You will be hungry, my lord."

He was, and gave no delay to sitting beside the table to eat. Katharine returned her attention to the gown that she had only the day before disdained to wear, and was silent. Senet's gaze moved over her, taking in her proud profile, the feminine line and flow of her body, her wet-dark hair.

"You've had a bath," he stated, tearing the loaf of bread in two. "That will have been more welcome than my feeble attempts to cleanse you of your adventures."

"You speak, I believe, of dirt," she said tautly, not turning toward him. "But that was not the cause. There was a small amount of blood this morn that I wished to wash away."

Senet straightened, filled with alarm before he realized what she meant. Then he laughed at his own foolishness. "I had forgotten," he told her. "Forgive me. You will think me witless, and perhaps be right in the thinking. I have told you that I had no experience with virgins. I am glad there was only the small amount." He cut a piece of cheese with a small dagger that was set on the tray. "I have not grievously wounded you, then."

"Nay, you have not." This was said in such chilly tones that Senet sighed and gave up hope of making conversation. He ate and drank in silence, until Katharine said, "Why did you bring that gown to Lomas?"

His hunger sated, Senet sat back more comfortably in his chair and regarded the expensive dress of burgundy velvet. It was trimmed with black fur and ornamented with fine gold thread, altogether a beautiful garment. He'd had it made for her in France, with no thought to cost, and had hoped that his bride would be able to wear it. Having no idea of Katharine's size or height, he had asked the seamstress to use her own judgment. It seemed to him now that she had done very well. Katharine would look very lovely in the gown, if she ever deigned to wear it.

"It was my wedding gift to you," he told her. "I could not come to my new bride without a proper wedding gift."

"You were very certain that you would wed me."

"I was very certain that I would have Lomas again, aye."

She turned to look at him, then, with glaring anger.

"I'll not wear it. *Ever.*"

Senet shrugged and took a sip of ale. He hadn't expected Katharine to become suddenly pliant and sweet simply because they'd shared so much pleasure the night before. Nothing would ever be so easy with her.

"As you wish, my lady. It is yours. Throw it in the fire, if it pleases you." Thinking of what it had cost him, however, he silently hoped that she would not. To turn the topic, he said, as pleasantly as he could, "You've changed these rooms a great deal. 'Tis very different from when they were my mother's."

The expression on her face softened slightly, but she said nothing.

Senet rose from his chair and began a slow perusal of the main chamber. "She loved being here," he said, "amidst the clutter of her beloved books and mathematical instruments." He glanced at his wife. "My mother had a great passion for numbers. I could never understand it." With a sigh he moved to a long, low table. "Her abacus was here," he said, touching the gleaming, spotless wood. "And her charts. 'Twas always a terrible mess, but she wanted it so. I can almost see her here again, bent over her work, scribbling and speaking to herself, smudged everywhere with ink." He smiled at the memory. "How often she tried to teach me numerical theories in this very spot." He tapped the table twice. "I was a poor student, I fear."

"Were you?" Katharine asked. He heard her rising from her chair.

"Oh, aye. I only wanted to go hawking with my father, or out for swordplay with some of the soldiers. My sister, Isabelle, was far more eager to take her place at our mother's knee." He glanced back at Katharine again, smiling. "It seems that only the women in my family have a love of numbers. I wonder if a daughter of ours will be so. Do you enjoy arithmetics, Katharine?"

"Only as I must," she replied. Her gaze fell away when he continued to smile at her. "I think there may be some of her things—your mother's things—somewhere in the castle. They were here when we arrived. I had no idea of what they were when I began to remake the rooms to my own purpose." She looked up at him with what seemed an almost apologetic gaze. "I cannot abide clutter, I fear."

"Nay, 'tis very good, what you have done," he said reassuringly. Did she think he would upbraid her for not leaving the chambers as he had remembered them? "You have made them your own, just as you should have done. They are your rooms, and you must always be in comfort here."

He continued to move about the chamber, touching the few articles of furniture, the tapestries on the walls, the lamps. Everything was in its place, neat and orderly. Just as all of Lomas was. His dreams of returning to his family estate to find it ruined and impoverished by some inept English lord—to find himself embraced by the people of Lomas as their rescuer—seemed more than merely foolish to him now. They needed no rescuing, not from Katharine.

She had done well. Very well, and without anyone else's help. If he'd never come, she would have continued doing well. The unsettling truth of it was, he needed *her* far more than she needed *him.*

"Senet."

He turned to her. It was strange to hear his name on her lips. She had said it the night before, in the midst of passion, but this was the first time she had purposefully addressed him without bitterness.

She seemed shy, nervous, and would not look at him. Her fingers plucked at the cords hanging from the girdle at her slender waist. He wondered fleetingly what she would do if he caught her up and kissed her, as he wanted. Would she shove him away? Strike him? Perhaps let him untie those same cords she played with and coax her back into bed? The very thought made his body begin to harden with desire. Letting out a breath, he forcibly relaxed and said, in as even a tone as he could manage, "Aye?"

Her chin lifted slightly, but her gaze skittered toward the fire. "I would have you know…certain things. I have no skill with a needle." She made that statement as if it were something dire and, having made it, began to speak more rapidly. "The kitchens I have always managed, of course, but only as concerns stock and supplies for the buttery and pantry. Well—" she made a fluttering motion with her hands "—perhaps I have not even done that, truly, as Ariette and Magan more often oversee such things. I have always seen to making payment for what goods are required. The castle is kept very clean, just as you see, by my command, but I do not know *how* 'tis done." Bright pink spots appeared on her cheeks and she turned away, moving back to her chair by the fire.

"Dorothea has had the ordering of the servants for as many years as I can remember. She is the one who makes certain that the rushes are changed and the floors washed and the tapestries dusted and…all of it. She keeps lists of what is to be done each month and week, but I cannot tell you even the least of what is on them. I know nothing of how to make soaps and candles, save what supplies are needed and which merchants in the village carry them.'' She stood by the chair, so clearly unhappy, lifting a hand to touch her forehead in a gesture of misery. ''I cannot embroider even the simplest design, or mend the slightest tear. I am all that is useless in a wife, and nothing that is wanted. If we lived in a mere hovel I would not even be able to make bread to feed you.''

She was truly upset, Senet realized, and he was thoroughly bewildered. What did he care of whether she knew how to make soap or not, or whether she could use a needle? And why should such foolish matters distress her so? He could do none of those things, either, save perhaps with the mending. Soldiers learned out of necessity to care for their clothes and tents. But her distress touched him deeply for, somehow, he was the cause of it.

''Others will make the bread, Katharine,'' he said soothingly, coming up behind her and setting his hands on her arms. She tensed beneath his touch. ''Do not worry o'er such matters. I will speak the truth to you, for I think 'twill give you ease. I did not come to Lomas for a wife, for I never wished to marry after my Odelyn died. It seemed wrong to take another in the place where I wanted only her to be. Katharine,'' he said when her head bowed, ''I do not say these things to hurt you. I swear by God that I would never do so apurpose. I mean only to give you peace in this matter.''

''Nay,'' she murmured, shaking her head, ''I understand you. There is no hurt.''

She thought of her own love, he knew. Of Lord Hanley,

whom she had risked death to find in the face of marrying another. If she had loved this man as dearly as he had loved Odelyn, then she truly did understand what he was striving to tell her now.

"To gain Lomas, I would have married any female—even if she'd been seventy years and a grandmother ten times over. I was fortunate, instead, to wed you, Katharine, for I would be a base liar if I did not admit that I find you more than beautiful and that I want you very much." He turned her to him. She shook her head, but gave no resistance when he pulled her into his embrace. "I'll not let myself feel shame for it. Or you. You are my *wife*, and Odelyn is dead, along with my heart. If 'tis a sin that I should so desire my own wife, then I am already a sinner without hope."

"Nay," she murmured.

"Aye," he countered. "We have only each other now, and if I am not the husband you wanted, or you the wife I thought to have, let us at least be as good to each other as we can." He lifted her chin until her gaze met his own. "And perhaps not overly demanding? If you cannot sew or make bread, I promise there are many more things that I likewise cannot do. But there is this, my little warrior." He kissed her softly. "This," he murmured against her lips, kissing her again, quickly, and yet again, more lingeringly, "we do most well."

Chapter Eight

The garden solar was filled with the light of the mid-afternoon sun, and the ladies sitting by the tall windows worked contentedly upon the large tapestry set before them, talking and laughing in a quiet babble of voices. Katharine, having paced the room half a hundred times since she'd entered it an hour earlier, at last fell into an unoccupied chair and gave a long, exasperated sigh.

"My lady," Ariette said from the chair in which she sat, "if you would but make a try with the needle..."

"I shall go *mad*," Katharine stated irately. "I shall wither away from lack of use within but three days' time, I vow."

"But if you will only..."

Katharine waved a hand in a gesture of refusal. "Nay, Ariette, leave me be. I have no skill with a needle, and less patience for it. And I am an *awful* student."

"Perhaps Magan will want your help in the kitchens, then?" Ariette suggested gently.

Katharine's face grew hot. "I went there first, but after a quarter of an hour Magan sent me here. I made the servants nervous, she said. And do not suggest that I attempt to run the household servants in Doro's absence, for I know very well that they would find me an intolerable mistress."

Ariette merely smiled and said, "I was not going to suggest such a thing, I promise you."

Katharine scowled. "Because you know I'm right." She pushed to her feet and began pacing again. "God above, how I pray that John Ipris will find Doro and bring her back to us safe. What will become of us, otherwise? We shall have no clean linens, and the dirt and vermin will overtake us completely. We shall be sitting up to our ears in filth, and what use will I be for it?" she demanded of no one in particular, shaking her head as she walked the circumference of the room, in and out of the windowed sunlight. "None at all, that's what. Useless and helpless—he'll understand the truth of that soon enough. Oh, God!" She pressed her fingertips to her forehead. "I have *nothing* to do, Ariette, now that he has taken Lomas from me. I have no value, no purpose. I might as well cover my head with ashes and go to sit with the beggars in the village."

"We have no beggars, my lady," Ariette reminded her with a smile. "You set them to work in the convent, if you will recall, when the sisters there needed help."

"Then I'll be the only one," Katharine returned irately. "Don't remind me of the convent, or I'll go mad with thinking of all that I promised the orphans there." She fell still and gazed out the nearest window, her mouth turning into an unhappy frown. "Those shoes I promised them," she said miserably. "He won't know about that, and even if I tried to explain it—how could I begin to do so? But they *must* have them."

"Aye," Ariette agreed calmly, exchanging a smile with the woman beside her, "they must. And new clothes, as well. And you did promise the sisters to send a mason to make repairs before winter comes. That one chimney in the main hall—"

"Is falling all to pieces," Katharine murmured, still gazing out the window, her fingers knotting together in frustration. "I cannot bear to think of it—with me standing here like a curst idiot and nothing to do—not able to even work a stitch of cloth, or knowing how to tell the servants how to keep the castle clean. I am only good for one thing. Only one thing…and if I cannot do that then I am truly beyond redemption." The truth of the words— her own words—struck sharply, and she turned to look at Ariette. "I *must* take care of my people," she said.

Ariette looked back at her serenely, as if this were the most evident thing on God's earth. "Yes, my lady. You must certainly do so."

Katharine straightened, casting her gaze at all the women present. "I have had the managing of Lomas since I was fourteen years," she told them. "It is the only thing I know—to manage the estate."

Needles held aloft, they all nodded.

Katharine turned her gaze to the door. "I will go now and tell him, as I tried to tell him before, though he would not hear me. But surely he'll recognize the truth." Of this, she wasn't entirely certain. She had come awake two hours ago to discover herself alone in her bed, after he had lulled her with his lovemaking. She had been furious to realize that he'd gone down to the great hall without her—in the presence of all her people. It had been awful to descend the stairs alone, beneath the knowing smiles of the servants and castlefolk. Katharine had felt the heat in her face long before she'd reached the sanctuary of the passageway that led out to the kitchens.

"I will go and tell him," she said again, still looking at the door. "I'll make him understand."

The matter, however, was taken out of her hands when the doors to the solar were thrust open. By Senet.

He took one step into the room, his angry gaze fixed on her at once.

"I thought to find you here," he stated with ill-contained fury, adding, with a latent glance at the others in the room, "madam wife."

His curt tone made Katharine's spine stiffen. Whatever softening thoughts she might have been forming toward him disappeared, to be replaced by indignation.

"I am here, my lord, as you see plainly. And as you already knew, for you earlier saw me entering." She thought of the brief, silent exchange they'd shared as she'd made her way from the kitchens, from which she'd been banished, to the solar. She had dared one look at him, sitting where he was in the chair of judgment that had been hers, to find him looking back, cold impatience written on his handsome face. He'd been surrounded by a group of unhappy merchants who were setting their complaints at his feet. Sir Aric had been sitting on his left, looking murderous, and Sir Kayne had been seated on his right, looking bored.

Senet had opened his mouth as she'd passed him, as if he would speak to her, but Katharine had ignored him and continued her course. She would not so lower herself as to behave like a whimpering minion to the man who was her husband, and if he wished to speak to her, he could step down from the dais and *request* her attention. But he did not, and Katharine had passed the dais with little more than a tight smile. She heard some of what the merchants were saying, and knew exactly what should be done in response to their complaints. But it was no longer her duty to solve such troubles.

"Indeed," he replied coolly, "I did allow you to come to the solar—"

"*Allowed!*" Katharine's hands balled into fists.

"—to continue this unseemly fit of childish vengeance—"

"Ch-childish!" Katharine sputtered, shocked and outraged. "I have done no such—"

Senet held a hand up into the air, silencing her before he finished his speech, "—but this is the end of it. I will have no more, Katharine."

"No more of what?" she demanded, taking a step nearer and lifting one fisted hand as if she'd strike him. "I have done nothing! And I will *not* allow you to speak to me in such a manner where it may be heard by others." The fist waved in the direction of the silent ladies at the other side of the solar. "Indeed," she continued, fully the lady of the castle, "I will not allow you to speak to me with such insolence at all!"

"Will you not?" he asked with raised eyebrows. Reaching out, he grabbed the fisted hand and dragged her toward the yet open doors. "Then we will speak in private, for there is nothing, I promise, that I should like better."

Katharine cast a frantic glance backward to Ariette, only to find her traitorous friend grinning.

There was little privacy to be had in the great hall, where everyone present stared at the spectacle of their new lord dragging their lady toward the kitchens. Katharine, suddenly thinking that Senet was angered because of something regarding the cooking, exclaimed, in a hushed, frantic tone, "I've already been there! Magan made me leave. Cease! I have been there, I tell you!"

"You speak in riddles," Senet stated bluntly, still walking and ignoring the attention about them. "But we shall have an end to that. Now." He came to a stop in the short hall that led to the buttery, which was hidden by a screen, and pulled Katharine to stand facing him.

Katharine looked behind him to make certain that the buttery was empty of servants, before whispering, "We can yet be overheard by those in the hall."

Senet tossed his hands out in exasperation. "I have no intention of engaging in a shouting battle with you for all to hear, Katharine. I only want you to explain this foolish behavior."

Her heart sank at his tone. He was clearly displeased, and why should he not be? She was useless and stupid, and only one day a wife. He would be sending her to Caswell with a good riddance before the sun had set, most like.

She gave him no answer, only closed her eyes and tried to turn away.

"Katharine!" His hands fell on her arms, turning her back. "Do you hate me so much? I know you are yet angered, and mayhap rightly, but I had thought—after last night, and this morn—" He seemed to cast about for the right words. "Can you still be so set upon this manner of vengeance? Have I not given you reason to trust me, even a little?"

"It is not vengeance," she said, fully wretched. "I told you that I am no fit wife, and now you have the proof of it. I wish to God above that you had simply let me deal with the merchants who were here an hour ago, for I could tell they vexed you greatly, and I have so often managed their minor complaints that I could have dealt with them were I half-asleep. At least then I might have been of some use to you, instead of this." She looked up at him finally. "It is not vengeance. I told you that I will fight you no more. I would not be so small-minded as to spite you now, having made such a vow. But there is naught I can do to correct my great lacking, though I swear, on my very honor, that I have tried."

He gazed at her with a measure of confusion. "Katharine," he said, his voice tinged with strained patience, "I believe we have crossed this path before, and I begin to grow weary of the journey. Let us have done with it. I told you not to worry o'er who makes the bread, or who does the sewing. I also told you that I require your aid in the managing of the castle. I did *not* mean in the kitchens."

Eyes wide, she stared at him. "Not in the kitchens? Or with the sewing?"

He shook his head, his crystalline gaze intent.

"But what *did* you mean?" she pressed. "Surely not..." She frowned. "Nay, but you could not have. 'Tis impossible. Men do not seek the help of women in such matters."

"Do they not?" he asked, patience threading away to a taut line. "Will you make me say it more plainly, then? I require your aid in managing Lomas as you have always done, because I cannot do it alone. What I remember of my father's teaching is dim at best, and we both know that he was not beforehand the most suited tutor for such learning."

His handsome face had reddened as he spoke, and Katharine knew that he'd suffered great discomposure at having to admit both his need of her and the lacking that his father had possessed as lord of Lomas. She understood this, that a man who was a proud soldier, now a proud lord, would dislike seeking any aid. She was much the same, herself.

"You would let me go on as before?" she asked. "To sit in the chair of judgment, as I have done, and to—"

"Nay, Katharine," he said firmly. "I am the lord of Lomas, and will sit in the chair of judgment. You will have a chair below me, beside either Aric or Kayne, and will serve as a member of my counsel."

She shrugged away his touch, suddenly angry. "I will not sit in so lowly a manner! Not when I was mistress of that chair only yesterday. It is too grave an insult!"

"And I will not give you my place, which I have only attained," he replied just as stubbornly. "You are too proud, Katharine. I offer you what I would no other woman."

"And you think I should be grateful?" she demanded, her voice rising. "Like some dog, given a place at his master's feet? Shall I also be made to lick your hand?"

"It is not like that!" he shouted. "God above, you willingly take insult where none is given."

Katharine crossed her arms over her chest. "Then we can reach no agreement. I have done naught but give to you since you have come, Senet Gaillard. My title, my estate, my people...even myself. I can give no more else I am become naught but a fool!"

"And I have taken nothing where I have not striven to return with equal value," he told her. "I'faith, with more. But it makes no difference with you, madam wife, for you want all or nothing." His voice rose. "There is no pleasing you!"

"Or you!" she returned hotly. "Were you in my place, Senet Gaillard, would you so readily—aye, even happily—accept so many defeats? *Would you?*"

That stopped him. He had opened his mouth to speak, then shut it and glared at her. Katharine drew in a slow, calming breath, and suddenly realized just how loudly they'd been shouting. There was a very still silence in the hall beyond the screen.

"There!" she whispered angrily, drawing closer so that she spoke directly into his face. "You've made me lose my temper and all the castle has overheard our words. Is it my reputation that you'll take from me next?"

Senet stared down at her with a fury unlike any he'd ever known. She was beyond maddening, talking him about in circles as if he were a fool, making him utterly crazed with but a few well-chosen words. The worst of it was that she was right. He would never accept so many defeats in the face of a conquering enemy, for there was only so much loss that a man could suffer before he would rather be dead. The trouble was that he hadn't thought that a woman would ever feel the like—for how could any female understand the humilities that only a man could know and fear?

Yet Katharine did. If she'd been a man, losing all that she had and being forced into every submission, he would have felt naught but pity for her. Because she was a woman he had assumed the wounds would be more easily salved. But it was not so. She was right to be offended, but he could not—*would* not let her go for anything so foolish as a chair.

"Your reputation," he said, reaching to take her hand, "is as safe as if it were fully armored. Come, Katharine. We *will* have an agreement on this matter."

He dragged her out into the great hall again, past the silent and staring castlefolk, and all the way up to the dais where Kayne and Aric yet sat.

"Up," he said to his two friends, then again, when they only stared at him dumbly, *"Up!"*

They stood, and Senet at last released Katharine, leaving her standing next to Kayne. Without another word, he moved to the chair that Aric had been sitting in and, with a powerful movement, lifted it up to the highest step, where the chair for the master of Lomas sat. The two chairs barely fit on the one level, but Senet shoved at them until they were meshed together, arm to arm. Then he turned to Aric and said, "You would be happier overseeing the men?"

Aric gave a single nod. "You know that I would."

"Then you are relieved of your duties here to take back your charge of the men."

Aric looked as if he'd just received a royal boon. Senet thought he almost saw his friend give one of his rare smiles, but the moment was brief, for Aric wasted little time in taking his leave.

Senet turned then to Kayne. "You will not be grieved or shamed to sit alone on this lower step?"

Kayne shrugged. "I am glad to sit anywhere if it be of service to you, Senet." He added, more meaningfully, "While I am yet here at Lomas."

But Senet didn't want to think of that now, for Kayne would leave them all too soon. He nodded his gratitude to his friend and then set his gaze upon Katharine, who looked fully stunned.

"And you, madam. Do you approve of this arrangement?"

Without speaking, staring at the two chairs shoved so awkwardly together, she nodded.

"Then we have an agreement." He moved closer to her so that she looked at him. "You will learn, Katharine, that I do not give way so easily. You and I will always find the way to meet on a common ground. Always."

She gazed at him with disbelief—as if he were some kind of wonderful man—and opened her mouth to speak.

Another voice sounded out first.

"M'lor!" Clarise came running from the direction of the stairs. "M'lor!"

By the time she reached the dais she was breathless, and Senet reached out to set his hands on her arms.

"What's happened?" he demanded, shooting an accusatory glance at Katharine. "Has someone offended you?"

She shook her head, answering in rapid French, pointing toward the great hall's front doors. Then she turned and ran in the direction she'd pointed, reaching the doors to open them before any of the servants could do so.

"Well?" Katharine, her voice chilly, asked from beside him. Senet turned to find that the beaming look she had set upon him a moment before had been replaced by one of cold anger. "Has Mademoiselle Rouveau been distressed by any of my people?"

"No," he replied, wishing that he hadn't so quickly assumed it had been so. He would have liked seeing more of that admiring expression on Katharine's lovely face. "She merely came to tell me that John has returned."

"John Ipris?" Katharine repeated, her entire body drawing instantly upright. "Has he—?"

Senet nodded. "Mistress Dorothea is with him. She is well, I think, for she is riding her own steed, and…" The words trailed away. Katharine hadn't waited to hear the rest of what he meant to say, but had hurriedly descended the dais and followed the same swift path that Clarise had taken.

Chapter Nine

"I want to sleep for a month. Leave me in peace, I pray you."

Katharine ignored Dorothea's pleas and continued scrubbing soap into her friend's unbound, raven-colored hair.

"Not until you're rid of all this filth. I learned only two nights ago how much better a good cleaning can make one feel. Especially after such an adventure. It's a good thing Magan fed you from the kitchen, for you'd never stay awake long enough for the evening meal. Ariette—" she cast a glance over her shoulder "—send one of the maids down for more water. Magan, where is that clean chemise?"

"Here, my lady." Magan set the garment on a chair near the fire. "And I've brought the towels, as well." She joined Katharine beside the tub in which a weary Dorothea sat, striving to keep her eyes open. "Oh, Doro," the younger girl said, rolling up her sleeves, "'tis so good to have you back at Lomas safely."

"Aye," Dorothea agreed sleepily, her eyes closed, "I'm glad, too. Now, please—"

"Wait," Katharine ordered sternly. Lifting one soapy

hand in the air, she ordered the serving maids from the room with the instruction that they could leave fresh hot water outside the door. When they had all gone, she said, "Now you may speak freely, Doro, with only Magan, Ariette and myself to hear."

"But I don't want to speak!" Dorothea wailed. "I only want to sleep!"

Katharine poured a bucket of warm water over her head. "Not until you've told us everything that happened from the moment you sneaked away from The Bull and Dog until you arrived back at Lomas," she said when Dorothea had stopped sputtering. "Here is a towel. Wipe your face and recount your tale, and then you may sleep as long as it pleases you." She reached into a nearby pot for another handful of the soft, scented soap and began to rub it over Dorothea's shoulders.

There was not much to tell. Katharine had already divined that Dorothea had left The Bull and Dog as soon as she and Magan and Ariette had fallen asleep. She'd taken her own horse and made good headway toward the place where Kieran FitzAllen was last known to be. She had only been waylaid twice, once by a group of laborers working in a field close to the road, and once by several men in a tavern where she had stopped to ask after Kie as well as to buy some food. Both times she had managed to avoid actual danger, and had continued on her way unmolested.

"But John Ipris must be blessed by the very angels," Dorothea said with a sleepy yawn as she was being dried and put into her chemise, "for he found me before the day was out. 'Twas at the inn at Saint Stephen, where I had convinced the keeper to give me a private chamber, though he took enough gold for it. But I had only sat down to take my evening meal when Master John came upon me." She willingly sat by the fire to have her thick, dark hair combed out and dried. "He was all that was kind and easy, though I threw my bowl and cup at his head."

"Doro," Ariette said chidingly, though with a smile, "that was ill-mannered."

"Aye," Dorothea admitted, "but even he agreed that 'twould have been wrong if I had submitted to him easily. Not after all I'd gone through during the day to avoid being found. And he readily forgave me the stains on his clothes. In all, I found him to be a fine and chivalrous man. And he was pleasant company, as well, on our return to Lomas, entertaining me with tales of the years he spent in France with Lord Lomas and Sirs Kayne and Aric."

"God's mercy," Katharine muttered from the bed at the other side of the chamber, where she was pulling down the coverlet. "You'll be falling in love with the man next, and then I'll have lost both you and Magan to our usurpers."

Dorothea opened her eyes at this and lifted her head to look at Magan. "You, Magan?"

Magan blushed hotly and stroked the comb through Dorothea's hair more quickly. "Oh, nay. Not me. Sir Aric has only been very kind. That is all."

Dorothea sat up. *"Sir Aric!"* she repeated with heavy surprise. "That hulking oaf?"

"He is no such thing!" Magan returned angrily, standing back and setting her hands upon her hips. "Perhaps he is not handsome as Sir Senet or Sir Kayne, or as charming and soft spoken as John Ipris, but he is most assuredly as fine and chivalrous!"

Dorothea swung her head about to look at Katharine. "I understand what it is that you speak of, my lady." She leaned back in her chair and closed her eyes again. Magan, giving her one last glare, went back to combing her hair.

"And what of you and John Ipris, Doro?" Ariette asked, combing the other side of the wet, lengthy hair.

"Naught," Dorothea answered with a sigh, "though I might wish there could be. His heart is already given elsewhere."

"In truth?" Magan asked. "But what of Jean-Marc? He is so terribly devoted to you."

Dorothea made a sound of aggravation. "Do not tease me with that horrid little rat, Magan, or I shall be merciless to you regarding Sir Aric. Though even he would be far preferable to Kieran FitzAllen's loathsome manservant."

Katharine laughed at this. "Poor Jean-Marc. He has loved you faithfully these past many years—indeed, since he set sight upon you—but you will have none of him. I cannot think how you can be so cruel."

Dorothea opened her eyes again, this time to spear Katharine with a frigid gaze. "Easily. And if we are to speak of men, my lady, why do we not make mention of your new husband? One night and day a bride, and you are seemingly in complete agreement with the man you would have gladly abolished the day before. Indeed, the two of you appear to have set every difference aside, if what I saw earlier is true."

"What did you see?" Magan asked with wide-eyed interest.

"Nothing," Katharine answered.

"Only our lord and lady with their heads together, involved in a very intent discussion. 'Twas most passionate, i'faith."

Katharine's face flamed, especially at the expressions both Magan and Ariette turned upon her. "You are demented from so long a journey, Doro," she said as calmly as she could. "Sir Senet and I were arguing, as we have done since he set foot in Lomas. He wished to interrogate you at once, and I insisted that you be allowed first to rest."

"I have watched you argue many a time before, Katharine Malthus—pardon me, for it is now Gaillard, is it not?—and have never seen such a look on your face. You are in love with him, I think."

Katharine, who had been fluffing the long feather pillow on the bed, stood upright. "Nay! I hate him, as I have done since knowing of him. My heart is not so easily won, and never by such a man as he is."

"You did wed him," Dorothea noted.

"Only because he tricked me to it! Magan can tell you the full of it."

Magan nodded, then leaned forward to say, confidentially, "But 'twas so romantic, I vow, and Sir Senet even took a ring upon his hand to mark their marriage."

"Magan!" Katharine cried.

"And today they did not come down from their wedding chamber until long past midday," Ariette added.

"In truth?" Dorothea asked, looking at Katharine, who had gone fully red in the face. "I see. Then mayhap Lomas is not all that Senet Gaillard has conquered."

"I will not speak of him!" Katharine said furiously. "Wretched fiends, the lot of you," she added with less heat as her companions laughed. She feared she had given away too much with her intemperate speech, but it would have been impossible to keep secret the tumult of her heart in regard to Senet Gaillard, especially from her closest friends. "I vow you will all drive me to madness, chattering about such nonsense when we have more important matters to discuss."

Dorothea, who had closed her eyes again, groaned aloud. "I only want to sleep! Please, I beg of you, let me go to bed."

Katharine sighed. "Very well. Perhaps 'tis not so pressing that it cannot wait until the morrow, when you have rested. And I must get belowstairs to the evening meal, as well, before my lord begins to wonder at where I have gone. I can only thank a provident God that you are home safe, Doro, especially as the journey was fruitless. But it is just as well that you didn't find Kieran, for 'tis far too late for him to make any difference now."

Dorothea's eyes opened once more. She sat up in the chair. "But I did find him, my lady."

Katharine shook her head. "You did not earlier speak of it."

"Because I did not bodily find him. But I discovered where he is and paid a man at Saint Stephen to take your missive to him. He will have had it by now."

"God's mercy," Katharine murmured, finding the nearest chair to sit in it, her gaze held on Dorothea's face. "If Kieran should come now—oh, God's mercy."

"Surely Sir Senet will merely send him on his way again?" Ariette said. "Just as he would do to the real Lord Hanley?"

"And Kieran FitzAllen won't tell him the truth." Magan lifted a hand to her throat in a nervous gesture. "Will he? Sir Senet would be terribly displeased to know that we had planned to deceive him in such a manner."

Katharine dropped her face into one of her hands. "God's mercy," she muttered again.

"I'm sorry!" Dorothea said miserably. "I didn't know that you had already been married to Sir Senet, else I would never have continued on the course we'd begun."

"Nay, it is my fault, Doro, and no one else's," Katharine told her, standing again and regaining her composure. "And if Kieran should arrive at Lomas parading as Lord Hanley, then I am the one who must take the consequences. We will speak of it no more," she said, moving to the door, "but let us agree to all pray mightily that Kieran never receives that missive. Sleep well, Doro," she said, stopping to look back at them, "and let your mind be easy on every matter. 'Tis so good to have you back at Lomas again. We should have been in desperate trouble had you not come home."

It was one thing to tell Dorothea and the others to be easy, but Katharine found it an impossible task for herself to accomplish. She made her way to her chamber to prepare for the evening meal with a heavy heart, contemplating whether she should tell Senet the truth now, rather than wait for Kieran to arrive. But perhaps, she thought, coming to a stop just before her door, Kieran wouldn't come, even if he did receive her missive. Then Senet need never know about the deceit she had planned, and then...perhaps...they might be able to make something of their marriage.

He had truly surprised her by setting another chair beside the one in which the master of Lomas sat. By doing so, he had as much as declared that he meant for them to rule Lomas together, side by side. The knowledge made Katharine smile, and set her heart to aching with a now familiar pain. She had ruled Lomas alone for such a long time, and more than once she had wished that she might share the heavy burden with someone she could trust—someone who would respect and value her skill at managing the lands and estate.

Leaning against the wall in the shadows, Katharine let herself smile. Senet Gaillard seemed to respect and value her. He was not like any other man she had met. And she, Katharine had no doubt, was unlike any woman he'd ever met, too. Her smile widened, and she was grateful for the darkness that hid her happiness. Perhaps…perhaps Doro had been right, if only a little bit. After all, Katharine thought, she suddenly found herself married to a man who was not only most handsome, but who was also kind and generous and unafraid of giving a woman a measure of power. And tonight he would come to her bed and love her again. It was, Katharine realized to her shame, something she'd thought about most of the day. Even now her heart began to beat more rapidly at the remembrance of the pleasure he'd given her, and she wondered if it would ever be thus with Senet Gaillard.

"You are foolish, Katharine," she murmured softly to herself, but still she smiled. Turning, she began to move to her door, only to be stopped by the sound of another door—the one that belonged to the chamber next to hers, which now was Senet's—opening just out of sight around the curving hall.

She could not see him, but heard his voice, though he was speaking in French too quickly and fluently for her to understand. Then another voice spoke, soft and feminine. Clarise.

Katharine froze where she was, her hand upon the latch of her own door.

The younger girl sounded distressed, pleading, and Senet was clearly trying to soothe her. The deep love in his tone was fully evident, and Katharine could almost imagine the look on his face, for she had seen him gaze at the girl with great tenderness more than once in the past two days.

Again the girl spoke pleadingly, and again Senet replied with comfort. Katharine swallowed and wondered if she could get into her chamber silently, without calling any attention to herself. She didn't want them to see her there, to know that she had caught her husband in a lie. He had promised, on his honor, to keep away from his French mistress, yet only a few hours after having given her his vow he had already broken it.

The conversation ended abruptly with the sound of a kiss, and Senet saying, in English, "Come, Clarise, before we are missed at the evening meal. All will be well," he was saying as he led the girl around the corner, his arm about her shoulders. "You must trust—" He stopped at the sight of Katharine.

"Good evening, my lord," she greeted coolly, then nodded at a terrified Clarise. "Mademoiselle. I hope you found my husband's chamber to your liking?"

"Katharine," Senet said darkly.

"Oh, milady!" Clarise uttered with trembling fear, tears streaming down her pretty face.

"Do not be troubled because of me, I pray you, mademoiselle," Katharine said, her gaze held upon her frowning husband. "I will not be at Lomas long enough to bring you any harm. I bid you good eve."

"Katharine," Senet said again, but she ignored him, opening her door and entering her chamber, shutting herself in with finality.

But he had the last word, shouting, as she stood on the other side of the door with both hands pressed against her cheeks, striving not to weep, "I'll not wait the evening meal for you this time, Katharine! You may go hungry with your pride!"

He gave her an hour to sulk, then excused himself from the high table and made his way to the kitchens. It wasn't what a proper lord would do, he realized, but despite his anger with Katharine for having so little faith in him, he was very aware that he was the one at fault for the current misunderstanding that stood between them. Aside from that, he didn't mind in the least escaping the grins and laughter that had been directed at him since he'd appeared—alone, again—at the high table. Kayne and Aric had lost no time in telling John every detail that he'd missed while he'd been absent from Lomas, and now Senet had to put up with teasing from all three of his friends.

He should let her go hungry, he thought as he made the short walk from the castle to the kitchens. He was far too soft where women were concerned—especially where Katharine was concerned, considering her unwarranted behavior. What he should do, were he a wise husband, was go up to her chamber and beat her soundly. It was what almost any other man would do, and was his right by law, as well. A disobedient wife was a woman mired in the gravest of sins, and it was his duty before God to save her soul by forcing her to obedience. Or so the church said. Senet had always been thoroughly revolted by the idea of a man raising his hand to any woman, which was most likely a legacy he'd inherited from his father, who hadn't had any better fortune in managing his wife than Senet did.

The maids in the kitchen were frightened by his abrupt appearance, a reaction that Senet was well-used to. His darkness and size often created fear in those who did not know him.

"I want something to take up to Lady Katharine," he told them. "Some of that chicken, and bread."

"Please let me be of aid to you, my lord," came a voice behind him, and he turned to find Mistress Magan, who had evidently followed him from the hall, blushing and

curtseying. Rising, she clapped her hands at the serving
maids. "Out! All of you. Go and have your meals." The
girls gratefully made a retreat, scurrying past Senet as if
he were bent upon causing harm. He scowled after them,
until he felt Mistress Magan lightly touch his arm.

"Do not let them disturb you, I pray, my lord," she
said before releasing him and moving to one of the long
tables where steaming platters of food were laid out, ready
to take into the hall. "We lived in great dread of you for
many months, since the day when Lady Katharine received Duke Humphrey's missive informing her of his
plans for your marriage. She was so terribly distressed, as
you might imagine, and though she strove mightily to hide
it from all of us—for she is the most considerate liege
lady on God's earth, I vow—we yet realized her great
dread of wedding you, and began to fear as well." She
took up a small basket from the end of one table and lined
it with a small linen cloth.

"Was I so detestable a choice for lord, then?" he
asked.

"'Twas not that, my lord, though we were indeed most
content beneath Lady Katharine's guidance." She set out
several more linen squares, deftly filling each with different foods—a succulent chicken leg, a thick slice of roasted
beef, a hunk of soft white cheese—and tying them into
small, neat packages. "'Twas more that we did not wish
her to be married against her will, for she is well-loved
by everyone at Lomas, in both the castle and the village
and, indeed, at every estate she oversees."

"I have seen with my own eyes that you speak the
truth," Senet admitted, wondering if he would ever be
able to lay claim to such love as his wife did. "Her father
was not so well-loved, I think."

The look Mistress Magan set upon him told him very

well what the people of Lomas had thought of Baron Malthus.

"I would not speak ill of my lord Malthus, may God assoil him," she said, setting each tied napkin of food into the basket, "but he was not, I fear, as concerned with the good of his people as Lady Katharine has ever been. I came to Lomas eight years ago, when I was but nine, being fostered here with my lord Malthus, and know well of what I speak. Ariette and Doro will tell you the same, for they were here before me, with Lord Malthus as their guardian. 'Twas unbearable until he gave over every burden to Lady Katharine—and her but ten and four. Ten and four!" she said again with great emphasis, looking at him only briefly before she produced a pewter goblet from a shelf beneath one of the tables, setting it beside the basket. "'Twas no easy thing for her, when her father had made every matter so impossible. There were debts—" she hesitated, then gave a shake of her head "—but I will not speak of that. And many troubles, my lord. Many troubles." She gave a great sigh. "'Tis hard even to think of those days, and what my lady suffered."

"Suffered," Senet repeated, feeling the heat of anger spreading within. He didn't love Katharine—he told himself that most firmly—but the thought of her suffering even the least amount of sorrow or pain made him feel murderous. She was strong and valiant, a warrior, but she was easily bruised, easily wounded—just as he had so foolishly and unwittingly wounded her this very day. She had let herself become vulnerable to him when he had made her his wife in full, when she might have fought him every moment. He had suffered once, as she had suffered, and had vowed that he would never again lay himself open to another being. But Katharine had trusted him, had opened herself to him, and now he couldn't bear to hear of such brave honor as hers being abused. "He did not beat her, did he?"

"Nay," Mistress Magan replied at once. "Never. No man could lift a hand to my Lady Katharine and know peace." She looked at him boldly, full in the face. "Not even you, my lord. Every man—and woman—in Lomas would rise up against you. I do not mean to speak with any manner of disrespect, my lord, but our Lady Katharine has kept us from years of hunger and misery—even to her own loss, for she never ate unless we all ate, and she would have no fire for her chamber if even one family in the village went without. All we have we owe to her, and to God's providence."

"An admirable woman in every way," he said, folding his arms and leaning against one of the tables. "How did Lady Katharine work such a miracle as to make Lomas into so prosperous a place? There is no lack here that I have yet seen, and 'tis certain 'twas no easy task to make it so."

"Nay, it was not," Mistress Magan admitted, filling a small stone pitcher with dark red wine. "Lady Katharine had no aid from any source, certainly not her father, and the merchants in the village were all at odds with one another. But she was so strong, and reasoned with them all, making terms and agreements so that all benefited. She began, as I seem to remember, with the baker, who was most unhappy with the miller for the quality of the flour he sold. The miller was unhappy as well, though with the quality of his grinding stones, but he could not buy new ones until all who owed him money paid it, and no one wished to pay for such poor goods as he delivered."

Senet grimaced at the thought of having to solve such

troublesome matters. "How did Lady Katharine deal with these fellows?"

Mistress Magan capped the pitcher with a small stopper, then carefully placed it into the basket alongside the goblet and packages of food. "She found a mason living in a nearby village and gained his aid in making new stones for the miller."

"And what did she have to promise this mason for his skill?"

Mistress Magan smiled at him. "I think that you begin to understand the difficulty of her work, my lord. Aye, indeed she had to promise him something, for he desired above all things a piece of land that he had long coveted."

Senet groaned aloud. Mistress Magan laughed.

"Aye, 'twas most vexing to my lady. But she went to the owner of the property—"

"Who made his own demands," Senet finished for her. "You need not say more, mistress, though I am grateful that you have told this much. I pray you will believe I speak the truth to you now, for I vow that I will bring no harm to Lady Katharine. My lady wife will have every honor, and more, that is her due."

Mistress Magan blushed again, so pretty and sweet a maid that Senet believed his stoic friend Aric would soon find himself a fallen man. Bringing forward the basket in one hand and a wrapped loaf of bread in the other, she gave him a shy smile.

"I believe, my lord, that if any man can bring happiness to my lady, you are him. Do not let her frighten you away with her outward manner, for she can be, at times, most stern. Beyond all she may wish you to think or know, she is yet a woman, and the heart within her desires far more than to be merely admired as a capable leader."

Senet touched the young woman's chin and smiled

down at her. "You may be certain, Mistress Magan, that I admire Lady Katharine in every way that a man can admire a woman, and far more. I will take all care with her heart."

He reached for the basket and bread, but she held them back.

"Shall I not take them to her, my lord? You would not wish to be seen walking through the hall bearing such as this, for all would know that you yet again gave way to my lady's ill humor."

He laughed. "Have no fear for my reputation, Mistress Magan, it will be safe." He took the bread and tucked it under one arm, then reached again for the basket. "There are many secret ways into and out of Castle Lomas, and I know each and every one of them."

Chapter Ten

Katharine was folding her clothes—every piece that she owned—making neat, angry piles of them upon her bed, when Senet suddenly pushed aside the tapestry that hid her chamber's secret passageway and stepped inside.

She took one look at him and turned to find something to throw.

"Katharine," he began calmly, "I only want you to listen to me before you—"

The small pewter box she took up from her mirrored table missed him by several inches, and Katharine inwardly cursed. He was moving closer, his hands held out placatingly, and she took several steps farther away, searching for something else to toss at his head.

"Go away!" she warned with all seriousness, looking about her. "God help me, where is that knife? What did you do with it?" She whirled to face him. "You may be the lord of Lomas, but you have no right to enter my chamber unannounced *and* uninvited. Now go!"

"Katharine, my sweet," he said reasonably, following her as she avoided him, "you have no cause to be so angered. Once you've heard me out, you'll feel most foolish."

She heaved a wooden bowl at his head. He ducked and kept coming, arms held out wide.

"Go away, Senet Gaillard! I want nothing to do with you! Liar! Knave! Do not dare to touch me! Senet! I mean what I say!"

He swept her up in his arms, ignoring her flailing fists, and carried her back to the secret passageway.

"I know that you do, little warrior," he told her, bending to fit the both of them into the passage—no simple feat as she made every effort to grab the sides of the opening. "I think that you always mean what you say. Just as I always mean what I say."

"Ha!" She folded her arms across her chest and glared at him in the torchlit passage as he carried her along. "Will you deny that you have broken the vow you made to me only last eve? And which you swore to me on your very honor?"

He nodded. "I have not broken it."

"With my own eyes I saw you do so!" she charged furiously. "By God above, you must believe me an utter idiot. Where are you taking me?" She struggled against his grip. "I have no time for such foolishness."

"What you saw," he said patiently, stopping near a brightly burning torch to set her down, "was a matter of complete innocence. I have not dishonored you with Clarise, and will not dishonor you with her or any other woman. Have you seen the hidden passage that begins here?" He indicated the slender wooden door set near the torch.

With a fulminating glare, she reached back to push the door open. "'Tis hardly secret," she said. "But there is no use to it, for it goes nowhere."

"But it does." He took the torch from the wall. "Come, Katharine." He held out a hand.

Ignoring him, she walked ahead into the new and far narrower passage, making her way with surefooted ease. Senet followed, carrying the torch high to light her way. In the space of a few moments the passage opened to a small, unremarkable chamber, where a large, uncovered opening looked out upon a tiny balcony.

"You see?" she said, sweeping an arm in a slow turning arc to indicate their surroundings until she came about to face him. "'Tis too small to live in, too high in the castle to be of use for defense, and too far removed from the main halls to make a useful place of storage. Your father was foolish to have it built."

He was busy setting the torch in the one holder that the room provided. "Nay," he said, "but you do not know the secret of it, my lady, for indeed it serves a very fine purpose."

"Secret?" Curiosity warred against her anger, and she looked at him warily. "There is no secret. I know everything about Castle Lomas. Everything."

He smiled. "But not this. 'Twill be our own secret, just as it once was to my father and mother. Come to the window, Katharine. Look, there."

She peered out into the dark night, at the small balcony just below the window. She had always wondered at the purpose the balcony served, and had finally decided that it was merely decorative.

"Have you ever stepped out onto the balcony?" he asked.

She shook her head. "Nay. 'Twould be foolish. There is nothing to be seen that cannot also be seen here, from this opening."

"But there is." He set one leg over the short wall that separated the opening from the balcony, then the other, hopping down until he stood upon the balcony itself.

Turning he held his hands out for Katharine, but she pushed them away and hopped across on her own. "'Tis very simple to reach," he admitted, though both his tone and expression were filled with admiration for her competence, "even for a lady in full dress. My father made certain it was thus, so that my mother could readily come and go as she pleased. But with privacy, as well. This—" he set a hand upon the wall that ran the length of the balcony "—is high enough to hide such activity from below. Now turn back to face the window, Katharine, and you shall see what cannot be seen except from out here. The secret of which I spoke."

She turned and looked. And gaped with surprise at what she saw. He had spoken rightly—it could not have been seen unless one made the short hop from the chamber outside to the balcony, but there it was. Another wall, jutting a little farther from the true castle wall, but only enough to hide the passageway that she now saw revealed behind it.

She looked at him. "Where does it go?"

He stretched his hand out to her once more, palm up. "Come, my good lady wife, and I will show you."

She was yet wary of him, gazing up into the dark, handsome face that was at once both proud and open, into crystalline eyes that beckoned her toward realms so totally unknown, but she set her hand in his, felt his fingers curl about hers and gently draw her forward.

It was not a long passage, only a few steps, leading to a closed door. Senet tugged the latch and swung the door wide, pulling Katharine into a beautiful candle- and fire-lit chamber. Ornate tapestries lined the walls and soft rugs covered the floor. Near the warmth of the chamber's small fire, several pillows were laid out beside a low table, which now was set with what appeared to be a small feast.

One wall of the chamber was lined with shelves, and on these were numerous bound manuscripts and an assortment of odd-looking instruments. All were covered in thick dust, just as the room was, save for the table where the feast was set and the pillows lay. Only that had been recently—very recently—cleaned.

"What is this place?" she whispered, filling with a strange numbness as she turned slowly about. "I never knew that anything such as this existed in Lomas. And I would have sworn by my own life that I knew all of it."

"Does it strike hard, little warrior, to discover that you did not?" he asked, setting a comforting hand on the back of her neck, touching lightly.

She was hot with sensation—anger, embarrassment, surprise—and hardly knew how to answer, save with the truth. "Aye," she murmured, and told herself that it was as well that she would be leaving this place that she loved so well. She cared far too much for Lomas if such a small, hidden discovery made her feel so wretched.

His touch grew warmer, his fingers more caressing. "I did not know of it, either, until the day before I left Lomas to be fostered with Lord Howton. I was but nine, then." He dropped his hand and took a few more steps into the room. "My father had this room made for my mother. 'Twas the place where she might come when she wished to be alone, to follow her study of numbers without being disturbed. And to be alone with him, I think." He glanced at her. "After I learned of it, I suddenly realized where it was they had so often disappeared to. They were both possessed of deeply romantic humors, I fear, though my father was far worse than my mother. She, at least, had a practical mind to go with the other."

"Did she, Senet?" Katharine still felt too stunned to think of any better reply.

"Here's proof of what I say." He moved to one of the shelves and picked up a small, angular instrument. "One of her toys. It's for measuring the distance between stars, I think." He lifted it to peer at it more closely. "'Twould make me go blind, I vow, just trying to understand how it works. My sister, Isabelle, could make sense of it, were she here." He put the instrument aside. "But she is as my mother was, just as I told you."

Katharine moved nearer to the fire, rubbing her hands over her chilled arms.

"There are no windows here to gaze at the stars. How is it that I never knew of this hearth? The chimney that serves it must surely have given it away." She shook her head. "I have missed it all these years. And my father, as well. So many years."

"'Tis why it is so full of dust and cobwebs." He moved nearer. "Come and sit here by the fire, Katharine, and eat. I brought you here because I wished to tell you of Clarise...and to make a gift to you of the chamber. 'Twill be our own after this night, and you must come here whenever it pleases you."

"Me?" she asked, resisting his attempt to draw her to the table. "What should I do here? I have never been allowed much time to myself."

"And neither have I, since I can remember," he said, touching her chin and smiling. "But mayhap we may give each other a few moments of such leisure, as a man and wife may do. Come, let me serve you, Katharine, and tell you about Clarise."

"I do not wish to hear of her," she said stubbornly, reluctantly sitting on the pillow he took her to. The food laid out before her looked wonderful, and smelled even better. Her empty stomach rumbled with aching hunger. "Nor do I want any more of your lies."

Senet sat on a pillow across from her. "'Twould be better if you first drink and eat before saying any more." He filled a goblet with dark red wine and pushed it toward her. "'Tis not poisoned, Katharine," he said when she only continued to glower at him.

"If it were," she muttered, lifting the goblet to her lips, "I would take it directly to your mistress and pour it down her dainty throat."

Senet's eyebrows lifted. "Would you, Katharine? Poor Clarise, to have made such an enemy. And her so sweet and innocent a child."

Katharine set the goblet down with such force that wine sloshed over the edge and dripped upon the table.

"Do not mock me with your whore, Senet Gaillard. I have said I will leave Lomas so that you may live with her openly, but I will not be humiliated before my people." She swallowed heavily. "Not when you gave me your word—" She could say no more without giving way to emotion.

Senet was silent for a moment, giving his attention to filling a napkin with food. "Can it be that my noble wife is jealous?" he asked at last, quietly and calmly. Before she could reply he continued, "Nay, do not answer such a foolish question, for we have already decreed that love can have no part in this marriage, and therefore no cause for jealousy on either side. Here." He tugged the napkin across the table until it lay before Katharine. "I am sorry it is so poor a meal, but pray you will enjoy it."

It wasn't poor at all, Katharine thought as she gazed down at the food he had assembled for her. She was half-starving, her mouth watering at the delicious scents that assailed her, yet she found that she could not eat. Or even speak. She merely closed her eyes and lowered her head, wretched with the knowledge that Senet Gaillard could hurt her as no one—not even her father—had been able to do.

"Katharine," he murmured, reaching across the table to cover her hand. "I have distressed you as I never meant to do, and beg you will forgive me. I wish, before God, that I had not deceived you, and cannot fully know why I've done so. I believe 'twas a mere vanity, and nothing better, because no other woman has cared to be angered on my account for such a cause. But there is nothing good in such deceit. I will give you the truth now, as I should have done before. Clarise is naught more than my ward— my foster daughter, i'faith. I vow on my honor that this is the truth."

She shook her head, even more unhappy. "That only makes the matter far worse. That you should dally with one so closely beneath your care."

"Nay, but you do not understand. Clarise has been as my daughter since she was but eight years of age. Her father was a French nobleman, a baron in Normandy who was faithful to England's king. He fell beside me on the field of war and begged me, before he died, to foster Clarise as my own, to care for her and her inheritance until she might wed. I was yet a young man, only eighteen and ill-prepared to give care to a child—most especially a girl child. But I gave Baron Rouveau my word, and Clarise has been with me since. The love I bear her is only that of a father. Nothing more sinful than that, little warrior. And nothing less fierce."

Katharine had lifted her head to look at him long before he finished speaking. She searched his face and saw that he spoke the truth—nothing was held secret behind that open gaze.

"Why was she in your chamber earlier?"

He at once looked aggravated, and stiffly sat back. "I

arranged a marriage for her before we left France to a man of suitable birth and fortune, whom I believe her true parents would have very much approved of. I thought to send for him, that he might come to Lomas and continue courting Clarise, perhaps even wed her here, but she insists that she will have none of him. 'Tis naught but a girl's foolish fancy—'' he waved his hand as if waving the idea away ''—for she will soon enough discover that I have done what is best, and will reconcile herself to her marriage. But when she came to my chamber in tears…'' He shrugged as if it were not so important, but his face told more, that her distress had touched him deeply. ''I tried to reassure her that all will be well.'' He looked at Katharine. ''And it will be, once she has left behind so many foolish and romantic notions. Why do you not eat?''

Katharine blinked, looked down at the food he'd prepared for her, and reached for a piece of chicken.

''You're hungry,'' he said with open satisfaction after she had nearly finished what was before her. He filled her goblet anew with wine. ''I knew that you would be.''

Sated, she reached across the table for a napkin that he had left in the basket, drew it out and delicately wiped her lips. Then she took a sip of wine, set her goblet aside, and, looking at him very directly, said, ''I find that I must offer you an apology, my lord, if what you have said is true. I was far wrong in my assumptions regarding your relationship to Mademoiselle Rouveau. I will not insult you in such a manner again. I make you this vow on my honor, which I hold as dearly as you hold your own.''

''I know that, Katharine,'' he said softly.

She nodded. ''In the morn, I will also make an apology to her.''

''There is no need.'' He sat forward and took her hand again. ''Indeed, 'twould be more seemly were I to make apologies to you, as well as to Clarise. She has feared you so greatly, and I am all to blame.''

Katharine pulled her hand away, feeling her own guilt regarding her deception with Kieran so deeply. "Not as much as I," she said, unable to look at him any longer. "I gave her little welcome, I…made every moment as unpleasant as I might. For you as well. I no longer know what I can say to you, my lord. It all seems wrong." She frowned. "And false. Just as I am, for I no longer know who I am, or where I belong. Even Lomas is become suddenly strange to me."

She shut her eyes tightly and set a fist against her forehead. "God above, I am so weary. Almost from the moment I heard of you, I have been weary." She pushed from the table, turning from him, and lay down upon the pillows, pressing her face into the softness of them.

He was beside her in a moment, pulling her up into his arms. "Don't be distressed, Katharine," he whispered, holding her tight against himself. "I meant to give you ease, but still I give naught but grief. You belong at Lomas more surely than I, and I will not let you so easily go." He kissed the side of her face, her cheek and ear. "I have yet six days to convince you that we can live together in peace and contentment. You will not leave before then."

She shook her head against his shoulder.

"'Tis well," he murmured, placing his fingers beneath her chin and gently lifting her face to his. There was no resistance in her when he kissed her mouth. Quite the opposite. She leaned into him, the tension in her body easing by degrees as the moments passed. His tongue pressed lightly at the seam of her lips, and she parted them, inviting the deeper caress with a soft murmur.

Senet lowered her to the pillows, and again she murmured, this time with a sound of relief.

"Shall I love you, Katharine?" he asked softly, one hand already pulling the laces of her surcoat free. "I want to give you pleasure." He lowered his head to kiss her neck, then the skin just above her breasts. "I want to give you peace and ease."

Her eyes were closed, her breathing heightened. "Yes," she whispered, lifting her arms so that he might pull the garments from her body. "Please." The word came out on a sigh as he removed her leggings in a slow, sensual caress, tossing them and her slippers aside.

When she was completely bare, he leaned forward to kiss her belly. "Nay, Katharine, but you must not say 'please' to me, for I am your husband. 'Tis your right, and my duty, to pleasure you." His big, callused hands moved lightly over her body, caressing her face, her neck, her breasts, moving downward over her limbs, stroking her arms and legs, even her feet, until she was restless with sensation. "Turn now. Onto your stomach. That's it. God above, you are so beautiful." His fingertips delicately traced the curves of her waist and hips, causing Katharine to shiver. He gathered up the heavy mass of her hair and spread it across the pillows, leaving her back fully exposed.

"Now," he said, leaning forward again until his breath was warm and moist on her skin, "relax for me, Katharine, and let me pleasure you."

His mouth touched her neck, first, in the spot just beneath her ear, lingering a moment before moving up to her ear, which his tongue lightly stroked.

"Oh," Katharine murmured, trying to turn away from the shocking pleasure of the caress. His response was to set a hand on the crown of her head to hold her in a gentle prison while he continued to delve and ravish the sensitive organ, drawing helpless groans and murmuring from Katharine. When he stopped, setting his warm mouth against her neck again, she said, "'Tis like torture!"

He laughed in a low tone. "Aye. Sweet torture. And there is more. Let me show you...."

He kissed and caressed every inch of her back, ignoring her faint protests and restless twisting, holding her down to receive the heated pleasure of his lips and tongue, even his teeth, which nipped lightly at her shoulder blades and down the length of her spine. He kissed her legs and licked the backs of her knees with quick, teasing strokes until she thought she would cry out aloud with the pleasure, then he suddenly turned her about, flipping her onto her back before she could make even a sound of protest.

She gazed up at him in the chamber's dim light, breathless and beyond protest, watching through half-opened eyes as he lifted one of her legs to his mouth, kissing the inside of her thigh.

"Oh, nay...nay," she pleaded softly as his mouth moved upward, his tongue licking at the too sensitive skin. She began to think that he did not mean to stop, and truly panicked. "Senet...oh, nay...do not...I beg you."

He was breathing harshly, and his touch had grown suddenly stronger, his grip fierce. With a sudden movement he lay on top of her, heavily covering her body with his own. His mouth greedily took hers and he pressed hard against her until she felt the strength of his arousal. His hand fumbled with the laces of his leggings, and Katharine helped, her movements desperate and clumsy.

"Aye," he murmured against her lips. "Open for me, Katharine. Let me love you."

He came deeply inside of her, thrusting hard, groaning aloud with a fierce pleasure that matched her own. She gripped him, moved with him, pleaded for release. She cried out when it came, not knowing what she said or what it meant, and heard, beyond the din of pleasure and the hard shuddering of his body, his deep answering groan.

There was silence then, save for the harshness of their breathing. Katharine's thoughts were disjointed and blurred. Senet lay atop her, seemingly lifeless. He made no attempt to separate their bodies, but covered her like a hot, heavy, damp blanket. Katharine didn't particularly mind. She lifted one hand to touch one of his arms, which was wrapped tight about her waist, and realized that he yet wore his clothes. He made a muffled sound of contentment at her touch, then sighed and nestled his head more comfortably on the pillow beside her head. Still he made no move to lift himself off of her, and when Katharine turned to look at him it was to find that he had fallen asleep.

"Senet?" she murmured, to which he gave no response. She smiled, thinking wearily that he had kept his promise to give her peace. With a sigh, she closed her own eyes, shifted as much as she could beneath him to be comfortable, and followed him into slumber.

Chapter Eleven

The candles had gone out by the time he woke, and the fire had died to glowing embers. He was lying on his side, Katharine tucked half beneath him, curled into him, naked and soundly asleep. Careful not to disturb her, he propped up on one elbow and gazed at her in the dim light. Images drifted through his mind, memories of war and blood and death, thoughts of France and what he'd known there during the past ten years. So much horror and ugliness, so much darkness. He had felt the scars of those days and events as deeply as the ones that marred his flesh, and had believed they would always be with him. Yet now, gazing at his wife, his former life seemed far away, as if it could no longer reach him in any palpable way.

What troubled him so much was that he did not know if this newfound strength had come from being at Lomas, as he had dreamed of for so long, or because of the woman who lay beside him. Being at Lomas gave him an almost overwhelming sense of happiness, but Katharine…she wrought altogether different feelings—and hopes—within. Hopes for, at last, a measure of peace in his life. And contentment. He had caught himself earlier in the day dreaming no longer of the past, but of the future, of living at Lomas with Katharine and whatever children God might bless them with.

Lifting a hand, he touched the soft curls that had fallen upon her cheek, gently wrapping a few of the silky red-gold strands upon one finger. He had not wanted to marry, but now he began to think that it was not so terrible a thing. He rather liked the knowledge that Katharine was his wife—his alone.

Releasing the curl, Senet carefully and slowly pushed up to his feet, dragging his leggings up over the cold flesh of his exposed legs and tying them. He looked down at himself briefly, amused to think that he had made love to his wife with his boots and clothes on. At least he had been able to keep Katharine warmer, lying so close upon her.

Leaving her shoes and leggings, he covered her with the heavy surcoat she had earlier worn, wrapping her in it as securely as he could before lifting her up in his arms. She made no protest nor opened her eyes, but, with a sigh, set an arm about his neck and nestled her head comfortably against his shoulder.

Only when he climbed back into the opening, jostling her slightly, did she murmur, saying, "I am too heavy."

Senet chuckled softly, drawing her into the castle. "I do not find you thus. You are a sweet burden. And a light one."

"You are a base liar, my lord," she muttered, yawning and snuggling against him as he carried her through the secret passageway toward her chamber.

"Nay, 'tis more truly said that I am a great warrior, far bigger than you, and far stronger."

She smiled against his shoulder. "I needs must ask Father Aelnoth to speak of the sin of vanity next Sabbath, I see.''

"He would do better to speak of the sins of lust and indulgence, methinks,'' Senet replied, pushing at the heavy tapestry hiding the secret passage to pass into the chamber. "I fear I have become a grave victim of such these past two days.'' He strode directly to the bed and, with one hand, tossed the coverlets aside. Laying Katharine upon the sheets, he found her mouth and kissed her. "I have never been so needy for a woman in my life, I vow. I have but to look at you and I want you, sweet Katharine.'' He kissed her again, then regretfully pulled away and stood, gazing at her naked beauty for a lingering moment before pulling the covers up to warm her. She smiled up at him in the darkness, but her weariness was so evident that he could not let himself take pleasure from her again.

He was weary, too. Moving to the other side of the bed, he began picking up the neat piles of clothes she had earlier made, tossing each of them on the floor.

"My clothes!'' she protested, sitting up. "Senet!''

"They will be just as well on the floor, and will come to no harm before the morn arrives. I cannot sleep with them taking up half the bed.'' He sat down to pull his boots off.

Katharine lay down again. "You might prefer your own bed, then.''

Senet smiled at the curtness of her tone, and stood to unlace and remove his leggings.

"I might,'' he admitted, crawling beneath the covers until he lay next to her. "But I think you will keep me warmer here.'' He slid his arms around her waist and drew her near. She must have felt the strength of his arousal, for she gave a soft gasp as their bodies touched.

"I seem to want you always, just as I said," he told her. "But we will sleep, for you are full weary, as am I. In the morn, I will make love to you again."

"Will you?" she asked.

He nodded against the top of her head, where he had comfortably settled his cheek. "If you will let me."

There was a great deal of tension in her now, so that Senet added, "I will never take you by force, Katharine. You need but say nay, and I will leave you in peace."

She was silent, some of her tautness eased. After a moment she said, very softly, "I will not say nay."

He tilted her chin up and kissed her, gently and lingeringly. "Then I will love you well and fully, and afterward, when we have broken our fast and finished with estate matters, mayhap you will go out riding with me, and teach me of Lomas all over again."

"I should be very glad to do so," she murmured, relaxing completely against him now, her head on his chest. She yawned loudly and set a hand about his waist. "Very glad. I will take you to the Convent of Saint Genevieve to see the children. And the sisters."

"Sleep, then." He closed his eyes and felt the deep contentment that he had so newly discovered wash through him, drawing him down into slumber.

It was just as he had imagined it would be, standing at the high table in the great hall with his noble lady at his side, the castlefolk of Lomas spread out at the long tables below. In the place of honor, near the salt bowl, Father Aelnoth gave the blessing for the meal, his voice loud and eloquent. Servants waited to place the many platters of food they held upon the tables. It was, Senet thought, a fine way to start a new day.

He was truly the lord of Lomas at last, after all his years of striving. He was here, in his rightful place, with Katharine at his side, overseeing his—their—people. It was a feeling like no other.

When Father Aelnoth was done Senet first seated Katharine, then waited for a servant to pull out his own chair. Following this signal, the rest of the feasters sat down to break their fast and begin the new day.

"The castlefolk are happy to see you in your rightful place again, Katharine," he said, glancing sideways to see her face. "And I am grateful to have you at my side."

She did not look at him, but smiled, clearly thinking herself unobserved. "'Tis good to be at table again," she said, her tone careful and dignified. When she lifted her face the smile had gone, replaced by a more formal expression. "And it is good to have you by *my* side, my lord."

"Is it?" he asked, biting back the urge to laugh. She would never give way, his Katharine. "It is good that we sit in equal stature, then, just as we shall do in the manner of judgment."

"Aye, indeed, that is so," she offered graciously, tearing off a piece of bread from the fresh loaf that had been set in front of them to share. "I am willing to share, so long as you take your part of the burden."

She was teasing him, he realized. And he was teasing her. God above, but it was wonderful. He hadn't smiled in the past ten years as he had smiled in the past two days. But there was something more he had realized...that Katharine was no longer so unhappy to have him at Lomas, as lord, and as her husband. She was yet a bit wary, for despite the intimate early morning loving they had shared, she had become stiff and resisting when he'd escorted her down to the hall. But when they had neared the high table she had behaved as demurely as any gentle lady might, deferring to him openly before the people of Lomas, keeping her hand upon his arm as if she needed his guidance. Allowing him to direct Father Aelnoth in the giving of the blessing, which duty she had before now performed for the past seven years, first in place of her father, and then as the lady of Lomas.

He was more than a little grateful, and could only pray that such good feeling between them would continue. Especially when the morning meal was finished and they took their places together in the hall to give audience and decide whatever matters were brought before them. The day before had proved to Senet how lacking in skills he was to care for such matters, but Katharine was clearly not. He looked forward to seeing how she ruled Lomas, and what practices she had used to so successfully make the estate lawful and wealthy.

"You dare to come before your new lord with such base lies upon your lips?" Katharine abruptly stood and descended the dais, so threatening that the men standing before her took several steps back.

"But, my lady..." the town mayor began.

"I will not have it!" she told him hotly, snatching the rolled parchment he held out of his trembling hands. "Snakes! Villains!" She shook the document at the small group of men. "Can you so insult the lord of Lomas by bringing such deceit before him as if you did not know how false and insignificant this matter is? Speak!" She pointed the parchment into the face of the village cobbler.

"You, Niall Radley. I want to hear what reason you have for visiting such grave insult upon your lord."

The slender man nervously cleared his throat. "My lady, we have only brought the matter to Lord Lomas with the hope that he might...might..." His hands fluttered helplessly before him.

Katharine stepped nearer, taller than he and forcing him to look up at her. "You thought to trick him into doing your bidding, when I have already decided upon this matter. Is this not the truth of it? You will not have forgotten my judgment regarding the land of John the Barber? Or is it simply that you hope to make null this same judgment in the hopes that Lord Lomas will make one more to your liking?"

"Oh, nay, my lady," the town mayor replied at once. "Never that!"

"What, then?" Katharine whirled about to face him. "If you lie to me again, sir, I will have you whipped! And will wield the instrument with my own hand, I vow! The truth," she said, her voice becoming dangerously low as she circled the man, "is that I was not to be here—" she pointed to the dais where Senet sat watching them "—or so you believed. You saw your chance to trick Lord Lomas into forfeiting my determination and ruling in your favor. *This* is the truth. Do you deny it?" She poked the rolled document at each man in the group. "Do you? Or you? Speak, base cowards! Your lord waits to hear what you wish of him!"

She threw the document onto the rushes with a sound of disgust and stomped back up the dais stairs. Sitting in her chair, she let out a taut breath and glared at the men below.

Senet regarded her for a moment with a look set somewhere between amusement and surprise, then he gave his attention to the town mayor, who appeared to wish mightily that he were elsewhere.

"Well, sir? You have elected to speak for the assembled. What have you to say? Present your case."

The mayor bowed nervously as the cobbler snatched up the rolled parchment.

"It is not so important a matter, my lord, as we may have thought," the mayor said, bowing again. "'Twas indeed but a fancy that brought us before you, and we will not waste more of your time."

"Nay, let me hear of it," Senet said. "I am most curious to see what has so angered my good lady wife, I vow."

A lengthy silence followed while the town mayor and the cobbler exchanged meaningful glances.

"They are too cowardly to speak of it now, my lord," Katharine said with disgust, "when their vile plotting has been so unhappily revealed. Did you not see how they hesitated when first they entered the hall and saw that I sat here beside you?"

"Indeed, I had wondered at it, when yesterday they were so eager to speak to me, and could not for all those who came before them."

"Aye, and how happy they would have been, could they have but attained audience with you then. They will not speak, therefore I will do so."

"My lady!" the mayor cried pleadingly. "You but misunderstand our intent."

"Do I?" Katharine asked. "Bring me the map and we shall let our lord decide."

The cobbler, bolder than the others, strode forward and handed her the rolled parchment.

"That land should belong to us!" he said with sudden anger, though his face was hot with embarrassment. "'Tis grievous unfair that you have kept it from us!"

"Do you dare to speak to your lady thus?" Senet asked angrily.

Katharine held out a staying hand, unwilling to let any man speak for her, no matter how sweet it was to have Senet rise as her champion. She had always wondered what it would be like to have a man support her authority, rather than fight against it. But she could only afford to anger the cobbler so far before he would refuse to make the shoes that the children in the convent so badly needed. As it was, she would have the devil's own time getting him to fulfill his bargain with her now.

"He does not. Niall Radley is an honorable man, and feels strongly that his case is right," she said, holding the cobbler's gaze. "I take no offense."

He was abashed and bowed, backing away. "I would not offend my lady Katharine for any reason. Forgive me if my words seemed to be what they should not be."

Katharine unrolled the map and held it out so that Senet could see it. John Ipris, who had taken Aric's place on the dais, rose from his chair to stand behind them and look at the parchment. Kayne, who sat on the other side of Katharine, held his gaze on the men below.

"Here." Katharine touched the document with one finger. "This field was the property of John the Barber, who held it completely and solely. 'Tis the most valuable land within the estate of Lomas, being blessed on one side by the main road and on the other by the river. Before he died, 'twas kept ready for crops, but never used—I was unable to discover why, for he ever stated that he would seed it each year. But 'twas well-maintained, and richly limed.''

'''Twould be a grave sin to let such fertile land go barren, my lord Lomas,'' the mayor added.

Katharine nodded her agreement of this before continuing.

"John the Barber had no living family, my lord, either wife or child, brother, sister or close cousin. There are distant relatives, but he did not want the land deeded to them upon his passing. He was a most Godly man—''

"And also a man of great civil responsibility, my lady,'' the cobbler interjected meaningfully. When Katharine looked at him he added, more respectfully, "Did he not always say that the people of Lomas were as his own family?''

"I cannot think it wise,'' Senet said with warning full in his voice, "that you should so continually interrupt the lady of Lomas.''

Katharine would have smiled at this if it wouldn't have been a disastrous thing to do in the midst of such an encounter. If Senet had any idea that the people of Lomas would treat either of them with the respect reserved for the nobility, then he was far wrong. Katharine had long ago abandoned such false sentiments for something far more real and valuable—the power to barter openly and honestly. Aside from that, the people of Lomas had proven their loyalty to her in a more compelling manner than mere posturing could do. When Senet Gaillard had threatened Lomas, her people had stood with her completely, right down to the children. Now, if he wished to win their loyalty as well, he would have to do more than play the noble lord.

"Shortly before John the Barber died, he made his will

quite clear on what was to be done with the land—"
Katharine paused to see whether she would be interrupted
yet again, but Senet's admonition seemed to have silenced
the others. "He desired that it be used to glorify God, and
also for the common good of the people of Lomas. I was
named as the overseer of his will, and 'twas lawfully declared—with Father Aelnoth as witness—that I alone
should determine how the land might be best put toward
attaining his wishes."

John Ipris, evidently having committed the map to his
perfect memory, straightened.

"There is neither monastery nor cathedral at Lomas,"
he stated. "Nor is there within many miles of here."

"Nay," Katharine admitted. "There is not. And thus
the difficulty in meeting the first of John the Barber's
wants. How to honor God through use of the land."

"*We* will honor God through it," the mayor declared.
"And John the Barber meant for the people of Lomas to
have that land."

"I do not see that this is so," Kayne remarked, breaking his morning-long silence. "'Twas to be for the common good of the people, and that is all."

Katharine nodded at the words. "This is verily so,
though the mayor and the cobbler would have the land
turned over to them, to farm it as they see fit."

"For the good of the people!" the mayor insisted.
"'Twould be available for all to use."

"Overseen by you," Katharine said.

"Aye," the cobbler admitted. "But each family would
have a plot, equal all, to plant as they wish. 'Twould be
fair and *equal*." He emphasized the last word.

Katharine frowned. "But only so long as one and all
followed your bidding. There can be no assurances that

you would not use the land to profit yourselves, or to further your own gain. You each have a great deal of family abiding in Lomas. With each member receiving a plot, you would shortly possess most of the land, and wield great power over those who had less.''

"It would not be so!" the cobbler replied adamantly, offense heavy in his tone.

"Truly?" Katharine returned with equal measure. "And if any in the village chose to go to Grenwald to use the cobbler there? Can you swear before God that you'd not hold the use of that land against them?''

"I would not!"

Furious, Katharine stood again, tossing the map to the rushes once more. "Indeed, sir? Just as you did not withhold your services from Alexander Bakewell because he merely let his own brother, the cobbler from Kingsmere, sell him the leather for a new saddle? Is that how you mean to be fair to one and all? Nay, there is no assurance that every manner of trouble will not arise should you and the mayor oversee the land as you wish.''

"Katharine," Senet said calmly, drawing her attention from the angry men below. "What did you earlier decide regarding this matter? I would know what deceit these men have attempted to visit upon me.''

She sat down again.

"It is clear that the charge of the land must be given in some manner to the church, and I have written to the archbishop in London to advise me as to how it might be done so that the people of Lomas will yet benefit.''

Niall Radley snorted aloud. "He will give it over to some distant monastery, which will take every profit for its own. How can the people of Lomas benefit from such as that?''

"However, Lady Katharine's decision seems to be a wise one," John Ipris said. "In such a matter as this, where so many have a great deal to gain or lose, a little patience is worth much."

"When will you hear from the archbishop?" Senet asked.

"Father Aelnoth thinks another month. The matter of our betrothal—of my reluctance to wed—" She flushed and looked away. "He believes that the archbishop may have delayed his answer until he discovered what the outcome of our marriage should be."

"As that is no longer a question," Senet said, amusement heavy in his tone, "we should have the archbishop's reply soon. I find your decision to be both just and prudent, my lady, and cannot believe that I would have made a better one. Indeed, were you not at my side, I would have given way to the deceit these men have brought before me today, most like, and committed the grave error of setting such valuable land into their care. You have kept me from such as that, and I thank you."

Katharine lifted her face to look at him, her earlier embarrassment forgotten in the pleasure of such lavish praise.

"My lord," the mayor said, wringing his folded hands toward Senet in a pleading gesture, "pray do not believe that our motives were so utterly base. Our cause is just, and we but came to plead with you on its behalf."

"Indeed," the cobbler agreed. "Our cause *is* just. John the Barber meant that land for the people of Lomas."

Senet stood, and slowly began to descend the dais. "But you would have gained it by methods that can only be seen as unjust," he said, moving until he stood very close, so much taller than the other men that he seemed to tower over them. "You are fortunate, indeed, that my good lady wife kept me from believing such lies as you meant to give me, for if I had discovered too late that she had already ruled upon the matter, and that you had basely caused me to alter that ruling, I would have been very, very angry." Reaching out, he grabbed a fistful of each man's tunic, drawing them nearer and speaking in a low, careful tone. "Lady Katharine's word is now as it was before, save that now 'tis strengthened, for I stand behind it, and will rightly punish any man who dares to defy it. Remember that." He released them and they stepped back, their eyes wide upon him. "'Twould be wise if you do not present yourselves before me for a goodly length of time," Senet advised. "I will not be so forbearing upon our next encounter. Now, leave."

The two men rejoined their friends, all of whom had remained silent throughout the confrontation, and who now, with the mayor and the cobbler, bowed repeatedly to both Senet and Katharine before turning about and fairly well fleeing the hall. There was a large silence in the room after the group had gone; even the servants had fallen still, which they had not done when Katharine had earlier raged at their guests. They were too well-used to their lady's fierce manner of dealing with such men to become agitated, but their new lord's quieter and more threatening skill had gained the attention of one and all.

Senet turned back to Katharine and held out his hand. "We have finished giving audience for the day, have we not? Come, my lady, let us make ready for our outing. I am weary of such as this."

Katharine stood and set her hand in his, letting him lead her down the stairs to where he stood. She felt yet dazed from all that had occurred, and murmured, "Thank you."

He smiled at her and began to lead her across the hall, ignoring the many eyes upon them.

"I am the one who should thank you," he said. "You saved me from making a grave mistake. But, God above, Katharine, I admit that you gave me much of a start this morn. I had thought you to be all noble lady before your people, regal and cold. But the heated manner in which you cowed them!" He laughed and shook his head. "Nay, do not bristle at me, sweet wife," he added when she stiffened and removed her hand from his arm. "I mean it for the most sincere compliment, I vow." He suddenly slid an arm about her waist and hugged her to him, right in front of all those who watched. Katharine gasped with both shock and surprise. "I have rarely felt such admiration for a woman," he said, "or indeed, for any man, as when I beheld you this morn, in all your fire and glory. I wish you had indeed had a whip at hand, for I have no doubt that you would have dealt with them even more handily." Turning, he shouted back to the dais. "Kayne!"

"Aye?"

"Find a whip among the men and buy it for my Lady Katharine. We shall keep it here in the great hall for her use, whenever she may want it."

"As you wish," Kayne replied with a nod and a grin.

"Senet!" Katharine whispered, horrified.

He laughed and bent to kiss her, lifting her off her feet and swinging her about before setting her down again.

"Senet," she said again, breathlessly, gazing up into his smiling face. "You are a crazed madman. A lunatic." But she knew that she was the one who had become crazed. A whip. He teased her for her temper, for the manner in which she ruled her people—she should be furious, and hurt. But she wasn't. Instead she felt as if she'd turned all to boiled oats inside, as if everything had become liquid and hot. Even her legs were weak, as if they could no longer bear her weight. And her heart was pounding so harshly that she felt as if it might beat a hole through her chest and fall right upon the floor. She was giddy and foolish, and sick...with love. For him. For this handsome, maddening man who had taken everything away from her and then, in but days, given it all back, and more. Oh, God above, but she loved him. It was a horror, a complete horror, and couldn't possibly be true. Yet it was.

"Indeed," he agreed, oblivious to her distress as he took her hand to pull her toward the stairs and their chamber above. "I think I must be, but the fault is all yours, my little warrior." He grinned at her. "May it ever be thus for, I vow before God, 'tis far better than any madness I have ever before known."

Chapter Twelve

The sisters at the Convent of Saint Genevieve greeted their unexpected visitors with the usual dignity and reserved cheer that Katharine ever expected of them. She had never seen Elder Sister smile—though the woman did display a great deal of warmth when with the convent's children—and to Katharine she had ever been stoic and dignified, but she unbent most amazingly when faced for the first time with Senet. Before accepting the introduction to her new lord, Elder Sister actually took his hand, held it quite firmly and looked him full in the face. Katharine had been too amazed to make any kind of comment, certainly not to say that she had never been treated to such deference. Senet, seeming to understand her thoughts, had cast a smug look at Katharine before giving Elder Sister his complete attention.

He was not, Katharine thought as she watched her husband being led about by a gaggle of younger nuns, possessed of the polished manners that his birth decreed. There was a soldierly roughness about him, a certain stiffness that she had seen in him during their first encounters, but which had disappeared in the past two days. But now it was back, this tenseness, as if he were constantly expecting some kind of attack to befall. He was clearly determined to know all of his people as lord, however, for he dutifully forged onward, even with Elder Sister, who was presently telling him of the many needs that the convent had. Senet gave Katharine one silent plea to save him as Elder Sister and some of the younger nuns dragged him off to view the repairs they so desired. She smiled at him sweetly and watched him go.

Sir Kayne and Sir Aric and John Ipris had come with them, as well as Katharine's ladies—even Dorothea, who had grumpily claimed that she had far too many duties to tend to after her brief absence, though she had given way after only a little persuasion—and also Mademoiselle Clarise.

"Come!" One of the younger nuns waved at them with great enthusiasm. "Come and see the children. They are meeting Lord Lomas in the courtyard."

The Convent of Saint Genevieve was comprised, in large, of the remains of an old keep, most of which was heading rapidly toward collapse. But the sisters, all of them very proud and determined, had labored hard to make it a livable and even admirable dwelling. With some help from Katharine in the way of bartering for help from the villagers, the women had rebuilt the castle's most essential areas, including the great hall where they and the children mainly lived, the chapel, the kitchens and the stables. The outer bailey, where the sisters had greeted their newly arrived guests, had been made beautiful with well-tended flowers and shrubs, as had the inner courtyard where the children often spent their afternoons if the weather—and their chores—permitted. The few small acres of land surrounding the keep had been planted with every variety of vegetable, bean and grain, and, as these were the main source of food at Saint Genevieve, the land had been tended with diligent care.

But all this was not enough to make Saint Genevieve a truly comfortable dwelling, especially for the children. Only two small hearths in the great hall were usable, and they were far from sufficient to provide enough warmth during harsh winter nights. And the sisters owned only a few meager cattle, both horses and cows, as well as enough chickens to provide eggs and, on rare special occasions, a little meat in the thin soup that was their daily fare.

Far more worrisome to Katharine than the living conditions at Saint Genevieve was the lack of decent shoes and clothing for the children. All her plans to provide such for them were so precarious. The town weavers would not provide the necessary cloth the sisters needed for new clothing if Katharine could not settle the trouble with the dye merchant; and the cobbler, now that he was angered anew over John the Barber's land, would probably find some cause for not making the shoes he'd promised. She didn't even want to think about how she was going to convince him to do so. And if she went away to Caswell, it would not happen at all.

"God's toes," Sir Aric said as they followed the sister into the courtyard, in which Senet stood surrounded by a gaggle of children of varying ages. "They care for all these?"

"These and more," Katharine told him. "There are six infants yet in swaddling, too young to bring out of doors. The children you see here should number, if they are all present, forty-six, aged from two to twelve years. There would be more," she said, smiling at the way he shook his head, "but all those who attain the age of thirteen are sent out to find their own way."

"Are they not fostered or apprenticed?" he asked. "Or given some manner of training before they are sent away?"

"Only what the sisters are able to teach them. They can read and write and work simple numbers. The girls are taught all they must know to serve as maids."

"And the boys? Each of these older ones here should be even now learning skills for which he might become a soldier, or mayhap even attain knighthood."

Katharine looked at him sharply, amazed to see that he meant what he said.

"You may have been born to a station that assured you of such as that, Sir Aric, but these boys can make no like claims. They are orphans, most of them bastards, with little to possess but their own names."

He turned his dark, fierce gaze upon her. "I am a bastard, my lady, and my mother naught but a whore. Kayne's birth was the same, and John's even less noble. He was found a naked babe in a muddy ditch just outside a London tavern—Ipris Inn, from which he took his name. Senet is the only one among us who can make claim of a noble birth."

Katharine blinked at him. "Oh, I..."

He looked away, his manner as terse and unfriendly as his words. "We were fostered by Sir Justin Baldwin, who had no care for our manner of birth and trained us for the knighthood. Just as these boys should be fostered and trained."

"This is so," Katharine began, but he had already walked away toward Magan, who turned and smiled as she saw him come.

"I remember coming here with my father when I was a boy." Senet lay back upon the grassy riverbank, pillowing his head atop of his hands. The sky above was blue, nearly free of clouds, and the afternoon pleasant and warm. Sitting beside him, Katharine gazed out at the wide, slow-moving river, a slight frown upon her face. "To fish, mainly, though he liked to practice archery beside the river, as well."

"'Tis shady," Katharine replied. "And cool."

He rolled over and propped himself up on one elbow, gazing at his wife. Her thoughts were clearly far away, and had been since they'd left the sisters and children at Saint Genevieve. Mistress Magan had instructed the kitchen servants to pack food and drink in baskets so that all those who were riding to the convent might later enjoy their midday meal by the river. It had been a good idea and a most pleasant experience.

Now, having eaten their fill, the feasters had wandered off in various directions. Mistress Magan had decided that she must search the woods along the river for mushrooms, and Aric had gruffly said that he should accompany her as guardian. Mistresses Dorothea and Ariette had declared that they would start their own search of the area, looking for wild roses, which possessed sweet-smelling flowers good for making perfume and soap. Kayne, ever a chivalrous gentleman, offered to go along and carry their baskets. Clarise and John had already drifted toward the riverbank, walking slowly away from the others, clearly involved in deep discussion. Senet could see them from where he lay, the two figures far-off now, but they had turned and were making their way back.

Katharine had shown no interest in either seeking out mushrooms or flowers or in walking. She had readily taken his hand and gone with him to relax by the river, and now sat gazing pensively at nothing in particular, her fingers absently pulling at long spikes of grass.

"Katharine," he said gently, reaching out to touch her hand. She looked at him, worry clear in her expression. "Have no fear regarding the children at Saint Genevieve. All that they require will be found, and all the repairs to the castle made—even if the funds for such must come from Lomas's own coffers."

She shook her head. "The sisters will not accept such charity, not even from me—us," she amended quickly. "But I am glad to have your aid in these matters, my lord. I have wanted to do so much for Lomas, but it has been difficult—"

He gripped her hand, squeezing it. "You have done a great deal for Lomas, Katharine. Indeed, from what I am told, you saved it from the abuses visited upon it by both your father and mine."

"Your father was not so guilty, Senet. I do not know what has been said to you, or what you have thought since you knew of your father's treachery, but the blame for Lomas's demise cannot be set at his feet."

"Not all of it," he admitted solemnly, "but enough."

"The fault lay first with the king's regents, who for too long a time set no one to oversee Lomas. The mayor ruled the town, but the castle was laid bare by a baron named Sir Myles Hersell, who left it empty and without care."

"My uncle," Senet said bitterly. "My mother's half brother. He took all that had once belonged to my parents and sold it for his own profit. 'Twas his daughter, Evelyn, who so foully murdered my sweet Odelyn."

Katharine's gaze sharpened and fixed on him. "Your own cousin?" she whispered with plain horror.

He nodded. "She and Sir Myles claimed my sister, Isabelle, after my parents had died, and made her as a slave. Isabelle, like our mother, is gifted with numbers, just as

I told you, and Sir Myles used her skills to make for himself a great fortune.''

Katharine looked at him with confusion. "But how could Lady Evelyn ever come to know your betrothed? And why should she kill her?"

Senet didn't like speaking of his past—any part of it, save those days of his childhood before his father's treachery—but Katharine had a right to know.

"The man who wed my sister, Sir Justin Baldwin, the lord of Talwar, was at one time betrothed—by order of the king's regents, and much against his will—to my cousin, Lady Evelyn. When he went to meet my cousin, however, he also met Isabelle, and decided that he would far rather have her for a bride. And as he would not be deterred by anything so foolish as a direct command from the crown, he kidnapped Isabelle and took her to a monastery for safekeeping until he could convince her to wed him."

Katharine's eyebrows rose. "Kidnapped her!"

Senet smiled and ran a caressing thumb over the back of the hand he held. "Aye. 'Tis the way of the Baldwins to take their wives in strange ways. Isabelle thought him mad at first, but then gave way and wed him, mostly, I think, to get away from Sir Myles and Lady Evelyn. At Talwar she was her own mistress, and she and Justin were happy together until Lady Evelyn suddenly appeared and sought to make Justin appear false in Isabelle's eyes."

"How so?"

"Evelyn made it seem as if she and Justin were bedding each other at Talwar, uncaring that Isabelle was so close by. 'Twas naught but lies, a plot of my uncle's to make Isabelle return to him and take care of his fortune again. But Isabelle—and all of us, to our shame—believed them rather than Sir Justin, to whom we owed everything, I far more than the others.'' He looked at her directly. ''I owe Sir Justin my very life, to this day. If he had not taken me away from Lord Howton, I would not have lived past my sixteenth year.'' He released a breath, pushing the dark thoughts away. ''Lady Evelyn proved not only false, but a murderer. She poisoned Isabelle so that she lost Justin's child, and killed my Odelyn in order to escape Talwar, where she had been made a prisoner after her foul deeds were discovered. Odelyn was a serving maid at Talwar, and had taken Lady Evelyn a tray of food in the chamber that had become her prison. My treacherous cousin took the knife that was set upon the tray and used it to gain her freedom. Odelyn's life was the cost.'' His voice thickened, and he closed his eyes. ''God, I vow I still cannot speak of it. Forgive me, Katharine.''

He felt her hand upon his hair, and she suddenly leaned close and kissed him on the mouth. ''Nay,'' she murmured, ''you must not ask forgiveness for speaking of such things, Senet. I wish I might take this pain from you, but I am full grateful that you told me all of it.''

He opened his eyes and gazed at her. ''I want no more secrets between us. I will tell you all of my past, if you wish it, though 'tis more than distasteful to me, and mayhap will be more so to you.'' Sitting up, he reached out to cradle her cheek, drawing her closer. ''If we are to make any kind of marriage, Katharine, it must be with the truth freely spoken. Always.''

She drew away, looking so troubled that he was afraid he had disgusted her beyond repair with his tale.

''Senet,'' she said, her tone tentative and nervous, ''there is something—'' She stopped, gazing at him with deep distress.

''What is it?''

''Naught.''

"You need not fear to tell me anything, Katharine. You must come to trust me in all things, for I vow that I will give you no reason for sorrow."

She shook her head, saying, "I am foolish. I only meant to ask if they are happy now. Your sister and her husband."

"Is that all?" He leaned forward and kissed her quickly, laughing. "You are a warrior, my Katharine, but you hide a gentle heart within, I think."

She reddened and he kissed her again. Then, setting back upon his elbow, he said, "They are very happy together at Talwar, Justin and Isabelle and their children, my six nieces and nephews—our nieces and nephews," he amended, "and have been for many years. Justin lets Isabelle work numbers and make fortunes to her heart's contentment, and she allows Justin to continue in schooling his many charges in the ways of knighthood. It is what he loves best, next to making swords. He is a skilled craftsman. Here. Do you see? He made this, and gave it to me the first Christmas I was at Talwar." He pulled a short, bejeweled dagger from the belt at his waist and held it out for her to see. "John and Kayne and Aric each have one similar to this. Sir Justin made one for each boy in his care that year."

Katharine turned the finely crafted dagger over in her hand. "How old were you then?"

"Sixteen. Nearly seventeen."

"It must have been a fine thing to have such a home, and friends. A master who cared for you." She looked at him. "Although I know 'twas not always thus. You suffered greatly while you were with Lord Howton."

"'Twas not a pleasant time," he admitted, taking the dagger when she handed it back to him. "But I do not think your early days at Lomas were so easy, either. How did your father come to inherit the estate? I have never heard the tale, but I think he had not before been landed. Is that not so?''

She nodded. ''The only lands he held, and these were quite minor, were those that he gained through marriage to my mother. May God be praised that she wisely held back the largest of them, Caswell, as her own, else I should have had nothing left to me after she passed. 'Twas only that he had wed her for, to claim that he was landed as a nobleman should be, though in truth, he was the youngest son of a knight, with no title of his own. My father,'' she said with a sigh, ''was a courtier, and very good at entertaining the nobility. He was handsome and charming and flattering, a perfect ornament to those at court, where we lived.''

''You disliked it? Living there?'' It was plain from her tone that she had.

''I *hated* it,'' she replied with violent feeling. ''I cannot tell you how greatly. 'Twas naught but a torment, especially for my mother, who was neither beautiful nor witty. She could not stand against such fine company as was ever at court, and certainly not against the blinding light my father shed. He treated her as if she did not exist—or worse, as if she did not matter enough to be recognized. He preferred the company of his friends, with whom he spent his days hunting and drinking and exchanging mistresses.''

''God above,'' Senet muttered. ''Did he mistreat you as well?''

She shook her head. ''Until we came to Lomas, he did not give me any more notice than he gave to my mother. She died from it, that lack of care. 'Twas as if she had faded into what he had made her feel she was—naught, and of no value—and one morn I found her lying very still in her bed, gone away at last.''

"Katharine," he murmured, "I'm sorry."

"Better that she was with God than with my father," she said bitterly. "'Twas her death, in part, that led to my father being granted such a boon as becoming lord of his own estate, for he was free to marry again and the woman who favored him was, by chance, the same woman whom Duke Humphrey wished to take as mistress."

"Ah," Senet said. "I understand."

"Indeed." She gave a nod. "Making my father a baron and deeding Lomas to him was far preferable to the duke than risking that the woman they both wanted would choose my handsome, charming father over himself. My father, of course, was quite happy to take what he was offered, and that is how we came to Lomas."

"You were young, were you not? Twelve?"

"Aye, and suddenly found myself mistress of an entire castle—one that was both empty and rotten with stench, for it had not been properly cleaned in the two years that it lay without use. I hardly knew how to go on—for as you have already discovered, I have no skill with managing a household, but my father expected me to do so. The day that we arrived, he took me and some of the servants to the great hall, commanded that it be made ready for his return, and then left us there before riding out with his particular friends to see what manner of hunting could be had." She smiled ruefully. "You may imagine, we were hard-pressed to fulfill his commands, and I was so frightened that I could barely tell the servants what to do."

"What did you do?"

"I went out into the village and stopped the first person I came upon—who was, as it happened, John the Bar-

ber—and asked if there were any in Lomas who had once
worked at the castle. He said there were, and I sent one
of my father's servants to go find them and offer goodly
wages if they would come at once and help to set the
castle to rights. Twenty-one who had served your mother
and father came that afternoon, most of them from the
kitchens. I was so grateful to them, for if they had not
come, my father would have returned to find the castle
far from what he had demanded it must be. But he was
well pleased with what he found, for the great hall had
been cleaned and set to rights, and the kitchen maids had
found enough provisions to present a fine meal to their
new lord. Since that day, I have loved the people of Lomas, and knew that I would do whatever I must to save
them from my father's foolishness and waste.''

Senet reached out to take her hand and draw it to his
lips. He turned it and gently kissed her palm. ''You leave
me all amazed, Katharine. Even at an age so young, you
were yet wise and strong.''

Her cheeks reddened with obvious pleasure and she
seemed suddenly shy, lowering her gaze, as if she was
not used to such flattery. But Senet knew that could not
be so. Surely her beloved Lord Hanley, if he had been
any kind of man at all, had told Katharine time and again
of how beautiful and rare she was. If he hadn't, then he
had been a complete fool, and not deserving of such a
woman.

''Was your father not angered that you had brought
new servants into the castle without his approval?''

''Oh, nay,'' she said, seemingly glad to turn their conversation back to subjects more familiar to her. ''They
were mine, as I had hired them, and I paid them as well,
out of the monies I had inherited upon my mother's passing.''

"God's feet." Senet felt a hot anger within, directed entirely at Katharine's louse of a father. "He was naught but a dog, to let his daughter pay for his own comfort."

"To let me?" she repeated with a laugh. "He *made* me do so, my lord. I paid to restock the kitchens, as well, or none but he and his friends would have had food to eat. What the castlefolk ate was my responsibility, but the accounts could not be held so separately without a great deal of effort. I found it far easier to pay for all until my funds were gone. By then, the lands had begun to return a small profit—enough to keep my father and his followers in food and drink, and the rest of us from starving."

"He was worse than a dog," Senet said tightly. "He was a *swine*."

"He was what he was," she said, shrugging, "and I his only child. He loved me in his own way, I think, especially when I took the burden of the castle from his shoulders, and mayhap 'twas best that he let me do so, for 'tis truly all I am good for." She held her hands palms up before letting them drop. "If he had not given me the charge of the castle when I was fourteen, I would have had little to do each passing year, save sigh with boredom."

"You might have learned to ply a needle," he teased.

She laughed. "Mayhap. But I am very glad that I did not have to."

They sat in a comfortable silence for the space of a few minutes, Senet lying upon his back and gazing up at the sky, Katharine staring at the river and pulling at the grass, until Senet glanced at his wife and saw that the pensive frown had come to her face again.

"Your friends are unusual men," she said, turning that face to him as if the thought troubled her. "They are not...well-born?"

Senet slowly sat up. "Nay, they are all base-born. All of those whom Sir Justin fosters at Talwar are thus. I was the only exception."

"Sir Aric told me," she said. "I had not realized before, and am filled with admiration not only for them, but for Sir Justin as well. 'Tis a very great thing that a man attain knighthood, and for men of such birth, 'tis the only way in which they may raise themselves above their station."

"Indeed, this is so. And Kayne and Aric attained knighthood with great honor, earning it on the battlefield with valor such as only few may hope to know."

"And John Ipris?" she asked. "He seems a valiant man, and was trained by Sir Justin just as you were. He did not seek knighthood?"

Senet answered the question with care. John was so much of a mystery still, even to those who knew him well, and seemed very pleased to remain that way.

"John could have easily attained knighthood, if he had desired it. Indeed, he was twice offered the honor after his efforts upon the battlefield in France. But his special skills led him down another path. He has been of great service to the crown, in many ways. I'faith, I do not know how we could have survived so well without him. You know better than I could tell you how valuable he was to me in gaining Lomas."

"Verily, you speak the truth." She lifted her head to look at where John and Clarise had stopped and were now gazing out at the river. "Mademoiselle Clarise seeks his company often, does she not?"

Senet looked at the couple standing beside the river. "She is probably wearying him with her many complaints of me, because I will not let her set aside the betrothal I have arranged for her. She often plagues John with her troubles. And he cossets her by listening. He has ever been the worst among the four of us, though Aric and Kayne have spoiled her, too.''

"But never you?" Katharine smiled at him in a teasing manner. "Were you always the stern guardian, then, Senet?"

He laughed. "Nay, I fear I was not. But never did I spoil her as John has done. She has depended upon him even more greatly since we left France, and you must not be surprised if you find them often in company together.''

"I cannot think I will," she said, so strangely that he looked to see what she meant. But her expression was all innocence. "And what of Sir Kayne?"

"What of him?"

She was thoughtful. "He is…sad, I think. He smiles and makes himself busy with good deeds, but there is a great restlessness there. A great sadness.''

Senet nodded. "You have seen well, Katharine. Kayne will not stay with us long. I do not know if he will be able to stay anywhere for a great length of time. I am sometimes troubled for him.''

"He is your friend," she said with understanding. "I have sensed that you are perhaps closer to him than Sir Aric and John Ipris. Only by a matter of small degree, but 'tis there, just the same.''

"I will miss Kayne when he leaves," he admitted soberly, "but I did not think he would make a home here at Lomas. He came to lend me his aid in regaining what was mine, and will stay only long enough to make certain of me here.''

"Where will he go?" she asked. "And why? Can he not find Lomas a goodly place to take a wife and settle?''

"Kayne is beset by troubles which cannot be known by another. He has seen too much death, killed too many.

There were things he suffered that I cannot speak of—horrors he alone knew. As to where he will go, I think he will find a quiet place where he can set the past as far behind him as he may. He has not spoken of it yet, but I think he may even put aside his knighthood.''

Katharine shook her head sadly. '''Twould be a great shame were he to do so. Knighthood is a rare honor, and he has shown himself truly worthy of it.''

Senet gave her a wry smile. "Aye, Kayne has ever impressed ladies with his chivalrous ways. No other man can compare, it seems.''

She laughed. "Do you think not? John Ipris seems to be a fine gentleman, as well.''

"But not Aric or your own husband?" he demanded with mocking sternness. When she only laughed the harder he reached up and pulled her down to the grass beneath him. "Such an unruly wife you are," he said, looming over her. "I am sure I must find the right manner in which to punish you." She didn't put up much of a struggle, especially when he began to kiss her, and was grinning up at him like a silly child when he lifted his head.

"The others will see us," she told him, not as if the thought particularly troubled her.

"Will they? Then we must give them something worth seeing." He kissed her again, more fully and deeply, then murmured, "Have you been properly chastised, madam wife?"

"If that is your manner of punishment, I do not think so.''

He smiled and ran a finger down the silk of her cheek, gazing at her as she lay upon the grass, her red-gold hair spread out beneath her. "You are so beautiful. I am the most fortunate man on God's earth, I vow.''

She began to look unhappy again. "Senet..."

He set his wandering finger against her lips. "Are you going to leave me, Katharine? Is that why you are so troubled?"

She held his gaze and murmured, "Nay, I am not going to leave Lomas. I will stay with you, Senet."

Relief, like a tide of cooling water on a blistering day, washed over him, and he felt, ridiculously, like pulling her off the ground and tossing her up into the air with a shout of celebration. But still she looked troubled, and even more unhappy than before.

"But this is joyous news, Katharine," he said. "Why are you yet so overset?"

"'Tis naught."

"Tell me," he murmured. "Trust me. There are no more shadows between us."

She looked even more distressed, and pushed up into a sitting position, away from him. "'Tis naught, just as I said." She rose to her feet, her back to him, brushing strongly at her surcoat to remove bits of grass and leaves. "Nay, that is not so." She whirled about, her countenance rigid. "'Tis Magan. I fear she has grown too fond of Sir Aric, and I am unhappy in the knowledge that I must warn her away from him. She is an heiress, as you know, and cannot marry beneath her station. Certainly not with a landless bastard, no matter what honor he may have attained in knighthood."

Senet stood as well, more slowly.

"Mistress Magan will marry Aric if she pleases," he told her. "I am the one who will approve the man she weds, and I will not gainsay the marriage if both she and Aric desire it. Indeed," he added, ignoring her angry exclamation, "I will both bless and be gladdened by such a union. I have never seen Aric so gentle and happy with a

maid before now, and cannot but think that his feelings
for Mistress Magan are of the most admirable nature.''

"My ladies are yet beneath my hand," she told him
furiously. "I alone decide their future, and I will not allow
them to make such disastrous alliances."

"I am the lord of Lomas," he remind her roughly.

Hot anger glinted in her gaze. "Aye, and so you are.
But my ladies are mine. I will not let you make a ruin of
their lives and fortunes."

She turned to walk away, but he grasped her arm and
pulled her back.

"You said that you would not leave Lomas, Katharine."

"Nay, I'll not leave—" she pulled her arm free "—but
if we can reach no agreement on this matter, you may
begin to wish that I had!"

Chapter Thirteen

Katharine rode back to Lomas in a state of fury, keeping her gaze straight ahead and her replies to questions short. Senet, a very fiend, refused to let her ride alone, and stayed beside her the entire way, easily managing his steed in the doing. Katharine could have outpaced him, but had far too much pride to do so. She would not give him such satisfaction as seeing her behave in such a lowly manner before others, no matter how greatly he overset her.

He would have the approval of who Magan married, would he? Nay, but he would *not!* Katharine might have been lulled by his kisses and soft words into setting her heart at his feet, but he would learn that her mind yet belonged to her. And even if that wasn't entirely true—for love certainly seemed to be a dreadful bewitching force—then she need only approach the trouble from another direction to settle it. She would speak with Magan and make her understand how disastrous a union with Sir Aric would be. Magan had ever been perfectly obedient and would accept that Katharine knew what was best for her. She would cease showing Sir Aric such favor, and that would be the end of it—of something that Katharine wished she'd never started.

It had been foolish beyond measure to use Magan as an excuse for not telling Senet the truth of her lies about Kieran and Lord Hanley, and she had only herself to blame for the anger that now stood between them. She had been so near to telling him, there by the river, the full of her sins, and to admitting that she had never intended to wed Lord Hanley, that she had never loved anyone until now. But, somehow, she had been unable to do so. She had not thought herself a coward, but now she knew herself for one. Senet's sweet kisses and tender lovemaking had made her thus. How could she lose what she had so recently gained? She could not bear to think of living with him and seeing distrust and dislike where there had once been respect and admiration.

"Katharine."

She didn't look at him. "My lord?"

Reaching out, he grasped the reins of her steed and forced her to slow. The others, ahead of them, rode on.

"You have no cause for anger."

She sat stiffly in her saddle, holding her gaze rigidly forward. "Do I not?"

"I have made you my equal as fully as I can, but in some matters I *must* be the lord of Lomas. You are a woman—"

Pulling the reins from his grip, she turned her horse about until she faced him. Glaring, she demanded, "What of it?"

He was stern now, the unbending knight who had taken Lomas from her.

"You could not have remained as you were forever, waiting for a dead man to return and wed you," he said angrily. "The king's regents would not have allowed it.

Lomas is far too valuable an estate to be held without ceasing by a maiden lady.''

"Valuable because I have made it thus!" she charged. "And if you had not so desired to hold it, Lomas would yet be mine."

"Nay, that is not so, Katharine. You would have had another year at most to grieve for your lost beloved, then a husband would have been chosen for you. If not me, then another, and you know I speak the truth. I was given the chance because Duke Humphrey had grown weary with your stubbornness, and I alone was ready to take you by force."

Tears of hurt and humiliation stung her eyes, but Katharine held herself as stone, as she would have so easily done only days before, when she had hated him.

"Because you wanted Lomas."

"Because I would let no other have it. Far better me than one who had no care for the estate. Or for you. Can you think another would have set you beside him in the place of judgment? Or that he would make you his equal even at table? Not even your perfect Lord Hanley would have done so, I vow. Nay, you will listen to me," he said tightly, reaching out and stopping her when she would have ridden away. "I have given you all that I can, and will ever do so, but on some matters I *will* have final say."

"Will you?" she challenged.

"In time, you will learn that I speak the truth." The words were a promise, spoken with deliberate care and meaning. Staring at him, seeing the strength of will he held leashed, knowing how easily he could turn that power upon her, Katharine shivered. Pulling free of him at last, she set her heels into her horse and rode on, rapidly closing the distance between herself and the others. Senet followed at a greater distance. After a few minutes, Kayne began to fall behind and eventually joined him.

There was a small commotion in the castle courtyard when they rode in, with several soldiers and townspeople milling about. So many fell silent and stared at Katharine as she dismounted with the aid of a servant that she asked, aloud, to no one in particular, "Is aught amiss?"

No answer came, but those who heard her began to look rather nervous. Some even turned away.

"What can it be?" Dorothea, standing beside Katharine, murmured. Ariette joined them the next moment, and they waited for Sir Aric to pull Magan down from her mount.

"I do not know," Katharine answered. "It is very strange."

Senet and Kayne rode into the courtyard, looking about at the unusual and silent crowd there. Senet gave Katharine a questioning look as he brought his horse to a halt, but she was yet angry with him, and turned away with a sweeping of her skirts and made for the castle's front doors, which a servant pulled wide at her approach.

The sound of laughter greeted her as she made her way into the great hall—the laughter of both men and women, loud and very merry. It had been a long time since she'd heard the like at Lomas. Indeed, the only person who seemed to fill the castle with such jollity, when he visited, was—

"Oh, God above." Katharine came to a full, sudden stop, bringing Dorothea and Ariette to a halt as well. "God above. It's him." She began to look about for a way of escape.

"Him?" Ariette repeated.

"*Him,*" Katharine said again, turning to face them in a complete panic. Magan and Sir Aric had only just entered the hall, and Senet and Sir Kayne wouldn't be far behind.

Dorothea's expression filled with understanding. "Oh, God save us, do you mean *them?*"

Katharine kept turning around, unable to think of what to do. "Him, them—"

"My lady!"

At the sound of the manservant's voice, Katharine turned about once more, steeling herself to be the lady of Lomas.

"Aye?"

The young servant bowed, but when he straightened, bewilderment was plain on his face.

"My lady, Lord...ah...Hanley has arrived?" It was more of a question than a statement.

Of course he would be confused to see Kieran FitzAllen appear in the guise of the long-lost Lord Hanley. Everyone at Lomas would be confused, something Katharine hadn't thought of, which only confirmed to her how utterly stupid she had been to conceive the idea in the first place. But she knew that her people would not betray her, for they were fully loyal, and would rapidly spread word of the pretense throughout the entirety of Lomas. Even the townspeople would do their best to treat Kieran as the stranger he claimed to be.

"Lord Hanley?" she repeated faintly. "I see. Thank you, Gareth. I hope he has been made comfortable?" None of which, she thought, was what any woman who'd been waiting so many years for her beloved to return would say.

"Katharine!"

She froze at the sound of the familiar voice. Kieran had probably just been told that she'd arrived. He was still at the far end of the hall, surrounded by a crowd of women, but she could see his tall, commanding figure striding toward her with his arms opened wide. Behind him his diminutive manservant, Jean-Marc, trotted in earnest to keep up.

Katharine could only stare, unmoving, as they neared. Kieran was more handsome than usual, dressed, somehow, miraculously, in the finery due a nobleman, all velvet and fur. His golden-brown hair had been trimmed around his face—though she could see that it was still lengthy, tied back now in a neat tail at the base of his neck—creating a perfect frame for his dark blue eyes. His utterly beautiful face—she had never known a man more well-favored—had been recently shaved. Not a bit of dirt or a single stain clung to any part of him. Even his boots, new and made of expensive leather, were perfectly clean. She had never seen her disreputable cousin look like this. She had never seen *any* man look like this. He was handsome beyond redemption, sinfully, perfectly, seductively handsome. And everything about his manner, the way he walked and smiled and held himself, told the world that he knew it.

The first thing people always noticed about Kieran was his eyes. Their deep-blue color was pleasant but not unusual—certainly nothing like Senet's extraordinary eyes—but he had long ago perfected the trick of directing them toward the object of his interest with a certain light and intensity that promised every manner of sinful pleasure. Katharine had used to tease him about felling so many hundreds of unwitting females with that look, but now, as he approached her, she saw with growing distress that he was directing it at *her*.

"Katharine, my own darling!" His voice boomed loudly throughout the entire hall, hearty and filled with gladness. "May God be praised! How I have longed and prayed for this moment—only to see you again!"

She raised her hands to ward him off, but too late. Kieran wrapped his powerful arms about her and lifted her off the floor, finding her mouth with his and kissing her with a feigned passion that left her gasping for breath.

"Kieran!" she whispered, both furious and horrified, trying to shove him away. He had often tried to sneak kisses from her, since the day she'd turned fourteen, always reminding her that, as they weren't closely related, they could be more affectionate than mere cousins. Still, he had never dared anything more intimate than a fleeting press of lips, knowing full well that she'd relieve him of several teeth if he did. She would have struck him across the face now if she'd been able to get one of her hands free. But her struggles were useless. He easily held her captive.

"Aye, my own love!" he cried, crushing her against him. "'Tis your Alexander come back to you, alive and well and waiting only for the moment when I can take you to wife. Kiss me again, my love. I have thirsted these many lonely months for the feel of your sweet lips upon mine."

Alexander? Katharine thought as he began to kiss her again. God's mercy, but he'd even gotten Lord Hanley's Christian name wrong. She tried to push Kieran away again, knowing that she had to get rid of him before Senet discovered the truth. She didn't care how much it cost her this time. Whatever he wanted, she would pay, although with the clothes and boots and everything else, it would doubtless be more than she—

"What is this?"

The roar was uttered at the same moment that Kieran was physically flung away from Katharine. So quickly did it happen that Katharine was dragged along, falling to the floor beside her cousin. Shaking her head, she looked up to find Senet unsheathing his sword with the clear intent of severing Kieran's head from his body.

"Senet, nay!"

Katharine was off the ground in but a moment, gripping her husband's arm.

"He is my—Lord Hanley." Senet tried to push her away, but she held fast, saying again, more sternly, "He is *Lord Hanley*. He knows *nothing*, not even that you are my husband."

"He will learn it," Senet said with fire-hot fury, lifting his sword. "I will teach him."

"Nay!" She held him back. She wouldn't let him kill her cousin because of her own foolishness.

"Husband?"

Kieran, shaking off his manservant, who had been striving to help him, had picked himself up from the floor. He was equal in height and strength to Senet, and showed no hesitation in stepping closer to face the other man.

"This cannot be!" he said with disbelief, playing the part of an outraged Lord Hanley to the full. "You have married another, Katharine? When you were betrothed to *me?* When you promised faithfully to wait for my return? I will not believe it!"

Katharine was hard-pressed not to laugh at the ridiculous portrayal he made. Kieran knew full well how she felt about the real Lord Hanley, and he had often entertained Katharine and her ladies with just this kind of mocking imitation.

"You will believe it," Senet told him threateningly, yet holding his sword at the ready. "You have no rights here, my lord Hanley. You left Lady Katharine waiting too long for your return, even to have word that you were yet alive.

Indeed, it was assumed that you were not, and the king's regents declared that Lomas could no longer continue without a proper lord, or Lady Katharine without a husband. I wed her but three days past."

Kieran looked at Katharine, his blue eyes wide.

"Three days past?" he repeated faintly. "Oh, Katharine, my darling love, can this be? Could you not have waited only three more days?"

My darling love? she thought with aggravation. Must he make the matter worse by spouting such sickening nonsense? The real Lord Hanley would never be so foolish.

"Indeed, my lord, it is the truth." She strove to soften her tone, to appear sorrier than she was. Senet would surely wonder at any coldness she displayed to the man she supposedly loved. "I waited for you as long as 'twas possible, but—"

Senet suddenly lunged forward, grabbing Kieran by the neck of his expensive tunic. "She waited faithfully, you filthy dog, for *years,* carrying every burden of the estate and her people, while you made not even the least attempt to let her know where you were, or even if you were alive." He shook him harshly. "Yet you would have had her wait longer? Forever, mayhap? While you took your leisure in coming back to her? What manner of love is this, you swine? I should *kill* you for the suffering you have caused her!"

"Senet, cease!" Katharine pleaded. "I beg it of you! Do not!"

"Never fear for me, my darling," Kieran said cheerfully, gripping the fingers that held him. Katharine could see the excitement building in his handsome face, but, then, he had always loved a fight. "I've lived through hell's own torment these past many years, only to return to you. I'll not leave you now!" With no little effort he wrenched Senet's hand free. "Certainly not with this lowly knave."

Senet easily ducked the fist that Kieran flung at him, just as Kieran gracefully avoided being sliced in half when Senet lunged at him with his sword.

"Senet, this is not the way!" Kayne shouted, storming up from behind Senet and pinning his arms to his sides with all the strength he possessed. Aric, likewise, shoved Jean-Marc aside and held Kieran in his place. When Jean-Marc removed the sword at his side with the clear intention of aiding his master, Aric snarled at him, "Do not, little rat, else you'll be dinner for the dogs."

"Lord Hanley," Kayne addressed that man, yet holding a struggling Senet back, "'twould be best if you leave Lomas. There is naught for you here."

"Indeed, you must go," Katharine agreed, relieved to think she might be rid of the awful situation so easily. She would send a missive after Kieran, explaining all, and including a goodly sum of money. Later, when she had found the way to confess her deceit to Senet, she would somehow let Kieran know that he could return to Lomas as his real self, her cousin. "I am sorry that you came with the hope of finding me as I was when you left, but there can be no turning back."

"Did you wed him of your own free will, Katharine?" Kieran asked, and Katharine heard real confusion in his tone. The missive she had sent to him had spoken frankly of her distaste in wedding Senet Gaillard. How could he— or she—possibly have known that she would fall in love with the man who had forced her into marriage?

"Aye," she told him, gazing at him very directly and praying that he would believe what she said. "I wed him of my own free will. Ask any at Lomas and they will tell you the same. Please, go in peace, my lord."

Kieran's gaze sharpened. "I do not believe this. You would have waited for me." He looked at Senet, whom Kayne had released. Senet, however, was staring hard at Katharine.

"It is not the truth," he said in a quiet voice. "Lady Katharine was forced to wed me. *I* forced her."

Katharine wanted to groan aloud. Must he suddenly become chivalrous *now,* when all she wanted was to stay with him?

"She would have waited for you for the rest of her days," he continued, "if I had not come to Lomas. But I am come, and have made Katharine my wife in both word and deed. You should have come three days ago, Alexander Hanley, for now you will never have her. Release him, Aric." This last he said as he at last sheathed his sword.

"I thought as much," Kieran said, straightening his tunic. He shot a look of disapproval at Katharine before giving way with one of his mischievous smiles. She had to tamp down the strong urge to plead with him not to play one of his games with Senet. All around them, silent and fascinated, the castlefolk stood, listening to every word. Within the hour there wouldn't be an ear in all of Lomas that hadn't heard the tale. "You merely wanted Lomas—" Kieran strolled to where Katharine stood "—and had to wed my darling Katharine to gain it. Is this not so?"

Senet nodded wearily, gazing fully at Katharine before admitting, "Aye. 'Twas only Lomas I wanted."

Her heart fell into her belly. Was he going to deny her now, after he had done everything possible to make her love him? Surely he wasn't going to step aside and give her over to the man he thought was Lord Hanley? But why else should he make such an admission? She stepped forward almost without thought to fight her own battle, just as she had always done.

"I was the unwanted trouble he had to overcome in order to gain Lomas," she told her cousin bitterly. "But for all that, I am Senet Gaillard's wife, and wed him of my own will. It matters not what he says, for I speak the truth. The marriage is fully legal, my lord Hanley, and cannot now be broken. You must go."

"Katharine," Senet said, his voice tight. She thought he would say more, but instead he looked away.

"But you are not a trouble to me," Kieran said. "You've never been a trouble, but only my whole delight."

"So much that you left her for so many years?" Senet charged hotly.

Kieran lifted his chin in a ridiculously dainty manner. "We shall come to that later, once my manservant and I have settled into our chamber."

"Chamber?" This came from Dorothea, who was artfully avoiding Jean-Marc's adoring gaze. The manservant had somehow sidled up to her and Dorothea was moving away even as she spoke. "Are you and your...servant—" she looked dubiously at Jean-Marc "—remaining at Lomas for the night, my lord?"

"Indeed," Kieran replied regally. "'Tis my duty—if I can but prove I have the greater right—to claim this marriage as false and regain the bride who was to have been mine. Katharine says that she wed Lord Lomas freely, but her heart is an honorable one, and she will not betray any oath that she has given—" he gave Katharine a sickeningly loving look that made her stomach churn "—while the lord of Lomas admits that he forced her to the altar. Nay," he said with full satisfaction, smiling at Katharine, "I'll not leave Lomas until I have determined exactly what the truth is, and whether I may petition the crown to annul this false union so that my love and I may yet be wed.''

"My lord," Katharine said, wishing beyond hope that she could make him understand, "I am well and truly wedded to Senet Gaillard."

Kieran moved nearer to her in a stately manner, clearly enjoying his role as the elite Lord Hanley. "Sweet Katharine," he said, chucking her under the chin as if she were the veriest child, "we shall see."

Chapter Fourteen

"**Y**ou wretched, unforgivable beast! I should beat you senseless!"

They were Katharine's first words upon greeting her long-unseen cousin the very moment they were alone.

Kieran FitzAllen, leaning against his chamber door, which he had closed as soon as Katharine entered the room, laughed.

"My own sweet cousin," he replied cheerfully, "how can you speak to me in such a dreadful manner? Especially after I've moved both heaven and earth in order to reach you as quickly as you bade me? And if you could only know what sacrifice I made."

"You?" she said incredulously.

"Aye, me," he returned, pushing away from the door. They were quite alone, as Jean-Marc was yet belowstairs, bothering Dorothea. "I was being kept by the most wonderful woman, Lady Pembroy, when I received your urgent missive. She was not only generous, but beautiful and talented as well. I was much aggrieved to leave her, sweet cousin, but did so when I received your missive. What else could I do?" He held out his hands. "Your words convinced me that you were in the direst need, requiring my presence at once.''

"I suppose this is true," Katharine admitted grudgingly.

"Indeed, it is. And I, being so loving a relative—" he gave her that deadly and practiced look from beneath his lashes, to which she responded with an exasperated tossing up of her hands "—came at once. Or as soon as I could. And at no small expense, I may tell you, sweet Katharine. Darling, you mustn't become so agitated," he admonished when she began to pace. "You've only yourself to blame for my presence here."

"I know that!" she cried, rounding on him furiously. "Why in the name of all that's holy couldn't you have left Lomas without creating trouble? And never say that you didn't understand what I was striving to tell you belowstairs," she warned, "else I'll pull the very ears off your head."

"God save me," he said with mock surprise, setting a hand dramatically over his heart, "but I can't begin to know what you mean, dear one. Did you *want* me to go away? Surely you haven't changed your mind about Senet Gaillard? Only days ago you wanted to be rescued from him."

"It was a mistake," she said irately. "I thought him to be a different man than what he is, and I have reconciled myself to...to being his wife."

"Have you?" Kieran folded his arms across his chest and slowly circled his cousin, gazing at her curiously. "I must admit, I had not thought the man existed upon God's earth whom you could become...reconciled to." He gave her a knowing smile. "But what of Lomas, Katharine? Your beloved estate, which you have tended these many years as if it were your own child?" At this, Katharine rolled her eyes, but Kieran went on. "Is Senet Gaillard so wonderful a husband that you readily handed Lomas to him?"

Katharine hesitated before replying, with care, "I have not abandoned Lomas to another, if that is what your words mean, Kieran. Senet Gaillard has taken much, aye, but he has given as well. We sit together in the place of judgment—side by side. Our place at table is likewise equal. 'Tis not what I wanted, but 'tis far better than what I expected."

Kieran's eyebrows rose. "Is it? Now, this I find interesting. You haven't fallen in love with the man, have you, sweet cousin? By the rood, Katharine, you have! You're all ablush!"

"That means naught!" Katharine cried, setting her hands over her burning cheeks.

Kieran circled her again, all amazement now. "It must, for the only other time that I've seen you turn so red was during my last visit to Lomas, when Jean-Marc entertained the guests at the evening meal with his song of the knight and the maiden who met in a field and...nay, don't begin to fuss at me, cousin, I'll not repeat it. God's mercy, but how brightly you bloom. How did you manage to get through your wedding night without dying of embarrassment? Or did you?"

"Kieran!"

He laughed. "I see the full of it now. God's toes, but Senet Gaillard has all my admiration. He's done the impossible and made a woman of my chaste and stubborn cousin. If you turn any brighter, Katharine, love, you'll explode. Now, don't—"

She swung a fist at him, but he easily jumped away, still laughing.

"I'll not speak of such matters with you, Kieran

FitzAllen! Only tell me how much money you and your rascal of a manservant require and be on your way. I'm sorry for ever calling you to Lomas. 'Twas a thoughtless, reckless act, and I should never have done so.''

"But if Jean-Marc and I go, Katharine, what will you tell Lord Lomas? Will he not wonder at your beloved Lord Hanley leaving so readily, without argument? Or will you tell him the truth of your deceit and reveal who I truly am?"

Katharine was silent, frowning darkly.

Kieran nodded, his expression one of satisfaction. "I had thought so. You do not want him to know that you lied to him about Hanley. Oh, Katharine. Such a muck and mire you've got yourself into." He sighed. "Nay, I don't think I can leave you yet. Not until I know that you'll be safe with this husband of yours."

Katharine gaped at him. "I'll only be safe if you do leave! Can you not realize what he'll think if he discovers the truth too soon? I must have time to find the way to tell him, and I'll not be able to do that with you here, making matters worse. Kieran, you *must* go."

"Not until I'm satisfied that all will be well for you. I want to be certain that Lord Hanley's sudden appearance—and disappearance—won't cause Lord Lomas to treat you badly. Until then, you must decide whether you wish to reveal me as your cousin, or to go on as if I were, indeed, Lord Hanley. I shall be perfectly glad to do your bidding, however you choose, Katharine. Although I confess a preference for continuing on as Lord Hanley. It's rather amusing to be a rich nobleman."

"Kieran, please, I beg you, don't take one of your fancies." She set a pleading hand on his arm. "If you bear me any love at all, *go away.*"

He patted her hand reassuringly. "I will, just as soon

as I can determine whether Senet Gaillard won't treat you poorly. How could I abandon my most dearly beloved cousin to such a fate, knowing that I had been the cause of it—though unwittingly. Nay, sweet Katharine," he said, ignoring her look of utter misery, "have no fears. I'll faithfully stand beside you during this strange, dark time. If you can rely upon no one else, you can at least rely upon me."

"Lady Katharine would not betray you in such a manner," Kayne said as he and Senet made their way up the stairs to the lord's chamber. "She is a woman of great honor, and this you know. She was magnificent when faced with the sudden return of Lord Hanley, most especially in the loyalty she openly displayed for you."

"Aye, she was magnificent," Senet said soberly. "I have never admired any woman more."

"She stated to one and all that you are her husband, as well as the lord of Lomas, and that the deed is done. I heard no regret or sorrow in her words, nor did anyone else present."

"I heard it," Senet told him. "I know, whatever her words may have been, that her heart must have died within her to say them. She loves him." His own heart ached at the statement. He had to draw in a long breath to steady himself. "She waited for him—did all that she could to escape me so that she might continue to wait. If she had only been able to manage three more days, she would have attained what she so greatly desired."

"And you would have lost Lomas."

"Aye," Senet said grimly. "I would have lost Lomas."

It came down to which of them had the greater claim—his for Lomas, hers for the love and happiness she had longed for. Only three days ago he wouldn't have cared in the least for what Katharine wanted—what anyone wanted—so determined was he to regain his ancestral home. Now, he could only think of the way she had looked, and hear the pain in her voice, when she'd told her beloved Lord Hanley that she was the unwanted trouble he'd had to overcome in order to gain Lomas. Senet had nearly thrown himself upon his knees before her and all those present, to tell her that he had been a fool to have ever thought of her thus. But she had stunned him utterly by the words she had uttered next, declaring—after he had admitted to forcing her to the altar—that she had wed him of her own free will and was his legal wife.

He had been suspicious, almost from the moment he'd made her his wife, that his feelings for Katharine were far deeper than the mere admiration and desire he had been willing to admit, but he had ruthlessly pushed the traitorous thoughts away. He could never feel for another what he had once felt for his beloved Odelyn. It was but the simple truth. What he hadn't realized, and never expected, was that he might one day come to love someone in an entirely different manner. The love he'd known with Odelyn had been tender and gentle, the first for each of them, and as sweet as only something so young and new could be. But what he felt for Katharine—God above, 'twas far stronger, fiercer, so overwhelming that at moments it took him aback. It was not the love that a boy felt for a girl, but that which a man felt for the woman he had claimed as his own, whom he had lain with in the union of marriage, bonding them together with a might that only death could sever.

All this he had known, and denied, in a secret place within, until that moment when Katharine had stood so proudly before all those assembled in the great hall and proclaimed, against the hurt he'd given her, that she was his wife and that their marriage could not be undone. Then he had known, without any doubts, that he loved her.

It seemed a fitting punishment for all his sins. He loved Katharine when he had never thought to love anyone again—and she loved Lord Hanley. Senet tried to view the matter with a measure of calm, but it was impossible. He felt only a deep rage against the man who possessed Katharine's heart...and envy, too. Lord Hanley was both handsome and charming, and Senet knew full well that he was neither. His body was ugly with scars, and his manner less than sweet. Only hours earlier he had well proved the latter to Katharine, informing her as if she were some menial servant that he would be master of Lomas regardless of what she might think. He had been angered with himself even as he'd uttered the words, but now he regretted them even more greatly. His intemperate, overbearing behavior had given her yet another reason to hate him, and to turn to Lord Hanley.

"Leave me be!"

The sound of the distressed, female voice brought them to a halt.

"But, Doro, my sweet love!"

"Argh! Don't touch me, else I shall be ill!"

Senet and Kayne exchanged glances as they hurried around the corner toward the sound of the confrontation, to find Mistress Dorothea backed into a corner and striving mightily to avoid the attentions of Lord Hanley's slight, wiry manservant.

"Only give me a kiss, Doro—hey!"

Senet had picked the smaller man up from the floor, and turned him, yet dangling, about to face him.

"You will not distress the women in my household," he stated tersely, giving his struggling captive a shake before dropping him to the ground. "Or any of the women in Lomas, i'faith, else I will kill you. Make your apologies to Mistress Dorothea.''

"Nay, I want none of him, not even that," Dorothea said with open distaste, lifting her skirts from the ground and moving around the fallen man so as not to even touch him. "Only keep him away from me and I will be glad. I thank you my lord Lomas." She gave Senet a slight bow. "I have just come from Lady Katharine's chamber with a message for you, my lord, to ask that you wait upon her as soon as you may." She bowed again and hurriedly took her leave.

"What do you do here?" Kayne asked Lord Hanley's squire, who, with easy grace, leapt to his feet. "How is it that you dare to trouble Mistress Dorothea in such an unseemly manner?"

"You are called Jean-Marc," Senet stated rather than asked, eyeing the small, slender young man warily. "You serve Lord Hanley."

"I am indeed Jean-Marc, my lord, " the young man said, making an elegant bow, "squire to Lord Hanley. As to what I am doing here, I happened to meet Mistress Dorothea while performing much the same task as she. I have a message to deliver to Lord Lomas. My lord Hanley has requested a meeting with you, my lord—" Jean-Marc bowed again "—whenever the time may be convenient. He is at your service. You need only call for him."

Kayne looked murderous. "Is it your habit, squire, to accost every maid you come upon who is alone and without help? You would have forced your unwanted attentions upon Mistress Dorothea if Lord Lomas and I had not come upon you in time, is that not so?"

Jean-Marc looked fully amused. He was a handsome youth, his hair straight and blond and his eyes blue and guileless. He looked like an angel that Senet had once seen in a painting in France, but smaller, shorter. Dorothea towered over him, and with the temper that Senet had already known of her, he had no doubt that she could have readily handled her unwanted admirer. Jean-Marc clearly felt the same, for he said, "Mistress Dorothea was about to break my nose before you came, or make the attempt, leastwise, just as she has attempted it many times before." He sighed and set a hand over his heart. "She is the most wonderful of all women, I vow. Such fire and beauty cannot be better found in any female." He looked at Senet and Kayne as if they, being men, must surely approve of such sentiments.

"You have met Mistress Dorothea before?"

"Many times," Jean-Marc said blissfully, his hand yet over his heart. "Each more wonderful than the last. 'Twould be heaven indeed if I could but convince my master to visit Lomas far more often than we—" He fell suddenly silent, and dropped his hand to his side. "Far more often than we used to do," he continued. "In the past, I mean. Long ago. Before we journeyed to the Holy Land."

"This was three years ago," Senet said slowly. "You were given to visiting at Lomas often before then? You would have been young to have conceived such a passion for Mistress Dorothea."

"I am older than I appear, my lord," was Jean-Marc's reply. "Much older."

Kayne made a grunting sound. "I readily believe that."

"How is it that your master never saw good cause during his journeying to send a missive to Lady Katharine, telling her he was yet alive and that his return to her was near at hand?"

The smile on Jean-Marc's face seemed to freeze there. He looked from Senet to Kayne, that smile rigid upon his face, then back again, uttering, at last, "Why, my lord, I am sure my lord Hanley will wish to explain the matter to you himself."

"I would rather hear you explain it, squire."

"Oh, but he tells the tale far better than I ever could, my lord. You will enjoy it a great deal more in hearing it from him. And—oh!" He seemed all at once to remember something. "Wine! My lord sent me in search of some, and I have left him all this while to wait for it." He waggled a finger at his forehead as if to indicate a mental insufficience. "Mistress Dorothea sent every other thought directly out of my feeble mind, but she ever has that effect upon me." He smiled and laughed and began to inch in the direction of the stairs. "Pray forgive me, my lord," he nodded at Senet, then at Kayne, "good sir. I must be on my way."

"Not so." Kayne set out a hand and easily dragged the younger man back before them.

"Nay, let him go," Senet said with a wave of his hand. "I will go and see his master and have the truth from his lips. Is Lord Hanley in his chamber now?"

"Aye, my lord," Jean-Marc said with relief, bowing as he backed away. "He will be glad to greet your lordship there, and I shall bring wine at once."

"What a strange little man," Kayne muttered once the manservant had gone. "I cannot like or think him trustworthy."

"Nay, I cannot either," Senet agreed. "Just as I do not trust his master. Lord Hanley has a great deal to explain."

"Shall I come with you?"

"Nay, Kayne, I thank you." He clapped his friend on the shoulder. "I wish to have Lord Hanley all to myself."

Chapter Fifteen

There was laughter coming from Lord Hanley's chamber. Loud laughter, enough so that Senet could hear it clearly as he stood outside the chamber door. Lord Hanley's deep, masculine voice made up part of the jovial sound, but the rest—most of it—was distinctly female, and plainly comprised of more than two voices.

"Kieran! Stop!" This came from one of the women. The next moment another said, "You've got six hands, I vow! Oh!" This was followed by a squeal and more raucous laughter.

Lord Hanley's voice was muffled as he made some reply to this, but filled with evident good cheer. He seemed to be intimately familiar with whoever was in the chamber with him, for after he spoke, the women giggled and laughed with even greater delight.

Senet banged loudly on the door, and the sound was greeted, to his great surprise, by more squeals.

"Never fear," Lord Hanley's voice boomed over the noise. "'Tis only Jean-Marc, returned with the wine. I sent him off before you came. God's mercy, but it's taken you long enough, you lazy—"

The door swung open, and Lord Hanley's handsome face filled with complete shock.

"My lord!"

"Lord Hanley," Senet greeted. The chamber beyond had grown rapidly silent. "You sent word that you desired to meet with me?"

"Indeed I did," Lord Hanley replied, a smile of greeting forming upon his lips. "I had thought you would send for me at a time more convenient to you."

Senet peered past him into the chamber. "Your servant assured me that you would be glad to receive me, though mayhap he was not aware that you were entertaining. I would speak with you, but it can wait for a more suited time."

"Oh, nay, nay. These maids have but come to lend aid in making sure of my comfort." He began waving at whoever was hiding within. "Come, good maids. Your services are not required at present. Come and be on your way."

There were two of them, pretty twin sisters whom Senet remembered well, for they had attempted to dally with him when he had first arrived at Lomas. He had firmly corrected them on the matter and had no trouble with them since. But he had heard, from Kayne and Aric, that the women were making a path through the fighting men, playing the whore for as many as would pay. Now, seeing their lord, they curtsied and hurried out of the chamber, casting glances at Lord Hanley as they did. Senet, watching them go, turned back to his guest with narrowed eyes.

"Please, my lord Lomas," Lord Hanley said with a sweep of his hand, inviting Senet into his chamber. "I am honored to receive you here, if 'tis comfortable for you. Jean-Marc has gone to fetch wine, and should return shortly. Please, take this chair near the fire."

Senet walked into the chamber, looking about at the luxurious furnishings. It was not as large as his chamber, or Katharine's, but it was just as comfortable, perhaps more so. It was the chamber kept ready for visiting nobility, and he supposed Lord Hanley was that, though his title was not one of high rank.

"I met your servant in the passageway, as I came," Senet said, moving toward the fire but not sitting. He turned to look at Lord Hanley as that man joined him. "He was behaving poorly toward one of my wife's ladies, Mistress Dorothea. I corrected him."

Lord Hanley looked at him with grave concern. "My lord, I pray you will forgive such bold and unwanted behavior on the part of my squire. Jean-Marc is an excellent servant, but given to much dallying, I fear. I shall punish him duly, you may believe."

"Keep him from Mistress Dorothea," Senet said flatly, "and all will be well. I will not tolerate it if she—or any of the castle women—should be overset because of your servant. Or you." He looked at Lord Hanley with full meaning. God help him, but he would kill the man if he dallied with the maids beneath Katharine's very nose.

"I understand you completely, my lord," Lord Hanley said with a handsome bow. Senet, seeing how polished and easy the other man was, felt his temper flare.

"I've come to speak of my wife."

"Ah," said Lord Hanley with sudden delight. "That is just what I wished to discuss with you, as well. I'm always pleased to discuss my darling Katharine."

Senet made a fist. "She is my *wife*," he said tightly, "and I will have no man speak of her thus."

"Certainly not," Lord Hanley agreed affably, as if that were an obvious fact. "Pray, forgive my thoughtless tongue. I cannot seem to help myself, so glad am I to see my…to see Lady Katharine once more. You may imagine how often I thought of my beautiful betrothed while I was imprisoned.''

Senet had to clamp his teeth together to keep his mouth from dropping agape.

"Imprisoned?" he managed at last, staring at the other man.

Lord Hanley sighed and cast his gaze toward the fire. "Aye. For nearly a full year, in Anatolia, where I was waylaid by vile, pagan Osmanli as I made my return to England.''

A brief knock fell on the door before it was pushed open, and Jean-Marc appeared, carrying a tray with a decanter and two silver goblets. He set the tray upon a table and in a moment was bowing to Senet and Lord Hanley, offering them the dark red wine that he had poured.

"'S'truth,'' Lord Hanley said as he accepted the goblet handed to him. "Jean-Marc and I both were taken as prisoners, and 'twas truly the darkest time we could ever have imagined.''

Jean-Marc, in the midst of handing Senet his goblet, stiffened and looked at his master. He blinked, glanced at Senet, then smiled and turned away.

"Just to think of it!'' Lord Hanley cried, setting the back of one hand against his forehead. "The horrid dungeon in which we were kept, the continual darkness, both day and night, and the food. God's mercy!'' He sighed loudly and sipped of his wine. "But Jean-Marc could tell you better than I of the food. I was too sick to eat for the first six months. Is that not so, Jean-Marc?''

Jean-Marc had been striving to make himself busy by folding his master's clothes and putting them away in the large wooden trunk set near the bed. The aggravated look he gave his master upon hearing his name, Senet thought, was not in the least proper for a squire. But the boy readily responded to Lord Hanley's question.

"Oh, indeed, my lord. So sick as you were, I should not desire even my greatest enemies to be likewise plagued. 'Twas the weakness that took him first, my lord Lomas. God's mercy, such a weakness as it was. I had to do all for him, for he could not even lift his head. And then, the boils. So great, my lord, and so many, and so fierce, that not a part of him could be seen beneath them!" Jean-Marc clearly seemed to be warm to the topic, and even left his folding aside to approach them, his hands held aloft as he described Lord Hanley's illness. "But that was not the worst of it, my lord. Oh, nay, indeed. Then came the strange blood-orange hue, covering his entire body."

"Orange?" Senet had never heard of such a thing. He had seen, during his soldiering years—men turn yellow in both eye and skin, but never orange.

"*Blood*-orange, my lord," Jean-Marc said insistently, rubbing his hands together as if he relished the thought. "Like a curse from the very Bible! And not just his body, but his eyes and hair, even the tips of his fingers and toes!"

"God's mercy," Senet murmured, much amazed by the idea of this. He glanced at Lord Hanley, who merely smiled and shrugged.

"Aye, m'lord, just so," Jean-Marc agreed, nodding. "But that was naught to compare with the shaking that o'ertook him when night fell and a chill set in. Such fits as he had! Please God, keep me from ever seeing the like! He shook so hard that I had to weigh him down with stones just to keep him from jumping all about the cell in which we were locked each night."

"Jean-Marc—" Lord Hanley began.

"And the screaming," Jean-Marc continued. "'Twas enough to make one mad, so loud and hideous as it was."

"That's sufficient, I believe," Lord Hanley told his manservant.

"Screaming, my lord Lomas, that could make a man tear his very hair out!" Jean-Marc moved ever closer, his hands held out before him as if he beheld the horror anew. "And then, of course, the rats came, as if his screaming had called them. *Huge* rats, my lord, hungry and vicious, the size of—"

"*Jean-Marc.*"

The squire looked at last at his master as if he had only just seen him standing there.

"My lord?" he asked innocently, dropping his hands.

"Lord Lomas understands fully." Lord Hanley made a dismissive motion with one hand. "You may return to your duties."

"Certainly, your grand lordship." Jean-Marc bowed low. "Only call if you require me further. I shall be here, fulfilling the small and meager duties which I ever pray will give pleasure to your great eminence, just as I always strive to do."

Lord Hanley cleared his throat loudly before turning to Senet, who was gazing at him questioningly.

"His mind became deeply troubled during our sufferings," Lord Hanley explained in quiet tones. "He's been a grave trial to me since, but I cannot let him go." He leaned confidingly toward Senet. "You understand, I'm certain. 'Twould be the basest of sins to abandon one who had kept me alive throughout such torment as we had in Anatolia. Now—" he straightened, his voice strengthening "—what did you wish to speak to me about regarding Katharine? You must know that I only want what is best for her, for I owe her much. 'Twas only the memory of my sweet betrothed—and my determination to return to her—that kept me alive." He sighed. "All those months, first suffering the torments of the damned in prison, then half a year's desperate journey to return to England, only to find, at last, that I was three days late. Three days," he repeated woefully, with a shake of his head. "'Tis almost more than I can bear." He wiped his eyes, which had begun to tear. "Forgive me, my lord. You wished to speak to me, not to hear of my great sorrows."

Senet hardly knew how to go on. He had come to demand answers of the man, to learn why Lord Hanley had been so negligent of Katharine. Now he had his answer. Lord Hanley hadn't been able to return to his betrothed, for he'd been imprisoned in a pagan land. And all the while he'd dreamed of Katharine, only to return to Lomas at last and find that another man had forced her to wife. Senet had never felt quite so badly about himself—or anything—as he did at that moment.

"You were imprisoned for a year?" he asked. "How did you come to be freed again?"

Lord Hanley was still wiping his eyes in an affecting manner. Senet began to feel worse than ever.

"We escaped, Jean-Marc and I. 'Twas either that or die, for our captors had decided that we had become too troublesome to keep alive.

Senet looked at him curiously. He knew something of escaping a prison.

"Were you not well-guarded?"

"Indeed, very well-guarded."

"There were many of them?"

"More than I could count, my lord. There must have been hundreds of them, both inside and outside the prison. And huge, evil brutes they were."

Senet regarded him more closely. "How then did you

escape? It could have been no easy thing unless you had aid.''

"'S'truth," Lord Hanley said with a nod. "Indeed, we never would have escaped at all save that we bribed some of our guards."

"Bribed them?"

Lord Hanley took a long drink of his wine. "Mmm, aye. 'Twas the only way to gain our freedom."

"But with what could you barter? Had they not already taken all you possessed?"

Lord Hanley stared at him, blinking. "Ah...yes," he replied slowly. "Certainly, they had indeed taken all we had. Even the gifts I was bringing back to Katharine from the Holy Land. We were left with naught but the clothes upon our bodies."

Senet set his wine goblet aside, having not taken even a sip. He looked very directly at Lord Hanley.

"How, then, did you bribe your guards?"

"What his lordship means to say," Jean-Marc interjected from across the chamber, "is that we offered our guards their lives in exchange for our freedom. *After* the riot. Is that not so, my lord?"

"Riot?" Senet repeated, looking from the manservant to his master with disbelief.

"Oh, aye, the *riot*." Lord Hanley set the palm of one hand against his forehead. "Did I not mention the riot? How foolish." He laughed heartily. "But of course, how could we possibly have bartered for anything save that which we took...during the riot. There was an uprising among the...ah...the..."

"Other prisoners," Jean-Marc supplied. "Led by you, my lord."

"Yes, led by me...." Lord Hanley gave his servant a brief look of consternation.

"You organized the other prisoners?" Senet asked. "To overtake the guards?" Lord Hanley certainly looked capable of doing such a thing, for he was a big, muscular man and Senet recognized a seasoned warrior from the measured grace with which the man moved. But even a skilled knight would have difficulty leading such an attack, having first been weakened by months of poor food and worse conditions, and without benefit of weapons.

"Just so," Lord Hanley said with a nod. "Just so."

"You would have waited for the right moment and sprung upon them—when? At what opportunity?"

"Ah...when?" Lord Hanley repeated faintly, glancing toward Jean-Marc. "Well, 'twas when..."

"When they brought us our evening meal," Jean-Marc said, as if the answer were obvious. "We were unshackled only long each day to feed ourselves, and in those brief moments, my lord Hanley bravely struck, leading all those prisoners who were with us and overpowering the guards, taking their weapons."

"Verily?" Senet asked with interest. "How many guards did you overpower?"

"How many?" Lord Hanley looked at Jean-Marc.

"A dozen." The manservant shrugged as if it were of little consequence. "At least."

"A dozen?" Senet repeated. "I see. And so you had twelve weapons for your use, once you had overtaken these guards. With twelve weapons, you managed to escape a prison which, by your own reckoning, was guarded by hundreds of men?"

"Aye," Lord Hanley said, clearing his throat. "Just so."

"I'll not ask you now for the many details of so successful a venture," Senet said, seeing the clear relief upon the faces of both Hanley and his manservant. "'Twould make far too entertaining a tale for my ears alone, and I am certain that Katharine and the castlefolk will wish to hear it at this evening's meal. You would honor us greatly by relating the tale—the entire tale.''

"I should be most glad to do so, my lord Lomas," Lord Hanley replied smoothly, making Senet one of the elegant bows that were beginning to set him on edge.

Senet began to move toward the door.

"My lord!" Lord Hanley stopped him.

Senet turned about. "Aye?"

"I had thought that you wished to discuss Lady Katharine?"

Senet shook his head. "I have heard enough. The rest I will learn from Katharine. Only tell me one more thing."

"Certainly."

"Was it dark when you escaped from your prison? You had said you attacked at the evening meal."

"Aye, 'twas dark."

"Then how, once you had made your escape, did you find your way to safety in that strange land? Even if you had horses and a guide, 'twould have been a very miracle to have evaded recapture with hundreds of guards close upon your trail.''

Both Lord Hanley and Jean-Marc stared at him in silence, until Senet nodded and said, with a measure of disgust, "Make certain you have a better answer for Katharine and the others this eve. I will not have her embarrassed by your feeble lies."

"Lord Lomas, you misunderstand—"

Senet took a step nearer, threatening. "I understand that you abandoned my wife for three years to follow whatever fancy lured you, that you left her to wait and worry while you pursued that same fancy. I can only guess at what truly occurred to keep you from returning to her, but I prefer the tale of your being imprisoned, foolish as it may be, for at least 'twill not break Katharine's heart with the truth of how falsely you have played her."

"I have not played her false!" Lord Hanley protested. "I adore my sweet Katharine!"

"God above!" Senet snarled, advancing further upon the man, though Lord Hanley seemed perfectly unafraid of him. "I cannot fathom what manner of man you are! If she had been mine, *nothing* could have persuaded me to leave her, but even if God had somehow ordained that we be parted, I would have done all I could—never ceasing—until I was once more by her side. But you—!" He looked at the other man with all the disgust he felt. "You cannot love or even care for her, as you claim. The great pity of it is that she yet loves you, and for that I will not allow her to be harmed. You will tell her what she wants to hear, that you were kept from her against your will—imprisoned by Osmanli or felled by some dread illness—but make certain that you tell the story well, for I will not have her humiliated before her people. Understand what I say, my lord. You will regret it if you bring but one tear to her eyes."

Lord Hanley regarded him steadily. "You care for Katharine."

"It matters not—" Senet said.

"Nay, but it does." Lord Hanley's tone was solemn, his gaze searching. "You care for her. Why do you let me remain here, knowing that I might take her from you?"

Senet sprang forward almost without knowing what he did, and struck the other man full in the face. Lord Hanley fell to the floor, nearly into the fire, but rolled away at once and shouted, "Leave him be, Jean!"

But it was too late. The wiry young man had come to

his master's aid, attempting to leap upon Senet's back. Senet, too long a soldier to be taken by any charge so foolish, had stepped aside and let Jean-Marc fall upon his face beside his master.

"I do not wish to fight you," Lord Hanley said, slowly standing, "more for Katharine's sake than my own, for I think we might match each other well and make a fair contest of it." He grinned and wiped the side of his lip, which was bleeding from Senet's blow. "I do like a good fight, I vow. But Katharine would not forgive me were I to behave in so base a manner, and, unless you force the matter, I will not fight."

Senet was breathing hard, his fisted hands held before him, ready for an attack. The other man's words came to him slowly, finding their way at last through the turmoil of his thoughts. Lord Hanley would have a swollen cheek now, because of him, and Katharine would know that he had been the one to strike her beloved. That she should love a man so false and unworthy was beyond his understanding, but love Lord Hanley she did, and Senet would not be the one to hurt her because of it.

"One tear from my lady's eyes," he said, striving to calm his rage, "and I will make you regret that you ever returned to Lomas. I vow it on my very soul. Do you not forget it. Please God," he said with full meaning as he backed away toward the door, "do not forget. For on my honor, I would be glad of nothing better than to be rid of you forever."

to oppose his ridiculous tale ... ... She had no

Chapter Sixteen

Long after the evening meal had ended, Katharine finally
found Senet. She had looked everywhere but in the place
where she thought he must be, and saved that until last,
unwilling to feel the despair of knowing he had so entirely
avoided her. She had waited all afternoon in her chamber
for him to come to her, knowing that Dorothea would take
her message to him at once, but he had not done so. She
had only seen him at the evening meal and, though he
had been polite and smiling, he had not made any effort
to converse with her.

Not that there had been much chance for talk. Kieran,
bearing a slightly swollen lip that Katharine assumed
Senet had given him, had entertained the assembled with
the most ridiculous tale of his supposed journey to the
Holy Land, of being imprisoned by marauding Ottomans
on his return journey, and of eventually escaping and
making his way back to safety and England.

It had been a captivating story, but also the most un-
believable collection of lies that Katharine had ever heard.
She'd sat in tense preparation every moment, waiting for
Senet or Kayne or anyone else to challenge Kieran's story
and expose him for the complete fraud he was. That no

one said a word, save for murmurs of amazement when Kieran grew particularly colorful in his telling, both surprised and distressed her. Surely no one really believed such nonsense? She never would have, if she hadn't already known the truth.

She was grateful, certainly, that no one had exposed Kieran, for then her own devious part in the ploy would have been revealed, and she could not have borne for that to happen before Senet in so public a manner. She had to tell him soon, tell him the full of it before the farce went any further, not only for his sake, but also for the sake of her people. It had been wretched beyond measure to sit through the evening meal, feeling the many questioning glances sent her way by the castlefolk who knew full well that Kieran FitzAllen and Lord Albertus Hanley were two different men. How had she ever thought that she could carry off such a deceit, when surely it must become obvious almost from the start? But, then, she had only wanted to fool Senet long enough to make him go away; never had she expected that she would be faced with carrying the lie on with him close at hand.

It was not yet fully dark when she found him, standing on the balcony that could only be reached by the secret passageway from her bedchamber.

She had thought that he might be in the hidden chamber that he had taken her to only the night before, but he was out here in the dark summer night, striving to make sense of the star measuring instrument that his mother had left behind. His pure black hair was alive with silver moonlight, which danced back and forth across the straight, silky strands as he moved the instrument about.

He had not heard her approach, for she had been as silent as she could make herself and now stood in the shadows, watching as he looked through the odd instrument at night's darkness, sometimes murmuring to himself and sometimes cursing, and she smiled against the tears that came, just to watch him thus and feel the deep love that she held for him.

But this love was too strange and hard. What would she do if he discovered the truth and began to hate her? How would she go on, day to day, if he would no longer smile and tease her, or share her bed at night? If he became the stern Lord Lomas only, cold and harsh as she knew he could be, she would not be able to keep her word and stay at Lomas. It would be worse than abiding in purgatory. Far worse.

"I waited for you this afternoon," she said softly, moving out of the shadows toward the small ledge that must be traversed in order to reach the balcony.

Senet did not turn, but continued to peer out of the strange instrument as if he'd already been aware she was there and had no care for her sudden appearance.

"I apologize. I was kept busy with other matters. I should have sent word to you, and am sorry that I did not."

"I thought mayhap you were angered with me." Sitting on the ledge, she lifted her skirts and swung her legs until she stood upon the balcony beside him.

He glanced at her, over his shoulder, before returning his attention to the instrument. "Nay, why should I be?"

"Because of Lord Hanley."

"He does not trouble me," he said, peering through the instrument. "So long as he does not trouble you, Katharine." He lowered his hands and looked at her. "Has he?"

Her heart was pounding in her chest, made worse by the directness of his gaze. She swallowed heavily and opened her mouth to make a full confession, but only said, "Nay."

Senet stared at her a moment longer, then looked away. "What would you have of me, Katharine? I cannot let you go to him."

"I do not wish to go to him!" She set a hand upon his arm, pleading with him to believe her. "I am your wife, and mean to go on as such. Is it not what you wish, Senet?"

He lowered his head. "Aye, 'tis what I want, but...I cannot think that it is what you truly desire, Katharine. I know that you love your Lord Hanley."

"Just as you yet love the one to whom you were once betrothed," she said.

"Aye."

"Then naught has changed between us. Lord Hanley will leave soon, and we will go on as we were. For the sake of Lomas."

One of his hands crept up to cover the one she yet held upon his arm, pressing hard. "For the sake of Lomas," he repeated. "If that is what you wish, then that is what we will do."

There was a brief silence, and then he said, "I have been looking over these odd instruments that were once my mother's. If you have no objection, I will send them to my sister, Isabelle, at Talwar. She will be glad to have something more of my mother than the few books she now possesses. And she will know how to work these foolish things," he said with a slight smile, lifting the instrument he now held to show it to Katharine. "I cannot make head nor tail of it. Can you?"

Hesitating, she took it, her heart yet aching with the knowledge that she had hurt him. She could hear it in his voice and see it in his manner. Somehow, she had hurt him.

"Shall I try?" she murmured, taking it. "I will be no better at it than you."

He looked so forlorn that she wanted to weep, though he pressed a smile upon his lips.

"Try it," he said, his voice a rough whisper.

She drew in a deep breath. "Very well." Lifting the instrument, she peered through it, seeing nothing beyond the blur of bitterly held tears. After a moment, she lowered the small, strange combination of metal plates and rods. "I do not understand it, either."

"Shall I send it to Isabelle, then?"

"Aye." She nodded. "And all that belonged to your mother. Whatever you do not wish to keep here at Lomas. For our children."

His head swung about. "Children?"

"Do you not think they should have something of their grandmother, even though they will not know her?"

He blinked, then said, "Aye, they should."

"Then keep this for them." She gave the instrument back to him. "If we cannot discover how it works, mayhap they shall do so."

"Very well." He seemed not to know what he should do with the thing, once he held it again. "Katharine...come into the hidden chamber. There is a fire, and wine. We can speak in comfort there, and I would not have you take chill in the night's air."

She readily followed him, sitting upon one of the rugs and making herself easy while he poured wine. She looked about the room, noting that it was much cleaner than it had been the night before.

"I am not skilled as a maid," he said, as if knowing her thoughts, "but I managed to rid the chamber of much of its dust. The rugs I shook over the balcony, expecting every moment to hear curses from below.'' He handed her a goblet and then sat beside her, reclining against a large pillow and stretching his legs out comfortably. ''I might have asked Mistress Dorothea to send maids to clean it better, but I did not wish for any others to know that the chamber is here. I thought to keep it a secret between the two of us alone.''

''That is just what I should like,'' she agreed. ''But I have disturbed your peace this night, have I not? You wished to be alone.''

''Nay, Katharine, 'twas not what I wished,'' he said gently, reaching out to touch her hand, which lay near his own. ''But I thought it best to give you time to speak to Lord Hanley apart from my presence. And I also wished to think of all that occurred today, to consider what is best. But I would have gone to search you out soon, for there is much we must say.''

''Senet...''

''Nay, please, let me speak first.'' He fingered the rim of the goblet he held, gazing at it consideringly before lifting his gaze to meet hers. ''I wished to tell you that I regret, very much, the manner in which I spoke to you this afternoon, when I told you that I will be master of Lomas. Do not misunderstand, for I meant what I said. I must take my place as the lord of Lomas. But I am sorry for the manner in which I spoke to you, Katharine. Forgive me, I pray.''

''We are both sorry, then, for I regret the manner of my response. You had the right of it, Senet. You are the lord of Lomas, and as such must have final word. 'Twas wrong of me to question and fight you, and I vow that I will strive never to do so again.''

He smiled. ''I do not mean to put such sweet words to

the test, my lady. In future, I will ask your opinion in all matters of import, and only after hearing you in full will I make a decision. I cannot promise that I will ever remember to do so, for I am a soldier used to the giving of commands, not to asking questions, but if you will remind me, I will not turn you aside. In this manner I hope that we may often be in accord, one with the other. Does this please you, Katharine?''

He was speaking of their future, and Katharine's heart filled with gladness. He meant for them to continue on together, just as she desired, and took no heed of Kieran's stupid threat to contest their marriage.

"Oh, aye," she said. "Very much, my lord. I thank you.''

He seemed pleased by this reply, and lifted his goblet to her in tribute. "Then mayhap we can discuss the matter of Aric and Mistress Magan more calmly?''

She sipped at her own wine before saying, "I would be glad to do so.''

"I have considered your argument regarding Mistress Magan, that she is an heiress and of good birth, and should therefore marry a gently bred man of equal standing and wealth. 'Tis true that Aric was born a bastard. That cannot be changed, even by his attainment to knighthood. But he is not a beggar. Far from it. When we fought in France, we all of us—Kayne, John, Aric and I—sent every groat and half groat we earned, also whatever boons we gained, to my sister Isabelle. She is, as I have told you, gifted in the way of money, and has made each of us wealthy beyond measure. I had thought to use what was mine to restore Lomas to its former glory, only to find that 'twas not needed. You have done far better than I ever could.''

Katharine smiled at the compliment, especially pleased because it was perfectly true.

"Sir Aric is possessed of a great fortune, then," she said, considering this new knowledge. "I need not worry that he would wed Magan for her inheritance. There is yet his birth to speak against the match. Howbeit," she pressed on before he could object, "I will indeed be moved to bless the union if you will likewise consider approving the same between Mademoiselle Clarise and John Ipris."

Senet nearly choked on his wine. Sputtering, he sat upright. "*What?* Clarise and—! What madness is this? There can be no question of any such union, for 'tis entirely ill-matched, and they would never wish it."

"No? I think, my lord, that there is nothing they would like better."

He laughed. "You do not know what you speak of. 'Tis foolishness complete. John is as a brother to Clarise, as we all are. And I trust him fully to ever treat her with the care and mind of a brother. If I thought, for even a moment, that he had betrayed that trust, I would beat him senseless and then banish him from Lomas. Forever."

She nodded. "I think this must be why they hide from you what is so plain to many others. John Ipris knows that you will never accept his suit, and Mademoiselle Clarise is afraid of what you will do to her beloved should you discover the truth."

"They hide *nothing*," he said, growing angry. "Clarise is a child, and John a man full-grown. The very thought of a union between them—when he has been as relative to her—is loathsome!"

"They hide their love for each other," Katharine said patiently, "and Mademoiselle Clarise is *not* a child. She might have already been married these past three years or more, if you had wished it. Indeed, you have recently betrothed her to a man she does not wish to marry, and must therefore believe her ready to wed. As to John Ipris, I cannot think that he is more than ten years older than she. Is the nobleman you have betrothed her to so much younger?''

Senet pushed to his feet, glaring at her. "He is older than John. But he is far more acceptable.'' Setting his goblet aside on a nearby table, he made his way for the door. "I will find John and discover the truth of this. If he has so much as dared to set a finger upon Clarise when I did not know of it—''

"Senet!" Katharine jumped up, throwing her goblet across the room to stop him. He turned, staring first at her, then at the mess she'd made.

"I have done my cleaning for the day," he told her. "You may care for that."

"You will not leave me in this manner!" she declared hotly, moving toward him. "I see now that your word has no strength to it, nay, no more than that of a tiny gnat!" Standing directly before him, she held her fingers up to show just how small.

"Katharine," he said in a warning tone.

"You gave me your vow, but a quarter of an hour ago, that you would listen to my counsel before making any determinations, yet already you forget your word. But I *will* have my say, and you *will* listen."

"Nay, in this you will have no say," he told her hotly. "Clarise is my ward."

"Just as Magan is mine!"

"No longer yours alone," he countered, leaning down to meet her face to face. "*I* am the lord of Lomas."

"Just as Mademoiselle Clarise is no longer your sole concern, for *I* am the lady of Lomas!"

He threw his hands up. "You do not know what you say! God above, but no other woman can make me so crazed. John is not acceptable for Clarise! Can you not understand?"

"Why? Sir Aric is clearly good enough for Magan, or so you say."

He looked at her as if she must be mad. "'Tis not the same. Clarise is the sole inheritor of her father's estates in both Normandy and England. She is possessed of lands and wealth beyond measure, while John is..."

"Aye?" she asked sweetly. "I believe you've only just told me that he's possessed of no small wealth of his own."

"That has no bearing." He ran a hand through his hair in aggravation. "Clarise is too highly born for one of John's stature. Her family can be dated to William, and has never fallen outside of nobility. Not once. In hundreds of years, Katharine." When she failed to be impressed by this, he grew even more aggravated. "John," he said frankly, "is so basely born that he does not even know who his own mother is. He is less than a bastard, knowing nothing of his people." Senet was fully pained, just speaking of such hard truth. "John was thrown into a ditch after he was born, a naked babe, left to die." He looked away from Katharine, but not before she saw his clear blue eyes darkening at the very words he spoke. "How can a man such as that wed a born lady like Clarise? 'Tis impossible, Katharine. Impossible."

Reaching out before he could move away, Katharine took his hand, holding it tightly. When she spoke, her voice was low and impassioned.

"You told me only yesterday that you would not have survived in France without John Ipris. Will you now deny that this is so?" She squeezed his hand until she knew it must hurt, until he looked at her. But this was the only manner of war she might wage with him, and she would not be sorry for using her woman's instinct, or her strength. "I have seen for myself that he is a fine gentleman, educated and worthy of every manner of respect. Tell me now—tell me as you look at me—and I will know you speak the truth. Is John Ipris not as a brother to you? Just as Sir Kayne and Sir Aric are? Would you give to Sir Aric what you will not give to him?"

"Nay." He shook his head, avoiding her gaze, troubled. "John is dearer to me than I can speak. There are not words for it. They are each like brothers to me. John, Kayne and Aric. But you know this, Katharine."

"Aye," she whispered fervently.

"I gave Lord Rouveau my solemn oath. I *must* see Clarise wed to one suitable. There is no other way."

"But there is!" she cried. "Only listen to me a moment, Senet, I pray." Her expression filled with eagerness. "John Ipris has performed great service for England. You have told me this yourself. Yet he took no honor for himself, not even the knighthood, which would have given a man of such birth great respect. But now, to gain Clarise for a wife, he may be persuaded to accept a boon. You will know better than I whether such a thing may be possible. Has he been of such service to England that he might possibly be given an estate? Even a very small one?"

Senet stared at her. "Katharine," he said her name very slowly, "you do not know what you say."

"'Tis an impossibility, I know," she admitted, "but I yet believe it can be done. If you and Sir Justin Baldwin request it. The Baldwins are a powerful family, and you have done as Duke Humphrey asked in gaining Lomas, so that he must now be well pleased with you. You might ask anything you desire and be granted it, while you are yet in his favor.''

He seemed not to know whether to laugh or frown. ''You're crazed. A man such as John? Become a *lord?*''

''John Ipris would make a far better lord than many men—my father among them. He seems to be most wise. Do you say that he is not?''

Senet turned away, his expression troubled. ''Nay. John is, i'faith, both wise and knowing. He would make a fine lord, but...it is too strange to consider.''

''But if it could be done?'' she pressed.

He continued to move slowly about the room, thinking the matter over, fingering his chin consideringly.

''Then, I suppose—not that I approve, understand me— I suppose it might make the difference. I do not think I could find legal fault with such a suit, if 'twere properly done. And if John wishes to wed Clarise—which I do not yet believe in the least,'' he said, looking at Katharine, ''but if he should, and if she is of a like mind...God above! I cannot fathom such a thing.''

''But it would do?''

A slight smile formed on Senet's lips. ''A small estate and a lordship—indeed, 'twould do very well.'' He nodded slowly, the smile growing as his tone warmed and his features began to relax. ''If it can be done.''

''Her relatives would be satisfied?'' Katharine asked eagerly. He was clearly beginning to see the possibility of the thing, to approve of it. ''They need not know the full of John's birth until the deed is done, and once they are wed, John will prove himself a worthy lord and husband.''

''He could not succeed to the title belonging to Clarise's estate,'' Senet warned, ''though I cannot think John would care for that. It can be held in abeyance for their eldest son.''

Katharine strove to hide the pleasure she felt. He was speaking of John and Clarise's future, as if it were going to be. "Or daughter," she said, "should they have no sons."

Senet smiled at this. "Aye, Katharine. Even a daughter. But how strange to think of it! John and Clarise! I have seen nothing of this love that you say exists between them. They have ever been greatly affectionate with each other, but I have thought 'twas because Clarise was so much easier with John than Kayne and Aric and me. Are you so certain of this?''

"I only discovered the truth this very day, for before that I truly thought Mademoiselle Clarise to be your mistress. You did not watch them as they walked along the river, but 'twas clear that they held each other in the deepest affection. Howbeit, I yet was not certain, until Dorothea told me that she saw the pair of them embracing— but an hour ago in the solar as she made her final round of the castle to make certain that all was in order before seeking her chamber. She told me of it before I came to find you."

He began to look angry again. "What manner of embrace?''

Katharine set a hand upon his arm. "A tender embrace, or so Dorothea said, but nothing more than that. They did not see her, and she did not remain long, only enough to know that John Ipris ended the embrace and put Mademoiselle Clarise away from him. He is a good and trustworthy man, and this I know because of you."

He smoothed his hand over the one she yet held on his arm. "You speak truly, Katharine, and I admit to a measure of shame. I would trust John with my very life, and

the more with Clarise's. 'Tis just that I am all amazed to
know that this thing is so, when I never knew or guessed
of it."

"But you will do all you can to lend them your aid,
Senet? Now that you know the truth?"

His fingers began to caress rather than hold her own,
and Katharine felt her chest tighten with wanting. She
turned her hand to give him access to the more sensitive
area beneath. He understood, and slid his forefinger lightly
over her palm, giving her a look that nearly made her legs
give way. She drew nearer, her breathing faster, counting
the minutes now until he would take her back to her
chamber and lay her upon the bed and make love to her.
Surely it would be soon. 'Twas dark outside, and she
could tell, by the heightened rhythm of his own breathing,
that he wished for that as much as she did.

"If it is true, my little warrior," he said, his voice low
and gentle, "I will do what I can."

Katharine smiled up at him, her heart filling anew with
the love she felt for this most amazing of all men. She
had never known a man so ready to listen, so unafraid to
change his mind or admit his own wrong. He had gone
from fury to understanding in but moments, just as she
had done, but he had not once raised a hand to her, or
treated her as his inferior.

"I thank you, my lord," she said, holding his gaze,
wishing that she might reveal all she felt for him. "I am
so grateful. 'Twould be a grave sadness if two who love
as they do were kept apart, for love is so rare a treasure,
and must never be taken for granted. Do you not agree,
Senet?"

It was all that she dared to speak of love, and if he but
said that she spoke the truth, she would dare to say

more…but he responded as if she'd poured boiling water upon him, instead.

"Aye," he said, setting her aside, turning completely away with an abruptness that left her chilled. "I understand you fully, Katharine. But 'tis no good, for I cannot let you go with him."

"Senet!"

"Nay!" He turned back to face her, violence in his face. "Do not speak of the man or I vow I'll—" He stopped, hands fisted at his sides. He drew in a long breath, then released it. "I cannot let you go, Katharine. Never. Not even for whatever love is between you."

"Senet, that was not what I meant," she said hurriedly, holding out a hand to him. "I promise it. Please—"

"It matters not," he said, his voice as stony as his expression. "I'd kill him outright before letting him take you away. If you love him, Katharine, you'll never forget that. You are my wife, and I keep what is mine."

He left the chamber without looking back at her, and Katharine stood where she was, staring at the gaping door. Swallowing, blinking, she nearly gave way to tears. Nearly.

"Damn him!" she swore furiously, wiping her eyes with a sweep of her fists. "Wretched man! I will teach him what it means to have Katharine of Lomas for a wife!"

Chapter Seventeen

Senet had only just slammed the door to his bedchamber when Katharine opened it again, storming into the room without invitation.

"I'm in no mood to speak to you further this night," he told her, far angrier at himself than with her. His body was hard with desire for a woman who loved another man, and the hurt of it was far more than physical. He ached *everywhere,* and would be damned to hell and back again before he'd let her, or anyone else, know the truth of that.

Her response, having given him a heated glare, was to slam the door harder than he had done and to throw the bolt.

"I did not come to speak," she told him, moving across the room. Before he could even begin to wonder at what she meant, she had thrown herself at him, wrapping her arms about his neck and setting her mouth against his own. She kissed him hotly, pressing her tongue against his stunned lips as if she'd force him to kiss her in turn.

"Katharine!" He turned his head aside, gasping for air, but she would not stop. Her mouth fastened upon his neck with such power that his skin stung from it. "Katharine, cease!'' He tried to pry her off, but she was a strong woman, and held fast with hands and arms and legs.

"You're going to make love to me," she said, her breath hot against the side of his face. "I've come to seduce you."

"You'll not," he said tightly, turning his face farther away to avoid her seeking lips. "I won't lie with you while you pretend 'tis him you're with."

Katharine stopped her attack and lifted her head to look at him. "I was a maiden on the night of our marriage. I knew nothing—know nothing, save what you've taught me." Sliding down his body until her feet touched the floor, she pressed fully against him, running her hands over his shoulders, his chest and lower. "But now you have taught me, and I have the right, as your wife, to demand more of you. You told me this yourself." Her fingers slid beneath his tunic, caressing, causing him to groan aloud. When she began to untie the laces of his leggings his entire body shuddered with wanting. He had taught her how to please him with her touches, and now she used such lessons against him.

"Katharine," he murmured. "'Tis wrong. You'll be angered in the morn...when you see him..."

"Oh, nay, Senet." Lifting up, she began to place more gentle kisses along the column of his neck. "You are my husband, and I will think of no one but you when we lie upon that bed." With her body, she pushed, backing him toward it until his legs came against the wood. "Kiss me, Senet," she whispered. "Please. I need you."

With a groan he gave way, knowing how deeply he would regret it on the morrow. Burying a hand in her hair, he pulled her up to meet him, kissing her with all the love and desire he felt. His other hand worked furiously to undo the laces of her surcoat, but when her clever fingers slipped inside his leggings to touch him intimately, he gave up the effort and picked her up in his arms, yet fully clothed. Turning, he set her upon the bed and lifted her skirts.

"You've driven me beyond madness," he muttered, his mouth against hers as he tore her leggings away and pulled his own down. "I must be inside you. Now."

"Yes, oh…Senet!"

"Is that what you wanted, Katharine?"

He thrust hard, deep, and she gasped with pleasure.

"More."

He gave her what she asked for. Harder, deeper yet.

"Like that? Tell me."

Her head had fallen back, her eyes closed as he moved within her.

"Yes," she whispered. "Yes."

She cried out when the pleasure overcame her, and he buried his face in her neck and followed, groaning and shuddering as sensation washed over him.

A long moment later, as they lay half on the bed, half off, waiting for their breathing to slow, Senet said, "You make me crazed."

She sighed and stroked a hand lazily over his shining black hair. "Good."

Lifting up upon his arms, he gazed down at her. "I do not understand you, Katharine. I do not know what to make of you."

With one finger she traced the line of his jaw. "How so?"

"Lord Hanley—"

Her finger pressed against his lips. "Do not speak of him. I do not wish to even think of him now. Please. Let this be only between the two of us, you and me, alone."

Because Lord Hanley was her beloved, Senet thought

bitterly, and she did not wish to discuss him with anyone else, certainly not her own husband. That she had followed him from their secret chamber—after telling him that she loved another!—with the intent of seducing him was no longer a mystery. He had taught her in the past few days just how pleasant their couplings could be, and her body was hungry for more of what he'd given her but a taste of. She meant to use him to sate that hunger—she was far too honorable to go to Lord Hanley and break her vow of marriage—and, though the knowledge pained Senet deeply, he would give her all that she asked for, and more. Because he loved her and wanted her as she wanted him. And that was enough for now.

"Very well." He lowered his head to kiss her gently, then pulled away altogether. "Let me love you more fully now, Katharine." He tugged her to a sitting position, as well, and began once again to unlace her surcoat.

She reached out and fingered his tunic. "Take this off."

The very idea made his heart twist. "Nay, Katharine, for I am very ugly, just as I have told you."

Without a word, she slid from the bed, and took hold of his tunic with both hands. Holding his gaze, she pulled until he at last gave way and lifted his arms, and then she tossed the garment aside.

"Sit," she murmured, placing her palms on his bare chest and pushing until he did as she asked. Kneeling, she removed his boots, one at a time, and then his leggings, until he sat before her completely naked. Then she rose to her feet and slowly, yet holding his gaze, removed the remainder of her own clothing. Senet watched, resisting the strong urge to cover his ugliness against the vision of her great beauty. Her green eyes held heated desire for him, but his chest was not so scarred as his back. She would be repulsed when she saw that part of him, just as

other women had been, and he did not know how he
would bear that. But when she came to him he could do
nothing more than open his arms and enfold her, his body
hardening at the warmth and softness of her.

"Now," she said, kissing his mouth. "Lie down."

He obeyed, reclining against the pillows as she climbed
onto the mattress. Leaning over him, she bent to kiss him
again, softly, a long, sweet kiss, and began to stroke a
hand over his bared flesh. Her fingers found the line of
one long scar and followed it, the touch so light that he
shivered at the pleasure. Groaning, he reached up to pull
her down on top of himself, but she resisted, lifting her
mouth from his and giving a shake of her head, causing
long, silky strands of her unbound hair to dance teasingly
over his skin.

"Nay, I have not tormented you enough yet, as you did
to me last night."

Senet understood at once what she intended, and drew
in a sharp breath. "Katharine, do not."

"Turn over," she said. "I am going to see these ugly
scars of yours, and then we need not worry o'er them
again. Turn, Senet."

Hesitating, he at last did as she asked, rolling to his
stomach and closing his eyes. Waiting for the exclama-
tions, the tears. Odelyn had been the only one who had
loved him as he was, but even she had been sickened by
her first sight of him.

Katharine said nothing, and the silence was worse than
what he'd anticipated. He forced himself to lie still, letting
her take in her fill of the misshapen lumps and valleys
that mapped his flesh. His hands curled into the bed linens, fisting, while he pressed his face into the mattress.

She moved at last, but toward him, not away. And then

he felt, upon his offensive flesh, the lightest of touches, warm and soft—her mouth.

He opened his eyes, pushing away the shock, certain that he was wrong. But she did it again...and then again. Tenderly, caressingly, placing kisses upon him just as he had done to her the night before. Not disgusted or sickened, but...*kissing* him.

Oh, God above, 'twas too sweet. It had been so long since anyone had touched him in such a way, giving him pleasure so openly and freely. For a moment he feared he might weep, so strong were the emotions tiding within, but he drew in a slow breath and gripped the bed linens more tightly, and lay where he was, letting Katharine have her way. His body ached with wanting, begging for release. Just when he had nearly humiliated himself by releasing his passion into the bedsheets, she mercifully stopped.

"Do you like this manner of torment?" she asked, her ragged breathing telling him that she was on the edge of desire, as well.

"Aye." He rolled to his back, grasping Katharine by the waist, lifting her up and then bringing her down on top of him, pushing her legs wide and melding their bodies together. She gave a gasp at the sudden, unexpected penetration, but after a moment closed her eyes with pleasure, letting her head fall back. "Now," he said roughly, teaching her this new manner of loving, "I get to torment you."

"How did you come to have so many scars?"

Katharine was lying in his arms, her head upon his shoulder, idly running a finger in slow circles over his chest.

"I was at Howton Hall when my father was judged

guilty of treason, and though I had been Lord Howton's favorite, I was at once stripped of all rights and standing, not even allowed to speak to the other boys, who had before been as my own brothers. Or so I had thought. The day that word came of my father's judgment, those boys who had stood as my closest friends—and who thus wished all the more to distance their names from mine— took turns beating me until I could no longer stand, or even crawl away from them. It pleased Lord Howton so greatly that each day after that, until the day of my father's execution, I was given over to the other boys for this sport, to be spit upon and reviled and beaten senseless. I wept, at first, not because of the pain, but because I had once held my friends so dearly. But in time, I stopped weeping or laughing or speaking—and that enraged them all the more.''

"Oh, Senet. How awful."

"Aye. 'Twas very bad," he agreed. "I was made a prisoner upon the day of my father's judgment—I will never forget Sir Howton reading aloud the missive that had come from my uncle, telling of my father's crime. We all of us stood in the great hall, listening, and at each word he spoke my very vision grew darker and darker. I had no care for myself, but for my father and mother and sister. Of course, I did not think that the master I had so honored would turn upon me, or, as I have said, my friends, but they did, within but moments. The beating came first, and then I was locked into a small cell and spent most of the following days there in constant prayer for the sake of my parents. 'Twas all I could do for them, and for myself. Then, on the day that my father was executed, Sir Howton gave a great, merry feast. He commanded that I should be made a part of it, to celebrate the death of my own father, and had me dressed in women's clothing and brought down to the great hall to dance for the guests.''

"God's mercy," Katharine whispered with horror.

"I do not remember much of it now, for it seemed as if every feeling had gone away from me. My father was dead, executed for a horrible crime that I could not believe him guilty of, for I loved him greatly, and my mother and sister had been thrown out of Lomas like the lowliest of serfs. Nothing mattered to me any longer, not even this added shame. I moved about in some manner of dance, I think, for I remember the feasters laughing and throwing coins, but I would not smile, as Sir Howton bade me do. He beat me with his fists to make me, but 'twas impossible. I could not smile. That was when he had me stripped, before one and all, and brought out his whip. It was to be the first of many such beatings, and 'twas a harsh punishment for a boy of barely thirteen. But I neither laughed, as he yet bade me, nor wept. Not then, nor upon any other such occasion. It was as if I had turned to stone, and there was naught anyone could do to hurt me. Katharine," he said, touching her cheek with his fingers and finding it wet, "you are not crying, are you?"

"Aye!" She made a fist and hit his chest with it. "I want to *kill* Lord Howton, and if I ever meet the unholy bastard I will!"

"My warrior." He smiled and kissed the top of her head, deeply moved by her desire to defend him. It was what she felt for the boy he had been, he knew, and not so much for himself, but he would hold the sweet knowledge dearly all the same. "I think Lord Howton will be fortunate indeed if he is never faced with such fury as you would show him."

"I will use *my* whip on him," she vowed, "and see how he enjoys the feel of it." This was followed by a

loud sniff. "If Sir Howton hated you so because of your
father, why did he not merely send you away? He had no
right to keep you a prisoner."

"Nay, he did not, but my uncle, Baron Hersell, would
not take me, as he had taken in both my mother and sister.
My mother had grown too ill to force her brother to take
charge of me, and, too, my uncle had told them that he
had made arrangements for Lord Howton to continue my
training for the knighthood. They assumed, then, that I
was yet treated well, and so made no attempt to bring me
to them. Later, after my mother died, my uncle used the
threat of removing me from Sir Howton's care as a way
to make Isabelle obedient to his will. 'Twas truly a crafty
threat, for Isabelle thought knighthood my only chance to
attain some honor after my father's deeds, and her lone
comfort was that her own suffering at least made certain
of my future success. Or so she believed."

"You should have left Howton and set out on your
own!" Katharine said hotly, yet weeping. He ran a hand
comfortingly over the curve of her back.

"I would have gone out into the world on my own,
gladly, but Lord Howton, greatly urged by my uncle,
would not release me, and decided to put me to use as
one of his servants—though more slave than servant." He
felt the bitterness of those years coming back to him,
could hear in his voice the anger and rage, but strove to
speak against them, not wishing to distress Katharine any
further.

"I was given the most menial and filthy tasks to care
for, being so greatly despised because of what my father
had done, and was locked, whenever I was not being used,
in my small cell. In those dark hours, I did not think of
my family, for that was far too painful. I thought only of
Lomas."

She sniffled again, lifting her head slightly. "Of Lomas?"

"Aye. 'Twas all I could dream of, being at Lomas again. I used to tell myself that if I could but escape Lord Howton and return to Lomas, all would be well. Do you remember the place where we ate our midday meal yesterday? By the river?"

She nodded against his chest.

"I dreamed often of being there, lying upon the grass as we did, in the cool shade, with the sound of the river flowing nearby. In my deepest misery, such memories would give me peace. But yesterday, even having dreamed of it so long, 'twas far more than what I had hoped. Far more. Mayhap that sounds foolish—"

"Nay," she said. "'Twould be my own dream...and was my dream, before I even knew of it."

He stroked her hair. "When you were at court? With your mother so unhappy and your life so unsettled?"

"Aye. And when we came to Lomas, I knew that God had at last heard my prayers.

"Ah, Katharine. How very like we are." He tipped her chin up to kiss her still-wet cheeks, then her nose, then her lips. With a sigh, she settled comfortably on his chest again.

"Sir Justin Baldwin saved you from Sir Howton? With John Ipris and Sir Aric and Sir Kayne?"

"They were not knights then, but with Kayne and Aric and John, aye. Sir Justin braved Sir Howton's mighty forces to take me out to freedom, and back to Talwar and Isabelle." He smiled at the memory, closing his eyes. "I remember the very moment when the door to my cell swung open, and there were Justin and Kayne, staring down at me. They seemed not to believe what they saw, for I was covered in filth and crawling with lice, the poorest creature you might ever dread to see. But they took me, even so, and my life was thereafter changed for the better.''

"How glad your sister must have been to see you."

"Aye, she was. But 'twas not the same for me. It had been so long since I had spoken, or let myself betray any manner of feelings, that I could not do so with her. 'Twas only later, many months, i'faith, when I at last knew how to weep, and laugh and share such things with others.''

"Because you were with Isabelle again?"

"Nay. Well," he amended with a slight shrug, "in part, mayhap."

Katharine was silent a long while, and Senet yawned, drifting comfortably toward slumber.

Her voice came quietly, breaking through the sleep that beckoned.

"Because of Odelyn?"

Senet drew in a breath and released it slowly. His eyes yet closed, he pulled Katharine closer, nestling against the warmth of her soft body.

"Aye," he murmured sleepily. "Because of Odelyn."

More silence, then Katharine asked, "Is that why you love her? Because she helped you to regain yourself after so many sorrows?"

He was almost too weary to reply, and wished that she would leave the matter be. It did them no good to speak of their other loves, or of what was in the past. But she would not rest until she had the truth.

"I did not love her for that. 'Twas because she loved me first, despite my ugliness and the darkness I held within. She loved me, and taught me how to love in turn.''

She was stiff in his arms, no longer soft and relaxed as she had been only moments before, and he slid his hand soothingly over her back, luring her back toward slumber.

Slowly, she began to give way, and he felt the flutter of her eyelids brushing against his skin as she closed them.

"She taught you how to love," she murmured, as if it were a very strange idea.

"Aye." He yawned and hugged her, resting his cheek against the top of her head. "'Twas not easy, but she would not give way, no matter how stubborn I was."

He felt her smile. "Were you very stubborn, Senet?"

"Very. Now let us sleep, Katharine. There is much to do on the morrow."

"Aye." She yawned. "There is. Much to do."

Chapter Eighteen

"Teach Lord Lomas to love you?" Kieran gazed at his cousin with clear amusement. "'Tis not possible, sweet. A woman can teach a man fear, pain and how to become utterly crazed. But love? Never. I'm afraid that must simply happen on its own. You can teach him to want you, but I doubt Lord Lomas requires any such lessons." He gave her a naughty look. "If the manner in which he kissed you this morn before one and all speaks for any kind of truth, then he is already an apt pupil in that regard."

Katharine's face grew heated, just as it had done when Senet had kissed her after the morning meal. It had been given as a parting gesture before he had taken John and Clarise into the solar for a private meeting, but Katharine knew that he had done it for Kieran's benefit rather than hers.

He had woken her this morn with his sweet and tender lovemaking, but once they had gone belowstairs to the great hall to attend the morning meal he had become quickly distant, giving his attention to Sir Kayne and Sir Aric and speaking of matters that Katharine had been unable to overhear. Kieran, sitting beside Katharine in the place of honor that would have been given to the real Lord Hanley, had soon gained her attention—and that of all those around him, as he usually did—and shortly had her laughing with his easy wit and humor. That was what had caused Senet to grab her up and kiss her in a thoroughly angry and possessive manner. The look he'd given Kieran after he'd put Katharine away from him had frightened her, and she knew that, more for Kieran's safety than her own, she must soon get her cousin out of Lomas.

Senet had invited her to attend him with John Ipris and Mademoiselle Clarise in the solar, but Katharine had declined. The moment they had gone, she'd dragged Kieran, much against his will, up to the castle roof—the only place where she knew they could be fully private. Standing now near the half-walled parapet that ran the length of the roof, they stood side by side, gazing at the land spread out below.

Ignoring his taunt about Senet, she said, "I knew you were the last man on God's earth to ask for aid. You've never loved anyone but yourself."

"Sweet Katharine," he said in deeply wounded tones, though he smiled, "how can you say such? I admit that I've not yet felt the finer depths of that tender emotion, but I have loved many women in my day. You among them, as you surely know."

"Aye, of course I do." She set a hand upon his arm, squeezing. "Just as I love you, and believed that I should never love any man better. I thought mayhap 'twas not in me to love differently. But, though 'tis a very sweet manner of affection to feel for a cousin, 'tis not at all like what I feel for Senet. Kieran, please—" she looked up at him, her hand yet upon his arm "—you must help me. Is there no way at all in which a woman might teach you to love her? I only need a few ideas to go by."

With a sigh, he covered her hand with his own. "I think I truly must be the last man on God's earth to ask, for I do not know if I even believe in this kind of love that you feel for your husband. I have often wished that I might know it. There have even been times when I've tried to force myself to it, to love the woman I'm with. But 'tis always the same. After a time I begin to grow weary of her company, and interested in that of another. I would change myself. I would," he insisted at her mocking smile, "but I cannot seem to do so. 'Twould be a good thing to love only one woman, forever."

This admission interested Katharine no small amount. Her cousin had ever been the most unstable fellow she'd known. He had treated every woman that he'd dallied with well, always gentle and kind while he was with them. But he was so easily distracted—usually by another woman—that he seldom remained in one place for more than a few days or weeks at a time. Even his visits to Lomas had been brief. But though he always left any number of broken hearts behind when he and Jean-Marc left, he was always happily received upon his next visit—especially by the women whose hearts he'd broken. But such was the measure of his charm and nature. He was too friendly and likable to invite hatred. Indeed, it was quite the other way around, and that was the problem. Kieran was always so well loved by those he met that he had become rather spoiled. If he ever did meet a woman who could resist his ample charms, he'd most likely be too shocked to run, and then his fate would be sealed.

"She would have to be very beautiful, the woman who might teach you to love her," Katharine said.

Kieran's expression grew thoughtful. "Nay, I do not think so, cousin. I've known a great many beautiful women, and they have each and every one bored me near to death. Save you, of course, my sweet," he amended with a smile. Katharine rolled her eyes. "In truth," he continued, "the woman I came closest to loving was not in the least a beauty. She was small and plump and merry and—God above, she was so witty." His voice was filled with tender remembrance, and his expression softened, as if he were seeing her again in his mind's eye. "I could listen to her speak for hours. 'S'truth!" he insisted when Katharine set a disbelieving look upon him. "Never have I known another woman such as Margery Talbot, who could say in but three words what others could not do in a hundred."

"Why, cousin," Katharine said slowly, much surprised by this new vision of the rascally Kieran FitzAllen, "I believe you must have truly cared for this intelligent woman. Who was this Margery? And why did you never wed her?"

"I might have done, for she was but the daughter of a poor squire, and my own birth, though illegitimate, was more noble than her own. But another man—a far better man, truly—wed her before I could so much as speak a word of my feelings. And now she has made him happy and content, lucky man that he is, with her merry company and intelligent speech. I have seen her since," he said, glancing at Katharine. "She's grown even plumper, having birthed three daughters who are just as plain and merry and witty as she is, and the man who wed her looks at her as if she is the most wonderful creature on God's earth. With all my heart," he said more softly, "I envy him."

"You'll find another such woman one day," she murmured hopefully.

He shrugged. "It matters not. I would have made a terrible husband, even to her, and that I could not have borne. No, 'twas all for the best that she wed the man she did, and not me, for I would have broken her heart a hundred times over by now. But you will never suffer such as that, Katharine, sweet.'' He squeezed her hand and smiled at her with affection. ''Your husband cares for you more than you know. You need not teach him to do so.''

''He has been kind and good,'' she admitted, ''but I would have his love.''

''Then you will surely have it, for I've never yet known Katharine of Lomas to set her heart to any task but what she fulfills it.'' Kieran ran the backs of his fingers across her cheek. ''I wished to make certain that you would be safe with this new husband of yours, and 'tis clear that you are. As Lomas is. He is a far better choice than that terrible fool your father betrothed you to, the real Lord Hanley. With all my failings—and though I would not have been a true husband—I would have been better to you than he.''

Katharine smiled. ''If you were possessed of a thousand more failings, Kie, you would have been better.''

''I am not sure how much of a compliment you mean that to be,'' he said with a laugh, then dropped his hand away and sighed. ''I'll leave Lomas, then, for 'tis clear you're set upon this marriage with Senet Gaillard, and I am but a great trouble for you.''

''Never that, Kie. You know how I care for you, far above any of our relatives.''

''"Tis not a difficult thing to best that sorry lot,'' he said, openly teasing. ''We've no dearth of lackwits and fools in the family branches, and that is God's own truth. But you and I came out well enough, methinks, and you have this now.'' He swept a hand out over the parapet. ''Lomas, and a man who is worthy to be lord of it and husband to you. You'll do very well, Katharine, I'm sure of it, and your children will be only like you and him—and mayhap one or two might be like your dear cousin. I should like that, to have at least one rascal continue on in the family line."

Katharine laughed. "Not my children, Kieran Fitz-Allen. You must marry and produce your own wily creatures, if you wish to carry on your tradition."

"Ah, well," he said. "Mayhap one such person, as myself, is enough in any family's history. I'm glad now that I came too late to stop your marriage." He patted her hand. "I have never seen you so content before."

"I have never felt so content," she admitted. "'Tis very strange, but lovely, Kieran. So very lovely. Will you go today? Or tomorrow?"

He lifted his eyebrows. "You wish to be rid of me that quickly?"

"Fool," she chided, lightly punching him in the arm. "I do not wish to be rid of you at all, if I could but find the courage to tell my lord who you really are. I only wish to make certain that you leave Lomas with a full reward for your efforts. I did promise, in my missive, that you would be well paid for wedding me."

"I would have come, Katharine, even without promise of payment."

"Oh, I know that, Kie," she said, setting her hand through his arm and hugging him. "But I will not let you go without making some manner of recompense. You'll let me?"

"Of course I will," he said cheerfully. "I would walk the world over for your sake alone, cousin, but I'd be a fool to turn away money for the task. Or to turn money away at all. And you've never known me to be such a fool as that."

"Nay," she agreed with a laugh. "I never have. Come belowstairs, then, to my chamber, and I will write a draft out for you now, which you may take to my banker in London. Then you and Jean-Marc may depart Lomas as it pleases you, tomorrow or today, it matters not. Though, much as I love you, Kieran, I do hope it will be today. I mean to make a conquest of my husband's heart as soon as may be, and 'twill be a far easier task to accomplish without you seducing half the castle maids."

The meeting with John and Clarise had gone well. Far better than Senet had expected it might. John had become very silent when Senet asked him whether Katharine's suspicions were true; Clarise, standing beside him, had gone completely white.

John had denied nothing, but had solemnly assured Senet that Clarise had not in any way been dishonored. Clarise had begun to weep and covered her face with both hands. But just as both Senet and John had started to reassure her, she had suddenly dropped her hands and declared, in French, "I love John! And I will marry no other! I have tried to tell you, but you will not listen!"

Senet was struck dumb by this. Clarise had never raised her voice to him before, but had ever been the sweetest and shiest of maids. She suddenly reminded him very much of Katharine—perfectly ready to do battle with him to gain her own way. John, however, shook his head, saying, "I've told her it's impossible, Senet, and that she must accept the marriage you've arranged for her. I will leave Lomas on the morrow and give you my word of honor not to see Clarise again."

"No!" Clarise uttered the word with open horror, grasping John's arm with both hands. "No!"

'''Tis the only way, my love,'' John told her gently. ''Senet will agree that this is so.''

But Senet hadn't agreed, and when he had told them what course he had decided upon, they both stood and stared at him as if he were an apparition. But only for the space of half a minute, after which Clarise shrieked and threw herself on him, weeping and laughing at the same time, and John took up repeating, ''You can't mean what you say,'' over and over again.

It had been a fine moment, and Senet's only regret was that Katharine hadn't been there to witness it, especially as she was truly the one whom John and Clarise had to thank for their happy future. He was eager to share it with her, and to warn her that the next time she saw John and Clarise she would be wept upon until she was soaked through and thanked until she was full weary of it.

He took the secret passageway up to her chamber, certain that he would find her there, smiling as he thought of her reaction to his news. Mayhap she would even kiss him, as she had done the night before when she had striven to...seduce him. He still could not believe that she had done so. It had been wonderful beyond words—and had given him hope. If she could not love him, she at least had no trouble in wanting him. It was enough for now, and if he could but get her with child, she might begin to forget Lord Hanley once he went away, as she seemed to have done before that man had suddenly reappeared.

He passed the place where the smaller passageway forked off to lead to their secret, hidden chamber, and then, shortly, was at the door that led into Katharine's chamber. He opened it with care, not wanting to give her too great a surprise, then pressed his hand upon the tapestry in order to push his way into the room. The sound of voices made him stop.

"Here you are, Kieran," he heard Katharine say. Senet stiffened. He had heard Lord Hanley called that before—Kieran—by many people in the castle, though he had given his Christian name as Alexander. "You'll leave tonight?"

"Aye," was the answer, and Senet knew for certain that it was Hanley. "Very late, I think, after all have sought their beds. I'll not wish to cause a stir. Perhaps 'twould be best if we bid each other goodbye now, my sweet, for we may not have so private a chance again."

Private? Senet thought with murderous rage. The man was *alone* with Katharine in her bedchamber?

"You make it sound so dire," Katharine said with a laugh. "As if we'll not see each other again. Surely you'll return to Lomas when matters have become more settled. You must, Kie."

Seething, envisioning just how he would kill the man for daring to be alone with his wife, Senet pushed the tapestry out with the flat of his hand just enough to peer into the room. They were standing close together—far too close. Katharine was gazing up at the man with a tender smile, while Hanley was busy stuffing what appeared to be a large, sealed document beneath his tunic.

"Nay, I will not."

"But, Kieran!"

"Listen to me, dearest Katharine." Hanley, having secured the document, reached out to set his hands upon her shoulders. "'Tis best for you and Lord Lomas if I do not come again—if we do not see each other again."

Her beautiful face filled with a distress that tore at Senet's heart. He drew in a breath to steady himself against the love she clearly felt for this man.

"But I'll tell him the truth! There is no need—!"

Lord Hanley shook his head. "Don't tell him. 'Twill only make matters worse, and far harder for you. You know I speak the truth. Once I've gone, Katharine, you must not speak of me again, but go on as if I'd never come."

Her eyes filled with tears that spilled over onto her cheeks, and she gazed up at Hanley with such love and despair that Senet felt the pain as if it were his own. He lowered his gaze to the floor, fighting for control. When he looked up again, Katharine had thrown herself into Lord Hanley's arms and was weeping against him.

"But I cannot bear to think of never seeing you again! Oh, Kie—please, do not say you'll never return." She sobbed and pressed her face against him. "'Tis all my fault," she managed to sob against her tears, the words muffled. "All my own fault."

Lord Hanley stroked her hair and kissed the top of her head. "My sweet Katharine, you cannot think I wish this? But 'tis what is best for you, and that is what I think of now. 'Tis not your fault in any measure. You love Lomas, and did what you could to save it. I expected nothing more of you, dearest." He kissed her again, then laid his cheek softly against her hair, murmuring, "I shall think of you often in time to come, and will believe that you are happy here, with sweet children all about you." He smiled. "Perhaps even one a rascally fellow." He grew more serious, as Senet had not yet seen him do since he'd come to Lomas. "Katharine, I do love you so very dearly. Never doubt that. I have not always been the kind of man I should have been, and I'm sorry if I've given you more grief than I should have done—but 'twas never meant to bring you harm or worry. Pray, do not think of me unkindly in years to come."

"Oh, Kieran!" she cried miserably, holding on to him the more tightly. "I cannot bear it! You must not go away forever! I'll tell Senet everything. I vow I will. Only give me time. Please."

Senet could bear no more. He stumbled back into the darkness of the passageway, not bothering to close the door behind the tapestry, and kept moving until he could no longer hear the sound of Katharine's tears. It seemed impossible to go on, of a sudden, and he knelt there in the cold blackness, pressing against the stone wall, his eyes tightly shut and one hand hard over his face, striving to force away the harshness of what he felt.

He did not know how long he knelt there, but in time he began to feel a needling ache in his knees and legs. The pain pulled him back from the darkness, and he heard himself breathing, felt his heart pounding hard in his chest, knew where he was and what had occurred. Slowly, he slid to the ground, sitting against the wall and setting his legs out in front of himself until the pain began to subside.

A long time he sat in that dark, chilled place, thinking of Katharine, remembering his parents and his love for Lomas, and wondering what he would do about all of them.

Chapter Nineteen

"Of course I will help you, Senet," Aric said, pulling his horse about to face his three friends. "You need not have even asked. But I cannot go with you afterward. I mean to wed Mistress Magan and remain with her at Lomas."

Senet nodded. "'Tis well. Lady Katharine will approve the marriage now, I have faith. She spoke most convincingly on behalf of John and Clarise."

They were all on horseback, the four friends alone as they had been much used to do during their fighting years, when they had trusted each other—and only each other—with their very lives. The field that stood before them in the heat of the late afternoon was the one that had once belonged to John the Barber. Senet had told Katharine after the midday meal that he and his friends were riding out to better survey the land and consider its possible uses. She had wanted to come, and had asked very sweetly if she might, but he had hardly been able to look at, much less speak to her, and had said more severely than he wished that her company was neither necessary nor desired. Now, thinking on the hurt that had darted across her eyes, he heartily condemned himself as a thoughtless, worthless bastard. She would be much better off without him. And much happier, too.

Aric shrugged at Senet's remark. "I do not care whether Lady Katharine approves or not. I will take Magan to wife. She has agreed to it, and to my plans. Our plans," he amended roughly, reddening. He had never before trusted a woman, or believed that a female could say or decide anything of import. But he was making the effort now, and his comrades were fully impressed with Mistress Magan's transforming power over their stoical friend. "I—" he stopped to correct himself again "—*we* mean to begin a school for the children at the convent. I will train the boys in the way of soldiering, mayhap even for knighthood, and she means to teach the girls all that will let them become maids for upper chambers."

"But she is a lady born," Kayne remarked. "Is she not possessed of estates of her own which will need tending?"

"Aye, and they will be cared for," Aric told them. "But I have no skills in such as that, and she less. Those who manage them now will continue as they have done, and when the time comes our children will take their rightful places." Looking at Senet, he abruptly changed the subject. "You should stay and fight for what is yours—you and the rest of us. For Lomas and Lady Katharine—and to kick that twittering Hanley off your land. I trust him not."

"Nor do I," John agreed. "There is much amiss in him and that manservant of his. He has called himself Alexander, for one, while the castlefolk and villagers call him by another name—Kieran."

"What of it?" Senet asked, settling his horse as the beast moved restlessly beneath him. "'Tis but a common name, methinks, while the other his Christian one."

"Lord Hanley's Christian name is Albertus," John said. "Not Alexander."

Senet looked at him sharply. "Are you certain?"

"Sir William told me a great deal about Lord Hanley. I'm certain."

The knowledge troubled Senet, for he, too, had wondered at not only the man's name, but also his many lies regarding his long absence from Katharine. But these thoughts could not overcome what he'd seen earlier in the day—Katharine's tears, her utter misery at the thought of losing forever the man she loved so well.

"It does not matter," he said at last. "Even if he is a fraud complete, I'll not change my mind. Kayne, you will lend me your aid?"

Kayne smiled at him as if the question were foolish. "As Aric said, you need not ask. Of a certainty, we will all of us stand with you, just as we have always stood together."

"This will be the last time, mayhap," Senet said, his voice shaded with a despondent tone. "John, will you do as I've asked and take Clarise to Justin and Isabelle?"

John nodded. "We will be wed there at Talwar, when permission comes from the king's regent. If it comes."

"It will, my friend," Senet vowed. "You will wed Clarise and become a fine and wealthy Norman lord, and when next we come together 'twill be to celebrate the birth of the first of your many children, pray God."

John's brows knit together. "But you will come to Talwar for the wedding, surely. Clarise will be brokenhearted if you do not, and for myself—how can I wed without my brothers standing beside me? You are my only true family, apart from Sir Justin and Lady Isabelle."

"If God allows," Senet said, "we will all stand beside you on that day, but I make no promise of it, for I do not know how matters will fall for me. This I do vow, that I will do whatever I must to see you and Clarise wed.''

"And I," Kayne assured.

"Magan and I will come," Aric said. "There will be naught to keep us away, as there may be with Senet and Kayne."

"It is enough," John replied. "I will pray that matters go well for you, Senet, as you desire. Though I yet wish you would choose another course, for I cannot think 'tis best for Lady Katharine."

Senet gazed out over the field, sitting barren and unused in the late summer heat. The harvest would begin soon, but this land would be untouched, yielding no profits. But next year, if all went well, the people of Lomas would not only reap profits from the land, but share in them as well.

"I cannot be swayed," he said. "There is no other course. Come, let us return to Lomas. I must speak to Katharine before the evening meal."

Something was wrong, but Katharine could not begin to know what it was. Senet paced one side of the solar, not looking at her even as he spoke to her, his manner stiff and cold and unyielding. He had been like this since returning from the ride he'd earlier taken with his friends, and nothing Katharine did or said brought a change to his strange behavior. He was as he had been on that first day at Lomas, a stern, harsh soldier, and not the tender, considerate man she'd come to so dearly love.

"I've considered what might be done with the land that once belonged to John the Barber," he said, still not looking at her.

"You have?" This surprised her. She hadn't thought

of the trouble with the land since Kieran had arrived—certain proof that love had left her addled.

"What do you think of deeding the land to the sisters of Saint Genevieve, with the stricture that they must rent out equal parcels to the people of Lomas for far less than would normally be paid for such fine land?" Stopping near one of the long windows, his back to her, he gazed out at the lowering sun. "The rent can be paid after the harvest, in equal portions. Or, if the sisters so choose, they may barter for services such as they require. In this manner John the Barber's wishes to benefit both the church and the people of Lomas may be met."

Slowly, Katharine stood from the chair in which she'd been sitting. "That is...perfect, Senet. I do not know why it never occurred to me, but 'tis *perfect!*"

He did not turn, even as she took a step toward him, but his stance relaxed and his head lowered slightly.

"Good. I am glad if you approve, for I think it a solution that will benefit all. The mayor and the cobbler may not be so glad to have the matter taken out of their hands, but all those at Saint Genevieve, and the people of Lomas, should be."

"Aye," she agreed, moving even nearer. "I cannot wait to tell the sisters. Can we do so on the morrow? Mayhap we can take our midday meal by the river again." Tentatively, she touched his arm. "'Twould be most pleasurable to do so."

He stiffened and moved away, keeping his back to her. "'Twill be too warm a day for such as that. I will send a missive to the sisters in the morn, and speak to the cobbler and the mayor in the afternoon. Will you write to the archbishop and inform him of our determination?"

"Aye, and gladly."

"There is another matter, as well."

"What is it?"

"Aric has decided to remain at Lomas, not only to be with Magan, but also to begin a school such as the one Sir Justin has. He wishes to train the boys at Saint Genevieve's for knighthood, if possible."

"And Magan wishes to help him," Katharine said. At this, he finally looked at her. "I know of their plans," she told him, wanting to touch him again, to lure him to kiss and hold her, but seeing in both his face and stance that he was unapproachable. With a sigh, she moved back toward her chair, pondering at what had happened to change him so from the man who had loved her so sweetly only that morn. "Magan spoke to me after you had gone, and told me that she will wed Sir Aric. I will not lie to you and say that I was glad, for I was not, and am not, but how could I deny my friend what is so dear to her? She will have that ugly brute of a man for a husband or, as she tells me, die for lack of him." Katharine lifted her hands in a shrug, and turned about to face him. "I gave her my blessing, and assured her of yours."

For the first time, a slight smile briefly crossed his lips. "Katharine," he said, then, again, more softly, "Katharine." Then he fell silent.

"What else could I do?" she asked. "She threw herself upon me and wept and thanked me, and then we told Dorothea and Ariette and spent a grand hour teasing her and laughing and drinking the good wine that Magan always keeps locked away. She is very happy, and if your Sir Aric ever does aught to change that, I shall slice his ears from his head."

Senet lowered his head into one hand. Katharine couldn't be quite sure, but she thought that she heard, for a few moments, the sound of muffled laughter. When he lifted his head at last, he had mastered himself into stone again.

"Aric is not an easy man to know or even to like, though I count him as close as a brother, but he is a man of honor and would never harm any woman, most assuredly not the only one he has ever loved. She will be safe in his keeping."

"Aye," she said. "I believe it is true, not for his sake, but because I know you would not speak falsely." She held his gaze and spoke more softly, saying, "I have come to trust you in all things, Senet."

Rather than please him, the words seemed only to make him the harder.

"That is as it should be," he replied. "We are agreed, then, upon the use of the land, and upon Aric and Magan. I have told you that John and Clarise will be wed at Sir Justin's estate, Talwar, as soon as the king's regent approves."

"Aye."

"There is but one more thing I wish to speak of. Something I wish to ask you."

"What is it?"

"Are you with child?"

Her eyes widened, and she uttered a surprised laugh. "I would not yet know, my lord. It has only been a few days since we wed." Then she laughed again, all amazed. His behavior was so strange, but if he was so eager to have a child, then all must be well. Mayhap he was only weary from all that had so recently occurred. She could hardly believe, herself, that so much had happened in only a few days—that she had fallen in love in so short a time. Or mayhap Senet was still overset because of Kieran, but that trouble would be solved within a few hours. In the morn, when Kieran was well away, she would strive to tell Senet the truth. He would understand, at least, that she had waited in order to spare him a public humiliation before all the people of Lomas, for now that Kieran had determined never to come again, there was no need for the deception to be spoken of out loud.

"I will know in a few days if I am to bear a child," she told him.

His gaze sharpened. "In truth?"

"Are you so eager, then, to have an heir? Is there some condition that I not know of in order for you to inherit the estate?"

"Nay."

"Lomas is yours, Senet," she said, wanting him to be fully assured. "I will not contest that truth for any reason."

"I want to know whether you are with child or not, that is all. Promise that you will tell me as soon as you know. No matter the answer, be it yea or nay."

She resisted the urge to press a hand against her stomach, hoping so desperately that, when the time came, she might tell him yea. But she had spoken the truth. If her courses ran true, she would know very shortly whether she was with child.

"I promise. You will know as soon as I."

He nodded, but did not seem gladdened by her reply.

"I will leave you, then, and go abovestairs to prepare for the coming night." He moved toward the solar's closed doors.

"The coming night?" Katharine asked, confused.

He stopped before setting his hand to the door handle. Just as he had done for most of the interview, he kept his back to her.

"I am going out with Kayne and John and Aric. We'll not be back before tomorrow's morning meal."

"Going out?" she repeated with a measure of distress. He had said nothing of this before. Not the least mention. She had meant to begin to teach him to love her this very night, but she could do nothing if he was gone. "But, Senet...I do not..."

"'Tis naught to worry o'er," he told her firmly, putting his hand to the door. "We are only going hunting, and will leave after the evening meal."

"Hunting for what?" she half shouted as he began to leave. "In the dead of night? For what?"

Still he would not turn, but stood in the open door, speaking in a low tone that she strained to hear.

"For game, Katharine. What else? For treacherous game."

Chapter Twenty

Seven days later, she knew.

She had promised Senet that she would tell him at once, that he would know as soon as she did, but it was a promise she was unable to keep. One could hardly tell a man who was seldom present anything at all.

In the past week Senet had behaved more like a ghost than the lord of Lomas. He appeared once each day to gather provisions, sometimes to partake of the midday meal, and to spend a few terse minutes with Katharine to discover whether all was well at Lomas. She had done everything she could think of to make him stay longer, to make him tell her what was wrong and why he was ever away, but he behaved as if he could no longer abide her presence, and took his leave as shortly as he could.

Each night he was gone, not sleeping in his chamber, certainly not in hers. They had been the longest nights of Katharine's life, for she had lain awake hour after hour, praying for him to come, striving to understand what had happened to keep him away. It could not be the farce that Kieran had played out as Lord Hanley, for her cousin and Jean-Marc had left just as Kieran had said they would, in the dead of night, with no one save the guards to remark their going. But Senet, who with his friends had been out hunting, had returned the following morn and made no remark upon the supposed Lord Hanley's absence. Katharine had told him that their guests had gone, and Senet had merely looked at her and said, "Good," in the same toneless voice that he had used ever since.

Ten days Katharine had been a married woman. Three of them had been the most wonderful she'd known, but the rest of it—she had never experienced such torment. Her life had become again much as it was before Senet had come into it. She sat alone at the high table in the place of honor during meals, and she sat alone in the chair of judgment each afternoon, save Sabbath day, and held audience to determine matters regarding the estate. And she lay alone in her bed at night and wept for what love and Senet Gaillard had done to her.

He asked her, each day, during his brief visits, if she knew whether she was with child. Today, when he came—if he came—she would at last be able to tell him. She did not carry his babe, and never would, if he continued on in this distant manner.

"My lady?"

Katharine looked away from the solar window, out of which she had been gazing at the lowering sun. Another two hours and it would be dark. Senet had not come yet today.

"Yes, Magan?"

"A messenger has arrived from London. From Duke Humphrey."

Katharine nodded. "I will see him. Give me but a moment."

"Very well." Magan bowed and began to leave the room.

"Magan?"

The girl turned. "Yes, my lady?"

"Has Sir Aric been at Lomas today?"

Magan sadly shook her head. "Neither today nor yesterday. I have been worried for him."

"But still you do not know where he goes with the others?" Senet's closest friends had disappeared with him, in a manner, for they all appeared at Lomas at different times, always to collect provisions and see that all was well and leave again. It was almost as if they were living elsewhere, and only visiting at the castle.

"Nay, my lady. He has said they are hunting, but will tell me no more, though I have pleaded with him. He promises that naught is amiss, and that he will shortly return to Lomas and not leave again."

"Hunting." Katharine sighed and pushed from the window to move toward the door. "They have been at it so long there could not possibly be any game left alive in the forest. Bring Duke Humphrey's messenger to me at the chair of judgment, Magan. I will receive him there."

Half an hour later Katharine was back in the solar with Mademoiselle Clarise. The younger woman was sitting near one of the windows, reading by the day's fading light a scroll that Katharine had given her.

"Do you understand it?" Katharine asked. "My French is not good, but I think I can translate it for you, if need be."

Clarise lifted her pretty face. "Does it say—is John to be made a lord, m'lady?"

"He is to be adopted into a noble English family, and given their name and an inheritance. Have you heard of Sir Justin Baldwin, the lord of Talwar?"

Clarise's eyes widened. "*Oui.* He is to adopt John? As his son?" She was clearly bewildered by the idea of this.

"Nay, it is his brother, Alexander Baldwin, the lord of

Gyer, who will bring John into the Baldwin family. 'Twill be legally done, and then John will have a noble family heritage to claim, as well as one of the Baldwin estates as his own. I do not say it will be a grand estate, such as Lomas is, but the Baldwin family is possessed of much land and wealth, and there can be no doubt as to the value of what John will gain. Once the deed is done, your relatives in France can have no objections, for only a complete pack of fools would turn aside the chance to ally their family with the Baldwins.''

Slowly, the girl began to rise from her chair, the document clutched in one hand, her expression one of fearful hope.

"And we will be married? John and me?"

Katharine nodded. "You will be married—no, please do not!" she said as Clarise threw herself at her, arms wide. "Mademoiselle, there is no cause...and I do not wish to be wet with any more of your tears." But the younger woman clung to her, hugging and weeping; and, with a sigh, Katharine gave way and began to pat her shoulder. "Very well, cry if you must. I suppose 'tis what I would do, as well."

All at once the girl pushed away, her face wet from her tears but glowing with happiness. "But I must tell John! At once! He will be so pleased!" She hurriedly moved toward the door.

"Mademoiselle!" Katharine stopped her. "How can you tell him if he is not here?"

"But he is!" Clarise told her happily. "Just above-stairs, with m'lor Lomas—oh!" She set a hand to her lips and gazed at Katharine with wide-eyed dismay. "I was not to speak of it," she stated more to herself than to Katharine. "Forgive me."

Katharine eyed her levelly. "Lord Lomas is above-stairs?"

Clarise nodded. "In his bedchamber. He and John returned an hour ago...but I was not to speak of it. *Grand Dieu*, but he will be so angry with me."

"Lord Lomas or John Ipris?" Katharine asked, fury rising up in a tide. "Nay, do not answer, for I know which it is. And they came up through the castle through one of the secret passages, I suppose?"

Silent, Clarise nodded.

"Not for the first time?" Katharine pressed. "Have they visited Lomas in secret before during the past seven days?"

Again, the girl nodded. "M'lady..."

"John Ipris is with him now?"

"Nay, for m'lor Lomas was to sleep...he was most weary, *oui?*"

"*Oui*," Katharine replied tightly, striding past the girl to reach the doors before her. "Most weary he should be, I vow, after so many days of deceit."

He was lying in his bed, sprawled upon his stomach, naked and snoring. His hair was damp, for he had recently bathed, evidence of which was a half-filled tub of water set by the unlit hearth. Katharine moved quietly to reach into the tub, and found just what she had expected—cold water. He would not have sent any servants to heat water for him, but someone in the castle must have known that he was coming and going, for he could never have had the water brought to his chamber, otherwise. Katharine would ask Dorothea if any of the servants had been behaving secretly, and discover who it was had kept the truth from her so long. She never would have expected that any of her people would serve her so basely.

A loud sighing sound came from the bed, then a great

commotion of twisting and turning as Senet flopped over on his back and, yet asleep, searched with a blind hand to draw the covers up about him. The next moment he was snoring again, deeply asleep, content as a slumbering child.

Katharine moved back to the bed to look at him, gazing down at his relaxed, cleanly shaven face. She was struck anew at how handsome her husband was, at how she had grown to love his every feature. But, God above, he could be so infuriating. She was tempted to drag the covers off him and dump a pitcher of the cold tub water on his head. But, though he deserved it, she could not. Instead, she sat beside him on the bed, and reached out to stroke a few strands of his silky black hair off his forehead.

He reacted as if she'd poured the water on him. With a shout he bolted into a sitting position, flinging a fist out and striking her full across the face. Katharine went flying helplessly backward onto the floor, landing so hard that the breath whooshed out of her and blackness covered her vision.

"Katharine! God's mercy!"

He was beside her in but a moment, his hand beneath her head, lifting her tenderly.

"Are you all right, love? I did not mean to strike you— never should I want such a thing. Katharine?"

Her eyelids fluttered open, and she drew in a breath, filling her lungs slowly.

"I'm all right," she murmured against the spinning sensation that was growing less disturbing.

He scooped her up from the floor and carried her to the bed. "You're not," he said, gently laying her upon the mattress and coming down beside her. "I'm so sorry, dearest one. I should have warned you never to wake me in any sudden manner. 'Tis always dangerous to do so with a soldier who expects an enemy at every moment, even in his sleep.''

"I'll remember that, in future," she said, groaning as he touched the place where his fist had struck.

"Oh, Katharine. Forgive me.'' He gently kissed the swelling on her cheek. ''Twill pain you a day or two, I fear, but should not show overmuch.''

"I'm glad to know of it,'' she said, touching the tender spot herself.

"How did you learn that I was here?'' he asked. "Nay, don't fuss with it, or you'll make it that much worse.'' He pulled her hand from her face. "Did Mistress Dorothea tell you?''

Her gaze fixed on him. "*Dorothea?* She knew that you were here?''

He frowned. "If she was not the one who told you, then who...?''

"It matters not!'' She struggled to sit up. "That treacherous fiend! One of my own ladies! Or mayhap they've all known of your comings and goings, and have been lending you their aid whilst leaving me to fret and wonder, knowing full well how overset I've been!''

With an arm about her waist, he pulled her down to the bed again.

"Calm yourself, Katharine,'' he commanded sternly. "There has been no plotting against you. Mistress Dorothea is my subject as well as your own, and I bade her send water to my chamber so that I might bathe. That is all.''

"You returned to Lomas only for that, then? To bathe?''

"And to sleep. I am weary beyond all measure.''

She tried to roll off the bed. He held her still.

"I should have gone to Caswell,'' she said bitterly, not

looking at him. "I wish—God's mercy, how I wish that I had done so."

"Nay, Katharine," he said. "You are the lady of Lomas, and this is where you must be. You could not be content elsewhere."

"I am far from content now. I thought you had come to Lomas to take your place as lord, but you are just as my father was, it seems. Or worse." She was horrified to hear tears in her voice. "You do not even bring back what you have hunted. If you have hunted at all."

His arm tightened about her, but still she would not look at him.

"In time, you'll know that I speak the truth," he said. "You will be happy at Lomas again."

"And what of you?" she charged. "You are not content to be here, as you first were. Oh, Senet, please," she begged, at last turning her head to look at him, "tell me what I have done to keep you away. If I could only know—"

"Naught, Katharine," he said with a fierce intensity, holding her chin to keep her eyes upon his own. "Naught. You must never think that any of this was your doing. 'Tis my fault alone, and I hold none of it against you. Never forget that. Promise me."

"I cannot promise what I do not understand," she replied.

He was silent, looking at her, his fingers loosening and beginning to stroke her cheek, her neck.

"I've kept away from you, but my nights have been filled with such dreams, Katharine." His movements grew softer, caressing. "I have wanted you so badly. I think it will be a madness in years to come."

"I hope it will be," she murmured, reaching up to

touch his face. "For both of us. I have missed you, Senet."

"Don't say that," he said harshly. "Never say that. God above!" He took her hand and pressed it into the pillows. "Are you with child?" he demanded.

She stared up at him. "Nay," she whispered.

Perhaps she only imagined the pain that crossed his features, the tightening of his jaw and lips.

"Are you certain?" he asked.

She nodded. "Aye. Only today."

"Very well." Slowly, he lay down completely, keeping his arm about her waist. "Very well."

"I'm sorry, Senet. I know 'tis a disappointment. Mayhap next month."

"Aye," he said. "Next month, Katharine. 'Tis all right. Do not worry o'er the matter."

"But you—"

"I'm content," he told her. "There is nothing more to say."

They lay in silence for a long time, until Katharine began to grow sleepy, too.

"I must go," she said, setting a hand upon his arm. "You will sleep better without me here."

"No, stay with me," he murmured, drawing her closer until their heads were nestled together. "Let me hold you this hour. You make a very good pillow. I shall never know a better one."

She smiled and relaxed, knowing that she would sleep. It was so good to be in his arms again, comfortable and secure, to be enveloped by the scent and warmth of him.

"I've not yet told you about John. A missive arrived from Duke Humphrey."

"I don't want to think of John now," he whispered. "Tell me on the morrow."

"Very well," she said, and yawned. "'Twill be the very first thing, on the morrow."

"Aye." He hugged her tightly. "The very first thing."

Chapter Twenty-One

When Katharine awoke, it was to find herself not in Senet's bed, but her own, still fully dressed. She came awake groggily, confused. The curtains to her bed were open, and an early morning light crept through her thick-paned window to tell her that she had slept through the evening meal as well as the ensuing night. How weary she must have been to sleep so long and so deeply! Her cheek, which she touched gingerly, ached, but she felt no swelling or tenderness.

Yawning loudly, Katharine stretched and sat up, swinging her legs over the side of the bed and shoving the curtains farther aside. Just as she was about to stand she heard a sound, "Mmm!", followed by several loud thumps.

It came from the other side of the bed, near the fire, and Katharine sat frozen, wondering what it could possibly be.

"Senet?" she asked aloud.

The same sounds came again, more urgently now.

"Uh...Doro?" She stood, wondering if one of her ladies had perhaps brought her something to break her fast. "Magan?" She moved slowly to the foot of the bed. "Ariette?"

Leaning to peer around the corner, she first stared, then blinked, then cried, "Kieran! God above!" Hurriedly she crossed to where he sat on the ground, his hands and feet tied and his mouth muffled by a cloth. Sitting beside him, in a similarly trapped state, was his manservant, Jean-Marc.

"What in the name of all that's holy are you doing here?" she demanded, to which Kieran responded with a glare and an angry sound. "Be still," she demanded, tugging at the knots that held him. "These won't give. I'll have to cut them. Stay here." As she rose she heard him making a muffled noise of mock amusement. A moment later she had found the sharp knife she'd used to bargain with Senet, and returned to cut their bonds away.

"Now," she said as she carefully sliced the gag about his mouth in two. "Speak."

"Arrrh!" he said, coughing and drawing in breath. "I'll murder that bastard!" More coughing. He shook his head as if to clear it, his unbound hair falling loosely on his shoulders. "I'll murder all of them!"

"You'll hang for it," Katharine said calmly, sawing at his bound hands. Jean-Marc, she saw, had closed his eyes and leaned his head back against a nearby chair. Both men looked exhausted, as if they'd traveled a great distance, yet their clothes were neat and clean and their faces freshly shaven. Whoever had tied them up had taken care to make them look their best before doing so. "There. You're free. Here, Jean-Marc, hold still while I cut this away." She set to work releasing the manservant, casting a glance back at Kieran, who was rubbing his sore wrists and ankles. "Who is it you want to murder?" she asked.

"Your husband," he replied, "and his friends. They're naught but fiends, the lot of them! Demented fiends!"

Katharine sat back, Jean-Marc's gag in her hand, utterly shocked. "*Senet?* He did this?"

"And his friends," Jean-Marc croaked, moving his jaw about with evident pain. "They fell upon us shortly after we had left Lomas, in the dead of night, and have held us captive since. God's toes, my tongue is growing wool."

"I don't believe you!" she said, staring at her cousin. "Why should he do such a thing?"

"You may believe it, for 'tis the truth," Kieran told her. "Jean-Marc and I have been held as prisoners this past week in a foul hovel in the deep of the forest. Your husband stood guard much of the time, taking turns with his friends. Surely you noticed him gone?"

Katharine felt faint. "Aye. He said he was...hunting."

"My hands." Jean-Marc held them out. Katharine ignored him.

"Hunting," Kieran repeated with disgust. "Indeed he was—for a husband for you."

"*What!*"

"What he means to say, my lady," Jean-Marc explained, "is that Lord Lomas sought for you a *new* husband. Apart from himself. And Lord Hanley was his choice. I believe he means to annul your present union on the grounds that he forced you to wed him against your will, and in this manner leave you free to wed the man you love. This is what he told us time and again while we were his prisoners. My hands?" He held them out again.

"But 'tis impossible!" Katharine cried. "He wed me so that he might have Lomas, and would never give it up. Not after all he suffered to gain it."

"He has given it up, for your sake," Kieran replied testily. "It seems you've taught the man to love you after all, my sweet. He's spent the past seven days, while I've been tied to a chair, instructing me in how to keep you happy. If I fail to do so, he vowed that he will return to Lomas and bullock me." He shuddered visibly. "I didn't dare to tell him who I really was, for he would have gladly killed me for the least of reasons. A madman is Lord Lomas."

"Nay." Katharine shook her head. "It cannot be. He's—Senet would not leave Lomas for my sake. You do not know what it means to him. What he has done to be lord here. I'll speak to him, make him understand...."

"He's not here," Kieran told her. "He brought us to your chamber in the morn, while you slept, through some damned hidden passage, and left us here, just as you found us. Then he and his friends took their leave."

"But why did you not wake me!" Katharine demanded.

"We tried!" he replied with equal heat. "God above, woman! We made noise enough to wake the dead, but you, in your comfort, slept on. What did your husband do to make you slumber so? Put herbs in your wine?"

"My lady?" Jean-Marc leaned forward, rocking his bound arms up and down in front of her. "If you please."

"Senet's gone?" she asked, yet shaking her head. "To where?"

"God alone knows," Kieran said irately. "But if he thinks I won't follow behind and give him his due, he's far mistaken. I'll want to borrow fresh horses from you." He jerked his head toward the table where Katharine's polished steel mirror was set. "He left a missive."

"My lady," Jean-Marc began again, but Katharine dropped the knife on the floor and rose at once.

She broke the seal on the folded parchment, sitting in her chair as she began to read. Behind her, she heard sounds of relief as Kieran cut away Jean-Marc's bonds.

"He's gone away," she murmured with disbelief, her heart pounding in her chest as she read his words. "He's giving up Lomas...for me. Oh, God." She blinked as tears filled her eyes. "He says he wants me to be happy with Lord Hanley, and asks me to remember him fondly and without hatred. He begs...begs me to forgive him for...any hurt he may have..." Her voice faded, and she lifted a trembling hand to her lips. "Senet's gone," she whispered, then sobbed. "He's left me. He's left *Lomas*."

Kieran and Jean-Marc were on their feet now, stretching.

"He did it for you, Katharine. Because he loves you."

She looked at him, tears streaming down her face. "But he doesn't, Kie. He loves Odelyn."

"Odelyn?"

She nodded, and wiped her cheeks with shaking fingers. "She was his betrothed, many years ago, but was murdered. He told me—he told me more than once that he would never love another."

"Well, he lied," Kieran said, looking about the chamber until he found a decanter of wine. He poured a goblet for both himself and Jean-Marc, who gladly took what his master offered. "Or mayhap he believed what he told you and then discovered, too late, that 'twas false. It gives me hope, i'faith. If a man like that can love a woman in the way that he loves you, I can believe that the same fate might one day befall me." He lifted his goblet to Katharine and drank.

"He left me...because he believes I love you," Katharine murmured, wonder in her voice. She could scarce take it in, this sacrifice that Senet had made on behalf of her happiness. "I told him, when he first came to Lomas, that I loved Lord Hanley, and would never love another. And then I could not tell him otherwise, when I knew that I loved him, because I knew Senet would never feel the same for me."

"It makes good sense," Kieran assured her, filling his goblet once more. "You believed he loved this Odelyn to whom he was betrothed, and were afraid of giving him too great a power over you by admitting your weakness toward him. I have experienced such as that many and many a time."

Katharine gave him a look of disbelief. "You have never loved in such a manner."

"Nay," he admitted, "but I have been loved, and 'tis in truth a terrible power to hold over another. But you need not worry o'er such as that now, my sweet, for Lord Lomas loves you greatly. You believe that, do you not?"

"Aye," she said, rising from her chair. "But what shall I do? He has gone away, and I do not know where."

"I'll find him for you, dearest, never fear. I'm quite looking forward to seeing how he likes being set upon without warning." He put his goblet aside and patted his belt, frowning. "Damn the bastard! He's taken my dagger. We'll need horses and weapons, Katharine, and a few of your men."

"You'll never o'ertake Senet Gaillard and his fellows, men the likes of Sir Aric and Sir Kayne and even John Ipris. They are all honored fighting men."

"John Ipris remained behind to make certain that all is well," Jean-Marc said. "I overheard that much, while they were carrying us into the castle. And Sir Aric means only to travel with them part of the way. He may have returned to Lomas by now."

"'Tis only Senet and Sir Kayne, then?"

Kieran nodded. "And they took no other men with them, but went alone. Lord Lomas thought it best to leave you as well protected as possible. A handful of those same men and a command from you, Katharine, my love, and we will easily overtake Senet Gaillard and his companion."

"And weapons and fresh horses," Jean-Marc reminded.

Katharine looked from one man to the other. "I cannot like it, Kie. You mean to harm him."

Kieran's expression was all innocence. "Harm Lord Lomas? Never, upon my soul, should I do such a thing."

"What do you mean to do, then?"

"I mean to bring him back to Lomas," he said with an angelic smile. "You told me that Senet Gaillard once made you his captive to force you to wed him. I think 'tis time that you had the chance to do the same with him. I shall bring your husband back, sweet Katharine, and make a wedding gift of him to you. Then you may make him your prisoner, and force him to do whatever you please."

how, His head ached badly, and he lifted a hand to rub it, yet above, but it hurt. He must have been wounded but could not remember. That much hurt a battle. But maybe he was no longer in France... and this... but where? The only thing he knew with a surety was...

Chapter Twenty-Two

"Senet."

He heard Katharine saying his name, but knew it was a dream. He had dreamed of her so often in the past many days when he'd been away from her that there was no surprise to hearing her now. For the remainder of his life, she would haunt him, a spirit joined with the memories that Odelyn had left behind, but without that gentle sweetness. Katharine's memory would only bring pain, and a longing so fierce that he would never know the end of it.

"Senet."

He turned to his side, burrowing his face into the pillow under his head, striving to make her voice go away.

"If you don't wake on your own, then you will never do so," Katharine's dream voice said. "I daren't come any closer lest you strike me again. I love you, but have no wish to meet your fist again, even for that. You told me 'twas dangerous to wake a soldier so unawares."

The words began to make their way through the heavy fog of sleep, and, with an effort, he lifted his eyelids a tiny crack. He blinked to clear his blurred vision. There was a fire nearby. Fur rugs. Pillows. He had been here before—it was familiar—but he could not think when or how. His head ached badly, and he lifted a hand to touch it. God above, but it hurt. He must have been wounded, but could not remember. Had there been a battle? But, nay…he was no longer in France, and this chamber was…where? The only thing he knew with a surety was that he had been away from war for many months.

The memories came back slowly, as he gazed at the fire, striving to make sense of his reeling thoughts.

He and Kayne had been riding through the forest. It had been midday, cool and shady among the trees, with a welcome breeze rustling the leaves. He remembered thinking, as they rode, that 'twas a strange, sad thing that he should be leaving Lomas on so a fine day, when he and Katharine might have spent it together by the river, talking, laughing, even making love there.

The attack had come of a sudden, but he and Kayne should have been ready for it. Never, in all their years in France, had they been taken unawares. It had been Lord Hanley—Hanley, God's mercy!—who had so easily unseated Senet from his steed. He'd been almost too shocked to defend himself, too surprised at discovering just how skilled a fighter the witty, mannerly Lord Hanley truly was. Kayne had been taken more gently, surrounded by a number of Lomas's men and made to surrender his weapons. Kayne had striven to remind them that Senet was yet their lord, that they owed him their loyalty, but they had replied that Lady Katharine had sent them, that their loyalty was with her.

Katharine had sent them, he thought again as the memory became more clear. Katharine had sent men after them—after him.

God above. He was at Lomas…in their secret chamber. He had heard her voice…

"Katharine?" It ached to move, but he began to struggle upward.

"I'm here. Nay, Senet, do not move."

With a rustle and a great deal of motion, she came down beside him where he lay yet on his side, a soft river of burgundy velvet tumbling into a mass against his chest and stomach. Her hand, cool and gentle, touched his forehead.

"You've been hurt. 'Twas not my intention that you should come to any harm."

"Hanley struck me." He groaned when she touched the painful bump.

Her hand lifted at once. "I know. I'm so very sorry."

"He took great pleasure in it." Senet remembered that most clearly. The man had been smiling as he'd brought his fist down on Senet's head, and Senet's last thought had been, even as darkness had waved over him, that perhaps Lord Hanley was indeed capable of leading a few unleashed prisoners in overtaking an entire prison guard of heathen Osmanli.

Gingerly, he rolled to his back and lifted his gaze to look at her. She was very beautiful, in such finery as he had not before seen her. Her red-gold hair was swept up into a soft arrangement and crowned with a circlet of gold and pearls. About her slender throat a necklace of gold and bloodred rubies reposed with one great, heart-shaped ruby dangling from the middle. She was wearing the wedding dress he'd brought her, and the burgundy velvet was more lovely upon her than he might have ever dreamed. She looked, now, as she might have looked upon their wedding day, if she had come to him willingly.

Seeing her thus, his confusion mounted tenfold.

"Why did you bring me back, Katharine? I meant to leave you in peace."

"I know," she whispered, her fingers lifting to lightly touch his chin. "But I can have no peace unless you are here with me, at Lomas. I love you, Senet."

He closed his eyes, his heart heavy and aching within.

"Nay, you do not. 'Tis Lord Hanley you love. I know this."

"I do not love Lord Hanley," she said. "I love you. Only you."

"I saw you with him," he told her, struggling to keep the misery he felt at bay. He could not bear to open himself to her in such a way. Not now, when her every word was like a dagger in his heart. "I was in the secret passage, listening, when you made your goodbyes to each other in your bedchamber. I know that he left you because you could not be together, and I heard you weeping...Katharine, I heard you weeping as if you would die from it."

"Oh, Senet." She lowered her head. "You have called me your warrior, but I am a coward. Naught but a coward." Her voice thickened with tears, and Senet struggled up into a sitting position.

"I brought him back to you, your Lord Hanley, so that you will be happy." His hand shook as he raised it to her cheek, cradling her. "It is little set against what I have taken from you, but 'tis all I can do. Katharine, I beg you, do not cry. I cannot bear to know the sadness I have given you."

She sobbed and set her own hand against his, pressing her cheek against the palm of his hand.

"I deserve to be wretched," she managed. "I have brought it all upon myself."

"Nay..."

"Aye!" Wiping her face, she lifted her head, yet holding his hand. "I lied to you in the foulest manner, Senet, and was too afraid to tell you because I thought you would hate me, that you would never forgive me, and that I could not bear, for I love you.''

He searched her eyes intently. "Lied to me?"

"Aye. I am not…I have never loved Lord Hanley. That is the first lie. I was betrothed to him, but I did not love him. In truth, I despised him, and was glad that he did not return from his journeys.''

"But I have seen with my own eyes the affection you bear for him, and he for you,'' Senet told her, confused. "He has told me from his own lips that he loves you dearly. I saw you weeping for him.''

She shook her head woefully. "What you saw, and heard, was all for one who is indeed most dear to me, but not for Lord Hanley. It is not Lord Hanley who came to Lomas, claiming that name. It is my half cousin, Kieran FitzAllen.''

Senet felt his eyes widening at the admission. His hand fell away from Katharine's grasp, and he stared at her.

"Your cousin,'' he repeated. "Kieran…''

"FitzAllen,'' she finished. "Before you overtook Lomas, when Duke Humphrey was insisting that we wed, I had determined that I would bring Kieran here and tell one and all that he was Lord Hanley, returned at last from his journeys. Lord Hanley was a stranger at court, and Kieran is base-born, completely unknown. We were to be married at once—''

"To your own cousin?'' Senet began to feel ill, and could hardly believe it was Katharine speaking of such things. "Do you love him so much that you would wed out of nature?''

"Oh, nay! Senet, I pray you, do not look at me so. He is not closely related, and 'twould not have been a sin. But that aside, 'twas not to be a true marriage. I do love my cousin dearly, but only as that—my cousin, and naught more. Never would our marriage have been anything more than one of necessity. I did not even mean to make him live here at Lomas. Once we had married and I was safe from you and Duke Humphrey, I intended to give Kieran whatever funds he required to live as he pleased, and then to send him on his way.''

''And you would remain as you were,'' Senet said dully. ''The lady of Lomas, just as you wanted to be. Untouched in every way.''

''Aye,'' she whispered, her eyes filled with sorrow.

''All this you determined to endure out of hatred for me.''

''Out of hatred for marriage to any man. I thought I would become as my mother had been, and could not bear such as that. I did not believe a man could be as you are—trusting and good and willing to let me be as I am. That is why I decided upon the farce with Kieran. I had sent him a missive asking him to come and help me only moments before you and your men made your attack upon Lomas, and that night—''

''When you ran away,'' Senet said. '''Twas to him that you ran. You thought to find and wed him before I could discover you.''

She nodded. ''It was the man whom I wed who would become lord of Lomas. Kieran would take the title but leave the estate to me.''

''I see.'' With an effort, he pushed first to his knees, then to his feet, nearly falling and thrusting Katharine's hands away when she tried to help him. ''Nay, leave me be.'' He knew he was behaving intemperately, but he was hurt, and hot with anger. Gaining his feet at last, he stumbled to the nearest wall and leaned against it, waiting until the spinning in his head stopped before opening his eyes and looking at Katharine, who yet knelt in the midst of the furs upon the floor. She looked even more beautiful from this distance. The burgundy velvet brought to life the gold strands in her hair, causing them to glitter and dance in the firelight. She was gazing at him anxiously, as if expecting him to fall any moment, her green eyes filled with concern.

"You told me, that night in the tower, when I held you as my captive, that you loved Lord Hanley and would always do so."

She paled. "Aye," she murmured. "'Twas the basest of my lies."

"Now you claim that you despise him?"

"I have always despised him. If you but knew him, you would not set that as a sin against me, I vow."

"And this cousin of yours. Kieran FitzAllen. Do you love him?"

"I do, but only as my cousin…as a brother. I hold him as dearly as you hold Sir Kayne or Sir Aric or John Ipris. No more than that, and no less."

He hardly knew what to think. She had lied to him about love, and he had nearly torn his heart out because of it.

"What do you want from me, Katharine? Why did you bring me back to Lomas?"

"You are the lord of Lomas," she said. "You love this land and these people. You must be lord here."

"I left them in your care because I knew they would be safe, which fact you know far better than me, for you went to great measure before we were wed to keep them in your hands. Nay, you did not bring me back for that. What," he repeated distinctly, "do you want from me?"

Slowly, she rose to her feet.

"I want you to forgive me."

He was silent, unable to give a reply to this. His heart throbbed in his chest as he gazed at her.

She lowered her head.

"I did not think, on the night when I lied to you about Lord Hanley, that I would wed you, for I thought no manner of violence could force me to it. It did not seem then so very great a sin. But afterward, when I wanted to confess the full of it, I could not forget what you had said of your Odelyn, that you would love her, and her only, for all of your days." She glanced up at him, then looked away again, turning first her head, then her entire body. "I felt foolish," she murmured, and he strained to hear the words, "for I had never known love before and I thought...of how greatly you would despise me, were I to tell you the truth." Katharine lifted a hand, a gesture that he had become familiar with when she was distressed, touching first her lips, then her bowed forehead, as if she could somehow comfort herself, like a child, with the movement. "And I could not bear that."

His heart throbbed harder now, not out of misery, but because he dared to hope. She was wearing the wedding gown that he had brought her, and had made herself beautiful....

"Why, Katharine?"

She sobbed and shook her head. He took a step toward her.

"Why?"

"Because," she sobbed, hard against her tears, "because I—I knew you could not love me." The hand went to her mouth, and she covered it tightly to keep the sound of her misery silent.

"You said that you love me," he murmured. "Do you, Katharine? Tell me."

She nodded, and lowered her hand. "I love you." Another sob. "I have never—never known—how hard 'twould be to love. And now you despise me, and I do not know—how I can live...." She could say no more, but covered her face with both hands and wept.

Senet was beside her in a moment, his hands on her shoulders, turning her about and into his arms, where he held her tight.

"If you believe I have reason to despise you, Katharine, then you have far more reason to despise me. I lied to you as well."

She clung to him as if she were afraid he would go away again, and Senet gloried in the feeling. Shaking her head against his shoulder, she made a sound of disagreement.

"Oh, aye, but I did," he told her, stroking her hair. "You thought you would never wish to marry, and I believed that I would never love again. But I was in grave error, for I do love again. Against all my stubbornness and foolishness, I love again, and thank God for it." He lifted her chin until she gazed up at him, her face wet with her misery, her eyes wide with disbelief and hope. "I love you, Katharine, my beautiful warrior."

"But—" she sniffled "—Odelyn?"

"I loved her, and will ever do so, but 'twas a boy's love, gentle and sweet, and not at all what I feel for you. 'Tis a man's love I bear for you, Katharine, and as fierce as any storm that could o'ertake me. Do you understand this?"

"Aye," she whispered, lifting trembling fingers to touch his cheek. "Oh, Senet. Can it be?"

"It must be," he said with a tender smile, turning his head to kiss her fingers. "I left Lomas because of it, and that I would have sworn, on my very life, that I would never do." He grew more serious. "I could not bear to think of you hating me for the loss of your Lord Hanley, and living with me here at Lomas, day by day, loving you so dearly and knowing that you wanted only him.''

''You sacrificed all you had striven for these many years,'' she said with wonder.

''It was as naught to me to leave Lomas behind. 'Twas leaving *you* that was so hard. You said that if I could not love you, then you did not know how you would live. When Kayne and I rode out of Lomas, I knew that same measure of woe. I did not know how I would live without you. Indeed, I feared very much that 'twould be like not living at all. I love you, Katharine,'' he murmured, cradling her face in his hands. ''With all my being, I love you, and I vow, upon my honor, that nothing now shall part us, save death.''

''May God keep us, then,'' she said, smiling up at him through her tears. ''For I wish to have a long, long life with you, Senet.''

''May God keep us,'' he agreed, and lowered his head to kiss her.

''Twill be time for the evening meal soon.''

Katharine snuggled against her husband and yawned. ''I don't want to leave here. Ever.''

He smiled and ran a caressing hand over her bare shoulder. ''We could have food and drink brought to us and remain here night and day,'' he suggested, ''but then 'twould no longer be our secret chamber.''

''Then I suppose we must go belowstairs,'' she said with a sigh. She ran her fingertips along one of the scars on his chest. ''Although 'tis not our own secret any longer, as it once was. Kieran knows of it.''

Senet pushed up into a sitting position, causing Katharine to roll onto her back among the rugs they lay upon. He looked down at her with a measure of consternation.

"You told him about it?"

She grinned at him impishly. "I had to. He's the one who carried you here after bringing you back to Lomas."

He was momentarily astonished, then slowly began to smile. "I had wondered how I came to be here. I should be glad, I think, that he did not toss me over the balcony when he traversed it."

"He did tease me at that moment," she admitted, "and offered to rid me of such a troublesome husband. 'Twas not well done of him, for I was already most angered that he had struck you so hard as to make you insensible."

"'Twas my just due for holding him prisoner a full week, I think. But why did you wish to bring me here, Katharine? Your chamber would have served just as well. Or mine."

"Oh, nay," she said, reaching up to touch his cheek. "I knew I must confess my sins to you here, where we would be fully alone, in the chamber which you made as a gift to me. 'Twas also where I meant to keep you—as my captive—if you refused to listen to reason."

He chuckled. "Your captive, Katharine? As you once were mine? But, nay, 'twas not needed, my sweet love, for I have been your captive almost since the moment I set sight upon you." With a gentle hand, he stroked the hair from her face. "How great a prize I gained when I o'ertook Lomas. I dreamed for so many years of returning to my home and taking up the title that my father had lost, but I could never have known how much more would come to me—so much more, and all that now matters to me. You."

"'Tis the same truth for me," she murmured, gazing up at him with all the love she felt. "I thought your coming would be the end of all my happiness, but 'twas not so. Not in the very least. It was instead the beginning of it, of a happiness and goodness such as I could never have dreamed of. How glad I am that you came to Lomas, Senet, and made me your wife.''

''As am I,'' he whispered, kissing her, ''more than I can say in words.'' He kissed her again, more lingeringly. ''Let me show you, instead.''

Two hours later the lord and lady of Lomas made their way down the stairs to the great hall, looking very pleased with themselves and as if they'd just spent the entire afternoon rolling about on the ground. Lady Katharine's hair was unbound, falling in a tangled river to her hips, and her circlet of gold and pearls was set precariously atop her head. Both their garments were heavily wrinkled and Lord Lomas's were even muddy. On his forehead was an angry red lump, which caused all who looked at him to wince in sympathy.

They were greeted by a raptly interested crowd of onlookers, including Katharine's ladies, Sirs Kayne and Aric, John Ipris and Mademoiselle Clarise, and—much to Senet's surprise and anger—Kieran FitzAllen and his manservant, Jean-Marc.

Katharine's cousin was reclining near a low table with his feet propped upon a chair, a tankard of ale in his hand and a lazy smile upon his face.

''I stayed to see how happy a conclusion came of the day,'' he told Katharine and Senet as they neared him. ''Also, to make certain that Lord Lomas took no permanent hurt at my hands.''

''I'm well, as you see,'' Senet told him tautly.

''Indeed,'' Kieran said, lifting his tankard toward him in a toast. ''But I did not truly need to see you with my own eyes. I realized that all must be well with you—very well, indeed—when Katharine did not come running back to the hall, shouting that you required aid. And if you were not arguing with each other all that time—'' he smiled ''—then it seemed likely that your wound was not in the least grievous.''

Senet's hands fisted, but Katharine held him back.

''You have not yet been made known to each other,'' she told the men. ''Kieran FitzAllen, I make you known to Senet Gaillard, Lord of Lomas. Senet, I make you known to my cousin, Kieran FitzAllen.''

''You should have told me who you were this past week,'' Senet said in an unfriendly tone.

Kieran smiled. ''While you held me captive, do you mean? And when should I have done so? While I had the gag in my mouth, or when you gave me ten minutes relief so that I might eat, while holding a knife at my head and warning me not to give you cause for anger?''

Senet began to look guilty. ''I am...sorry for that.''

''Oh, nay,'' Kieran replied easily, pulling his feet from the table. ''It left me without doubt that you would kill for my cousin's happiness, and I can ask no more than that from the man who took her to wife. And 'twas at least a restful week, I vow.''

''The most restful of *your* life,'' Jean-Marc observed. ''There were no women about.'' At this, the castlefolk around them laughed.

''None of that, now,'' Kieran said pleasantly, rising to his feet. ''I mean to make a proper toast to the lord and lady. All join.'' He lifted his tankard, and looked around as all surrounding them made murmurs of approval.

''To the Lord and Lady of—''

''Lord Lomas!'' A servant pushed his way through the crowd, his face alight with distress. ''Lady Katharine!''

"What's amiss, Gareth?" Katharine asked.

The young man pointed in the direction of the great hall doors, which now stood open.

"It's—it's Lord Hanley, my lady."

"What!" Senet had been standing with his arm about Katharine's waist, but dropped it now to step forward and gaze searchingly over the crowd. "Kayne, go and see who dares to..." But Kayne had already gone.

Katharine touched the servant's arm. "What manner of jest is this?"

Gareth looked at her with wide eyes. "'Tis no jest, my lady. It is Lord Hanley, only just arrived and demanding to see you."

Kayne pushed his way through the castlefolk until he could see Senet. His gaze was somber. "You'd best come."

The crowd parted and Senet and Katharine moved forward. There, standing in front of the open doors, stood a small group of men, all of whom, save one, were clearly fighting men, soldiers standing ready to protect their master.

The one who was not, and who stood before them all, was a short, plump, balding man of perhaps fifty years, dressed in a manner of finery befitting a king.

"Oh, dear God," Katharine murmured, a hand covering her lips. "Dear God. 'Tis *him*."

Senet glanced at her before facing the newcomers.

"Who are you? And for what reason do you come to Lomas in this manner, with men-at-arms?"

The balding man stepped forward. "I am Albertus Hanley," he announced loudly, "baron of Hanley and the betrothed of Katharine Malthus, lady of Lomas."

Senet turned to Katharine, a look of full exasperation

on his face. "How many Lord Hanleys must I suffer," he demanded, "before I am done with them?"

Katharine pointed faintly at the newcomer. "Senet, he *is* Lord Hanley. 'Tis not a jest. I cannot imagine how...or why...he has returned after so many years."

"Indeed, I am Lord Hanley," the short, balding man said in an imperious tone, "recently come from the Holy Land to claim my bride. Who, sir—" he gave Senet an assessing look from head to toe "—do you profess to be?"

Senet's hands fisted again. "I'll tell you who I am—"

"I am the one who can best answer such as that," another voice interrupted. Kieran FitzAllen, yet carrying his tankard, pushed his way to the fore. "My lord Hanley," he said with a bow to that man, "men and women of Lomas—" he swept his free hand toward the crowd behind him, turning to take them all in "—let us drink the health of the lord and lady of Lomas, and pray God's blessings upon them!"

A loud, raucous cheer filled the hall, drowning out Lord Hanley's indignant protestations. Kieran moved to the man, setting an arm about his shoulders as if he were a close friend, then called out to Senet, "Kiss your good lady! This is a celebration!"

Senet shook his head, laughing, and turned to Katharine. "Your cousin is mad, but right—'tis a great celebration, and I will kiss my wife." He pulled her near and kissed her long and fully, increasing the cheers of all those around them. Then he set his hands about her waist and lifted her high into the air, shouting, "The lady of Lomas!"

The cheers grew even louder, and Katharine threw her head back and laughed as Senet twirled her about in a dizzying circle. Happiness was hers, echoed in the loud pleasure of her people, and she would never let it—or him—go again.

* * * * *

If you enjoyed what you just read,
then we've got an offer you can't resist!

Take 2 bestselling love stories FREE!

Plus get a FREE surprise gift!

HARLEQUIN®
Makes any time special™

WIN A DREAM

In celebration of Harlequin®'s golden anniversary

Enter to win a *dream!* You could win:

- A luxurious trip for two to *The Renaissance Cottonwoods Resort* in Scottsdale, Arizona, or

- A bouquet of flowers once a week for a year from **FTD**, or

- A $500 shopping spree, or

- A fabulous bath & body gift basket, including **K-tel**'s *Candlelight and Romance* 5-CD set.

Look for **WIN A DREAM** flash on specially marked Harlequin® titles by Penny Jordan, Dallas Schulze, Anne Stuart and Kristine Rolofson in October 1999*.

FTD

RENAISSANCE. COTTONWOODS RESORT
SCOTTSDALE, ARIZONA

K-TEL

*No purchase necessary—for contest details send a self-addressed envelope to Harlequin Makes Any Time Special Contest, P.O. Box 9069, Buffalo, NY, 14269-9069 (include contest name on self-addressed envelope). Contest ends December 31, 1999. Open to U.S. and Canadian residents who are 18 or over. Void where prohibited.

PHMATS-GR

Celebrate **15** years with

Every Man Has His Price!

HEART OF THE WEST

At the heart of the West there are a dozen rugged bachelors—up for auction!

This August 1999, look for *Courting Callie*
by **Lynn Erickson**

If Mase Lebow testifies at a high-profile trial, he knows his six-year-old son, Joey, will pay. Mase decides to hide his son at Callie Thorpe's ranch, out of harm's way. Callie, of course, has no idea why Joey is really there, and falling in love with his tight-lipped father is a definite inconvenience.

Each book features a sexy new bachelor up for grabs—and a woman determined to rope him in!

Available August 1999 at your favorite retail outlet.

HARLEQUIN®
Makes any time special ™

COMING NEXT MONTH FROM

HARLEQUIN HISTORICALS